A Can of Worms
A Sam Jenkins Mystery

Wayne Zurl

Published by
Melange Books, LLC
White Bear Lake, MN 55110
www.melange-books.com

A Can of Worms ~ Copyright © 2016 by Wayne Zurl

ISBN: 978-1-68046-329-3

Cover Design by Lynsee Lauritsen

To Bitsey,
One of the toughest, most loyal individuals I've ever known.

Chapter One

I wore my navy blue suit with a pale yellow shirt, striped tie, black wing tips and a pair of black wool socks. I was neat, clean, shaved and sober, and I didn't care who knew it.

My apologies to Mr. Chandler for the obvious paraphrase. But since I've already committed what some might call blasphemy, I'll continue to hover slightly above plagiarism and refer back to Philip Marlowe's first thought from a page of hardboiled fiction and embellish my own story.

It was about one o'clock in the afternoon, mid-June, with the sun not shining and a look of hard, wet rain in the clearness of the foothills.

Only my foothills were those of the Great Smokies, not Marlowe's Hollywood Hills.

I wasn't a private detective. I was a police chief, and I only owned a new suit because my wife insisted I needed something more up-to-date than my closet full of thirty-year-old Harris Tweed sport jackets.

The similarity I shared with Philip Marlowe or Doghouse Reilly, the name Marlowe used when he introduced himself to Carmen Sternwood in that famous opening scene, was that I too intended to call on four-million-dollars.

In 1939 when Raymond Chandler published *The Big Sleep*, four-million bucks could set the world on its ear. Today, that's only a little more than Warren Buffet's lunch money. But power isn't measured in cash alone. The man I planned to visit looked extremely well off. He was, by no means, the wealthiest man in Blount County, but he ranked among the most powerful.

Retired Judge Minas Tipton lived in a sixty-year-old brick home in a beautiful section of Maryville, Tennessee. Two days earlier, he invited me to have lunch with him.

Generally, when the judge and I got together, it happened because one or more of the local politicians were upset with my official shenanigans. That day was no different. I knew exactly what the topic would be.

I used the big brass doorknocker to announce my presence. In sixty seconds, the judge's housekeeper, Loretta, opened the door.

"Good mornin', sir." She spoke with a soft East Tennessee accent and gave me a friendly smile. "Come on in an' I'll git the judge for ya."

I stepped into the living room, a place Loretta called the parlor. The furnishings were all early Federal period antiques, class all the way. If I didn't know who I had an appointment with, I might have thought I'd be visiting Rhett Butler.

Loretta stepped into the hall and looked into a private office across from the parlor. "Judge, Chief Jenkins is here."

I heard him stand and send a swivel chair sliding away from his desk. A moment later, I saw him.

He greeted me with a big and genuine smile. "Sam, good mornin'. It's good ta see ya again. Very good indeed."

I shook hands with the dapper old man. He was pushing ninety, but could have passed for fifteen years younger.

"Good to see you, Judge. Here, I brought you something I think you'll like." I handed him a bottle of white wine.

I'd been on a Viognier kick ever since a friend who knew his liquor suggested it. I thought my twenty-dollar bottle of Napa Valley wine was just the cat's ass, and since the judge was never at a loss for a supply of tasty hooch to go with lunch, I knew he'd appreciate the gesture.

"Damn it, Sam, ya didn't have to do that, but I'm glad ya did. I've had this before and just love it. Love it indeed. Now why don't we sit down, and I'll have Loretta fix us a couple o' drinks."

We sat in his elegant living room. Loretta brought us drinks, his bourbon, mine scotch.

The judge held up his glass and toasted me. "Well, here's to ya, Sam—all the best."

"Cheers," I said.

We both took a sip.

"I saw that scotch yer drinkin' and was just taken with the label," the old man said. "I thought of ya and bought a bottle. How do ya like it?"

I swished the scotch over two ice cubes in a short glass. Loretta remembered how I liked my whisky. I took another quick sip.

"Excellent," I said. "Famous Grouse is a great blended whisky. I like it as much as that moonshine the Chivas brothers have been peddling for centuries."

"Ha, ha, ha, ha. You've got a way with words, Sam. Ya surely do."

The judge always provided his own laugh track during a conversation. When I first heard it, I wasn't sure if he was putting me on or it was genuine. I'm still not certain, but it's his way, and it's always there.

"You made a good choice, Judge. Thanks for thinking of me."

"My pleasure, Sam. My pleasure indeed."

The old cutthroat smiled and sipped his bourbon. That day it came from Buffalo Trace.

"Sam, I've been told you're kickin' up some dust in the barnyard again. I don't suppose ya give a hoot, but you've ruffled some important feathers."

Since childhood, I've worked on perfecting a look that silently said, "Gee whiz, I'm really not that bad, am I? Don't you think I'm just so damn cute?" I tried it on the judge before answering.

"I'm sure you remember I have these silly ideas about doing the right thing," I said.

The judge closed his eyes and nodded. He knew what he'd be up against.

"I know the boy we're going to talk about is personable, and he's a serious, hardworking, conscientious individual." I shrugged and took a pull on my scotch. "At first I didn't want to hire him because he'd been thrust upon me by a group of political hacks who didn't care if I had good personnel in my police department or just a bunch of well-hung ya-hoos who needed jobs. You know that."

Tipton opened his eyes, continued nodding and listened as I spoke.

"But I ended up liking him. I was even prepared to tell people I'd been wrong. But all that aside, now I have the reputation of my department to consider, and he owes someone a serious debt."

I thought my look would be as effective on Minas Tipton as it always had been on my mother, she being as tough as any criminal court judge with thirty years experience. I figured he might roll over and let me off the hook. I thought wrong.

"Sam, I sympathize with ya. I truly do. I didn't want ta touch this with a ten-foot pole, but a good friend asked me ta speak with ya. Why do ya suppose they'd ask me, Sam?"

I shook my head and shrugged again. "Because you and I have gotten to be good buddies?" I hoped that didn't sound overly sarcastic.

He sat forward and nodded. "Exactly, Sam. They know damn well ya don't respond to threats, especially when ya hold more ammunition than they do."

I dipped my head an inch and waited.

"I want ya ta understand, Sam, I'm not takin' their side here—not takin' their side at all. Why don't ya tell me the whole story—what's happened so far. You know I'll believe ya. You're an honest man. And Lord knows, believin' some of those politicos I hang with is a fool's errand."

I settled back in the overstuffed chair, took a sip of Famous Grouse and considered the old judge. He had aged well. He stood about five-nine and still kept himself in the middleweight division. I've never seen him without a jacket and some sort of tie. Today he wore a light blue blazer, white shirt and yellow and navy bow tie. I took another sip of whisky and began my saga.

"So far everything leads me to believe the kid is guilty of forcible rape."

Tipton's eyes widened at my blunt statement.

"The girl's mother sounded outraged when she learned I hired Dallas Finchum as a policeman. At first, the victim didn't want to get involved. But after a little gentle persuasion, the girl told a credible and compelling story. This seems to be a date rape gone terribly wrong. The victim's ex-roommate corroborates her story."

4

Other than raising his white eyebrows the first time I used the word *rape*, the judge sat patiently.

"The way I'm looking at it now," I said, "aside from Dallas losing his job at Prospect PD, there are a few people in a shitload of trouble for covering up the crime. That goes from the sheriff's polygraph examiner here in Blount County to the people at the Hamilton County DA's office for *misplacing* the case file. It's a long story, Judge. How about I freshen up your bourbon and add some more Grouse to my glass?"

"A fine idea, Sam. A fine idea, indeed. Now believe me, son, I'm inclined ta side with ya on this. The reputation of your police department is very important. If this boy, nice young man or not, is guilty of such a crime, he must answer for it in some way."

I felt a little trickle of relief when I heard the judge say that. I wanted to believe he meant it when I handed him the refill.

"You may know," I said, "that when I received approval to hire an additional officer, I planned on advertising the position, doing some objective screening of candidates and after that choosing the best person for the job."

He nodded, sipped his bourbon and waited. The judge was one of the best listeners I knew.

"I ended up having the mayor tell me that with approval of the newly created position, Dallas Finchum had been earmarked as the person to fill it. As you can imagine, I was not a happy police chief."

He used his right hand to smooth down a perfectly groomed head of white hair. Then he looked over the rim of his glass, lowered his eyes a little and focused on me. "Ha, ha, ha, ha. I expect not," he said. "No, sir, I surely expect not. That maneuver got ya New York temper up in the air, didn't it?"

I smiled, nodded and continued to tell him the whole story. Some of what I'm sure he already knew, but restating facts never bothered me, and he seemed content to hear me out.

* * * *

At his pre-employment interview, I had all intentions of meeting Dallas Finchum and disliking him. His uncle, Albert "Buck" Webbster, was the former Prospect police chief—my predecessor. Some people still don't know the true story of Buck Webbster and thought he just retired to Florida. Anyone who watched the news one day in early 2006 may have seen the story of a police official caught by agents of the Tennessee Bureau of Investigation selling confiscated handguns in the parking lot of a Knoxville gun show. But Buck, who had political connections up the wazoo, was allowed to retire, avoid jail time and lie about the end of his career to anyone who'd listen.

Enter Sam Jenkins, ex-detective lieutenant from a great metropolitan police department—one on Long Island, to be precise—who had been lolling away his retirement in the sleepy little community of Walland, Tennessee.

A couple of years after Webbster's exit from Prospect PD, I was the guy about to be handed a ration of grief from the local politicians for calling PO Dallas Finchum onto the carpet about his past conduct, and if I had my way, giving him the sack.

As I told Minas Tipton, when I met Dallas I liked him. I liked him a lot. The kid looked like the perfect police applicant—well groomed, in good shape, intelligent and respectful, almost to a fault. Dallas said all the right stuff.

Being the softhearted schlep that I occasionally am, I decided to forget my preconceptions and overlook the possibility that Dallas might have the same dishonest streak present in his Uncle Buck. I'd even overlook my injured self-esteem and swallow an employee I didn't personally choose. That last one would be a big concession on my part.

So, in February of 2007, I hired young Finchum. Mayor Ronnie Shields swore him in. The mayor's secretary, Trudy Connor, notarized his signature on the oath of office, and I handed him one of our large oval silver and gold badges.

For the months that he worked as a rookie cop, before a police academy class had been scheduled to kick off, I assigned him to work alongside the best cops Prospect had to offer.

Sergeant Bettye Lambert showed him our police station and taught him the daily duties of a desk officer. Sergeant Stan Rose, my night patrol supervisor, started his education toward being a street cop. I kept my eye on him and was pleasantly surprised.

Patrolmen like Bobby John Crockett, Junior Huskey, Will Sparks and others each gave him a week of their time and experience. Even old Vernon Hobbs, Prospect's 'blue knight', allowed him to ride along and learn by example. Everyone said the kid did just fine.

Then I received a phone call destined to turn Dallas's world upside down and, to a large extent, mine, too.

Chapter Two

"Sam, I've got a woman on the line." Bettye sighed before continuing. "You really need to talk with her."

She transferred the call, and I answered my phone.

"Chief," the woman said, "do you normally hire rapists to be po-leece-men in Prospect?

I'm glad no one was watching me. I felt my eyes pop open, and I'm sure my jaw dropped. I knew exactly who she was talking about.

"That's a disturbing question, ma'am. Would you explain a little more?"

"I'll explain a lot more. Will you do somethin' about it?"

I had the option to tap dance and keep a disillusioned citizen on the line or take offense at someone thinking I might not be the best police chief Prospect ever had. Compromise is everything.

"Ma'am, I've believed in something important ever since I got sworn in as a police officer a long time ago," I said. "I think a cop's reputation is one of the most important things he or she has. If what you say is true, my reputation and that of Prospect PD are in jeopardy. You bet I'll do something about it."

There was a long moment of silence.

"You'll listen ta me then?"

I thought I hooked her attention. "Of course I will."

"My daughter was raped by a man y'all hired."

I remembered back all those months to when I met Dallas and thought, why me?

I gave the caller a few options. "Would you like to do this over the phone or at the police station? Or would you like me to come to your home?"

There was another moment of silence.

Then, "On the phone is aw rot fer now."

"Sure, that's okay—for now. Will you tell me your name?"

"I guess ya need ta know that, don't ya?"

"It would help. I'll need to know your daughter's name, too."

"My name's Asher—Jodelle Asher."

"Thanks, Mrs. Asher. If you didn't hear Sergeant Lambert or me say so before, I'm Sam Jenkins, the police chief in Prospect."

"They's a bunch o' Jenkinses here in Blount County. You from a local family?"

"No, ma'am. I'm from New York."

"Ya didn't sound like you's from Tennessee."

"No, I guess I don't, do I?" I knew the answer to my next question, but I asked anyway. "Mrs. Asher, which policeman are we talking about?"

"That Finchum boy, Dallas. He's the one raped my daughter, Dorie."

I remembered my reaction when Dallas first told me about an incident that both the UT campus police and Chattanooga detectives summarily dismissed as unfounded. I worried about it then. Now it felt like something was waiting to come back and bite me in the posterior.

"When did this happen?" I asked.

"More'n three year ago, but that don't make it no less awful, does it?"

I silently blew out a little air. "No, ma'am. I can't think how rape can ever be forgotten or looked at as anything but awful."

Bettye Lambert walked into my office and sat in one of the guest chairs in front of my desk. She held a sheet of paper. Her little granny glasses rested low on her nose. She reached forward and handed me a Tennessee Department of Safety printout for Jodelle Asher, showing her personal information, address and driving record. Bettye had listened in on the conversation, then checked on our complainant

9

"Dorie was in school at UT, Chattanooga," Jodelle Asher said. "So was Dallas, but I suppose you already know 'bout him." She waited a few seconds for a response, but I didn't offer one. "They knew each other ever since high school." She pronounced the last words hi-skoo. "They's seniors in the college school when the rape happened. Dallas had asked her out a couple times, then one night he ups and attacks her. I believe my daughter, Mr. Jenkins. If she says she was raped, then she was raped."

I had already heard Finchum's account of what Mrs. Asher just said and the rest of what she was about to tell me, but I asked a few basic questions and allowed her to talk so I'd have two stories to compare.

"Did your daughter report the rape?"

"Yes, sir, she shore did to the college po-leece."

Bettye took off her glasses and sat there swinging them back and forth listening to the one-sided conversation.

"Campus police usually don't investigate serious crimes," I said. "Did they refer it to the local police or the sheriff's office down there?"

"They did. Hamilton County Sheriff. Little good that did."

"What did the Hamilton County detectives tell your daughter?"

I looked up at Bettye, waiting for Mrs. Asher's explanation. Occasionally she wears a hint of green eye shadow. It goes well with her blonde hair and hazel eyes—matches her uniform pants, too.

"A lotta noise is all. They called her a couple o' days after it happened. Then he, this detective, told her how hard it was to prove rape and how tough a lawyer would make it fer her when she got ta court. That man made her feel like she'd be the one on trial, 'stead o' Dallas."

The story began differing from what Dallas told me.

"Did your daughter report this immediately after it happened?"

"Yes, sir, she did. Same night."

"And a *couple of days later* a detective tried to kiss this off?"

"Yes, sir."

"Did Dorie see a doctor?"

"Yes, sir. Same night. A woman from the college po-leece took her."

"Were there any witnesses? Did anyone see her right after she was raped? A roommate maybe?"

10

"Yes, sir, Dorie had a roommate. Nice girl, name o' Laura Jean Hensley."

I wondered how much of this behind the scenes action Dallas Finchum knew.

I looked at Bettye again. She tilted her head as if to say, "This sounds like a fine can of worms you've picked up, Sammy."

"Mrs. Asher, I plan to investigate this, but I'll need to meet your daughter and speak with Laura Hensley as well. When do you think I can do that?"

"Dorie don't much like talkin' about the rape. Bad memories an' all. Laura, she lives in Knoxville. Works there, too."

"I believe all you're telling me, Mrs. Asher, but I can't arrest Dallas Finchum or fire him for what he did based on our telephone conversation. I need to see Dorie, get a statement from her, see Laura, record what she saw and then find out why the people in Chattanooga didn't do more."

"I unnerstand."

"Before we hired Dallas, my investigator and I listened to his side of this date rape story. A detective named Gallagher spoke with your daughter, and she refused to make a statement. She said the incident was over, and she wanted to get on with her life. She more or less reaffirmed that she decided not to press charges."

"I know Dorie was terrible upset over the whole affair. I can pitcher her sayin' that. That mean nothin' can be done now?"

"No, it doesn't."

"Good."

"May I speak with Dorie now, or will you have her call me?"

"I'll ask her. Don't know if she'll talk with ya though. She might not've changed her mind."

I began to feel a serious frustration.

"I promise you, Mrs. Asher, if I can do something to help your daughter, I will. But it's important for me to speak with her...and with Laura Hensley. They have to cooperate."

"I'll have ta call ya back."

"Okay. Do you live in Prospect?" I asked, wondering if the driver's license information was up to date.

11

"No."

"Where do you live?"

A little more silence.

"Mrs. Asher?"

"We live in Maryville." Like most local people, she pronounced it Murr-vull. "East end o' Murr-vull, not fer from Walland."

"Tell Dorie I'll meet her anywhere she wants. Here at Prospect PD, at a public place, anywhere—doesn't matter."

"I hear ya."

"Can I call you back to find out what she says?"

"I'll call you."

"When? Tomorrow?"

"I 'spect so."

"Alright then. Good luck with Dorie. And, Mrs. Asher, I promise I'll help you."

"Uh-huh. I'll call ag'in."

She hung up. I needed a drink.

Chapter Three

Detective John Gallagher isn't really a detective. He was, but not in Tennessee. John worked for me back on Long Island—for nine years; then we both retired.

Just before I hired Dallas Finchum, John called looking for a job. You'd really have to know him to understand why. John retired with over twenty-five years of police service, received a good pension and, at his age, had long been eligible for Social Security. But John's wife spends money like a soldier just before a suicide mission. That pair always lived above their means.

Before coming to Tennessee looking for work, John tried to sell his expensive home in Boca Raton. He sold his boat, his Cadillac, his lawn mower and still needed a job to make ends meet.

So, with a suitcase in his secondhand Saturn and his wife in Florida to close the sale of their house, John came to Prospect PD to take a job as a clerk-typist. But after a little gentle persuasion, I convinced the mayor to change his job title to police operations aide. And out of respect for John, I bought him a badge and made him an honorary detective. In reality, he's been deputized and is legally an auxiliary cop with a civilian's concealed carry pistol permit. He's Bettye's assistant and my Man Friday. John conducted the pre-employment investigation on Dallas Finchum.

Bettye heard a sector car call in and returned to her desk to answer the radio. I yelled into the file room behind the front office, "Hey, John."

"Yeah, Boss?"

"Come back to your desk so the three of us can have a talk."

I told John about my recent conversation with Jodelle Asher. Bettye listened and made a few notes.

"He told me about that, Boss. Remember?" John said, looking a little defensive. "Wasn't a rape, according to him. A date rape, maybe...if you stretched things. You know the deal. She said, 'Okay, okay, okay,' then 'maybe not, maybe not', and when it was all over, she claimed rape."

Bettye sat quietly, but I saw her expression change. She didn't care for John's dismissal of Dallas's conduct.

"The local cops resolved the situation," John said. "She didn't want to prosecute."

"Yeah, I remember. Are you sure about all this," I asked. "Nothing else important that didn't get into a report?"

"I had them confirm it on the poly."

John stood next to his chair. His large belly strained the two shirt buttons just north of his belt line.

"The polygraph examiner never said he specifically addressed this in detail. His report was sketchy," I said.

"I called, and he said he did. You remember?"

"Yeah. Think back to the interview, John. Did Dallas sound truthful to you?"

He shrugged and scratched his short reddish-brown hair. The bastard was five years older than me and had less gray.

"He was embarrassed, but he didn't hide anything."

I remembered Dallas mentioning the incident to me, and he did sound truthful.

"And all the paperwork came back from Hamilton County to corroborate Finchum's story?"

"Yep. That's why I didn't go any further with the investigation. The campus cops, the county dicks and the DA there all said the same thing."

"The girl's mother had quite a story," I said. "We need to see the victim. There's supposed to be a witness from the incident, too."

"Okay, Boss, but when I found her back then, she didn't want to say anything."

I nodded. "Refresh my memory. Exactly what did the polygraph examiner say about this? Charlie Dietzen did the test, right?"

"He's the man. I'll get you the report, but I remember he said the kid was truthful. No doubts and no bullshit about qualified truthfulness. Charlie said he was satisfied."

John finally sat, straightened the tie that was too short to reach his waistline and seemed a little tense.

He wasn't the only one feeling uneasy. I signed off on the completed background investigation and recommended that Dallas be hired.

"Okay, Betts," I said, "iron up some civilian clothes. As soon as the victim calls and sets up a meeting, we'll hit the road. She'll be a lot more comfortable if I take you instead of John."

"Okey dokey, darlin'. I've got a new pants suit that makes me look like a TV detective."

"I can't wait to see it."

"What's wrong with me, Boss?" John asked.

"What's right with you? You'd scare me away from making a complaint."

"How can you say that, Boss? I'm *compassionable* and sympathy-minded."

He tried his best to look hurt, but ended up smiling.

"Of course you are. You're just not understandable to most of the English-speaking world. Stay tuned, John."

* * * *

Before I confronted Dallas Finchum, I wanted to hear the victim's story and see what the witness had to say. I waited for Jodelle Asher to start the ball rolling.

What I received first was a call I didn't need. Well, I always like hearing from that particular person, but the timing and subject of our conversation was all wrong. I watched the letters WNXX, a Knoxville TV station, appear on my caller ID. Even without the station's symbol showing, I knew the number—I dial it often enough.

"Hi, Sam," she said.

"Hey, Rachel, how's my favorite news girl? You haven't called in a while."

"That's television journalist and senior news anchor to you, mister. Hey, I've missed you."

Rachel Williamson is the evening anchorperson on one of the Knoxville stations. For as long as I can remember, she's been voted East Tennessee's best-looking female celebrity in some newspaper poll.

"Yeah, you, too. You sound good. Everything okay?"

"Sure, I'm doing well. Thanks."

I thought this would be just a friendly chat without getting into any business. As usual, we'd talk about nothing in particular. I'd flirt. She'd giggle, and we'd be good for another three thousand miles.

"I've been watching the news every night. I see you're letting your hair grow."

I turned my chair to the left and swung my feet up to rest on my desktop.

"Oh, good, you noticed. Do you like it?"

"Of course, I noticed. I'm a cop. I notice everything. I know everything."

"Gimme a break, Jenkins. So, do you think you'll like me with longer hair?"

"Hard for me not to like you."

She's got the cutest little dimple in her chin.

"That's no answer."

She does that just like a cop.

"You'd look nice bald. Well…I guess that was a stupid thing to say."

"Sam."

Trapped.

"I guess I liked your hair the way it used to be."

"Oh."

"Don't give me *oh*. You wanted an answer. I always thought your hair looked perfect."

"And now it's not?"

"I didn't say that. I just have strong preferences. That's all. If you had something perfect, why argue with success?"

"My husband likes it."

"I'm sure he would."

Of course, he would, the yuppie asshole.

"But you don't?"

"Jeez! If you were here I'd spank you."

"Oooo, that sounds kind of kinky."

Saved by the bell.

"Do you love making my life difficult?"

"Of course not, Sammy. You're my best friend. Would I do that to you?"

"You're a woman. I can never figure out you people."

"It's nice to be something of a mystery."

Okay, time for a new subject.

"So, what's happening in the world of a big-time news girl?"

"Actually, I called to ask something about your police department."

"Really?"

"Yes, I called because I've heard one of your cops is being accused of rape."

"Oh, Christ! Who told you that?" I dropped my feet to the floor and sat upright.

"Sam, you know I can't—"

"Yes, you can. Don't give me that confidential sources crap. This is me you're talking to. It was the girl's mother, wasn't it?" I didn't wait for an answer. "Don't I call you with everything interesting, important and newsworthy that happens in this jerkwater town?"

"Yes, but—"

"Do I call anyone else? Do you not learn about everything that creeps and flies in Prospect as soon as I confirm it's true?" She didn't answer. "Well?"

"Wow. You're getting all emotional on me. This is your best friend you're talking to. I'm just asking."

That was the first time I remember getting annoyed with her. I took a breath and regrouped.

"I'm sorry. There's no reason for me to yell. You're right. I got a call about this earlier today. I guess just before Jodelle Asher called you."

"I guess."

"I hope she only called you and not any of the other stations. Especially that moron Allen Peters. I'm waiting for her to call back before I'll know if her daughter will speak with me. So far, we believe that the kid, Dallas Finchum, has been truthful about this. He says it was all consensual until after the fact. But I need to hear the girl's story and speak with her ex-roommate," I said, cooling down considerably.

"Will you call me, and keep me in the picture?"

"You know I'll call you with what I know as soon as I know something. Know what I mean?"

She laughed. "Okay, I know."

"I hate to grovel in front of someone so much smaller than me, but please, please, please don't say anything until I call you."

"Do I make you grovel?"

"You just did."

"That makes me think I may be short, but I'm tough."

I laughed.

"Hey, don't laugh. I *am* tough."

"Yes, you are. Tough is good in your business. I'm just more interested in sexy."

"Really?"

"Forget I said that."

"Coward."

Chapter Four

At ten-past-eleven the next day, Dorie Asher called. She sounded less than eager to discuss the incident that occurred in her dorm room at the UT, Chattanooga campus. She insisted on not coming anywhere near the Prospect municipal building where we have our offices for fear of meeting Dallas. We finally agreed to meet at Tibbs' restaurant, a local beanery on US 129 just south of the Knoxville Airport.

If you could overcook it or deep-fry it, you just might find it on Tibbs' menu. I wished my victim had picked a better place to eat. I didn't even have high hopes for the coffee.

"Hey, John," I said as I put on my sport jacket," try and act like a cop while we're gone. Okay?"

"Hard to do, Boss. I'm only a clerk-typist."

"An unemployed clerk-typist if you don't watch your step."

"You know, Boss, you don't scare me with your *unflammerary* remarks. You couldn't fire me. The mayor likes me."

"Nobody likes you, John. And while we're gone, please don't type like you speak."

He grinned at my comment and made the stupid face he always makes. "See you later, Boss. Bye, Sarge."

Bettye and I left through our private back door.

* * * *

Tibbs' restaurant is a low, white-painted, stucco building on the west side of route 129. A narrow horizontal blue stripe ran across the exterior walls, four feet from the ground. It made Tibbs' look like an architectural sanitary pad.

I found a spot in an already crowded parking lot, the local populace no doubt looking to bolster their cholesterol levels. We met Dorie Asher sitting in a booth near the back of the dining room.

After getting our introductions out of the way, Dorie looked relieved to see the Sergeant Lambert I said would accompany me turned out to be a female.

Dorie Asher was a pretty, dark-haired girl dressed conservatively. I couldn't help thinking she and Dallas would have made an attractive couple.

She was using her lunch break to meet with us. I suggested we order as soon as the waitress stopped at the table. Bettye and I asked for coffee. Dorie wanted a burger, fries and a diet Dr. Pepper.

When Bettye and I interview a female, especially a victim of a sexually oriented crime, she begins the dialogue. I try my best to stifle any male-chauvinist-pig comments until they become absolutely necessary.

Once Bettye got her talking, Dorie explained a simple date that had gone out of control.

"Dallas and I went out to a movie," she said. "After that, he took me to a local hangout he knew for pizza and a couple of beers. I can't remember the name of the place. It wasn't where I'd usually go. It was, like, further from campus than I'd drive just to get a pizza."

The waitress interrupted by dropping off Dorie's meal and our coffee. I noticed a round wall clock off to my left. It must have had a quartz movement, the second hand snapped sharply into position every time it moved. I wondered why clocks intrigued me so much.

"What happened after you left the pizza place?" Bettye asked.

Dorie took the raw onion rings off her burger, pushed them to the side of the plate and added mustard and ketchup to the beef patty.

"My roommate, Laura, was out on a date, too, so the dorm room was, like, empty. Laura usually stayed out pretty late when she went on dates, so Dallas and I could be alone until, like, much later. So, Dallas asked if we could go back there. He wanted to pick up some more beer, but I, like, don't drink that much, and he let it go. We went straight back to the room."

"Did anyone see you two go into your room?" I asked.

"No, I don't think so, and no one ever told me they did."

"What happened next?" Bettye asked.

Dorie took a bite of her burger, a sip of Dr. Pepper and hesitated before answering.

The twelve-inch round clock ticked away. After sixty seconds, the minute hand advanced with the same snap that marked off the seconds.

"I put on some music, and we started to, you know, uh, like…get friendly," she said.

"That was all okay with you up to that point?" Bettye asked.

"Yeah, I mean, I liked Dallas."

She nibbled a couple of fries and sipped more soda. We waited for her to proceed to the next logical topic.

"Look," she said, as if we were too old to understand her story. "If Dallas had played his cards right that night, we probably would have hooked up, ya know? I mean, like, I don't know if I loved him, like, loved him to marry him, but we'd been friends for a long, long time. I like, liked him, like a lot."

"And what happened to make you change your mind? Where did Dallas start going wrong?" I asked.

"Well, like, we never did it with each other before. I didn't know what to expect from him. I mean, I knew what I'd like, but I didn't know what Dallas would do."

She dipped a couple more fries in ketchup, and we watched them go down the hatch.

"So, he says he wants…" she began to explain and paused. "Oh, man, I'm, like, really embarrassed to say exactly what he wanted, but it wasn't my thing, especially for the first time. Can I just leave it at that?"

I nodded.

Bettye said, "Sure you can, Dorie. You tell your story any way you're comfortable."

She began again. "So when I said no to what he wanted, he, like, got kinda insistent and told me again what he wanted me to do." She started to attack the fries again but stopped and dropped them back on her plate.

21

"I'm, like, really not comfortable talkin' about this again. Do I have to?" She wiped her fingers with a paper napkin.

"Would you be more comfortable if I left you two ladies alone?" I said.

"I guess so," she said. "I'm sorry." She looked as if she was.

"That's not a problem," I said. "You two take as long as you want. I'll be out in the car if you need me. It was nice to meet you, Dorie, and please believe us, we will do anything we can to help you."

I slid a twenty under my coffee cup next to Bettye. The coffee, by the way, sucked—big time. And Dorie's burger patty looked like the sole of a combat boot.

Thirty-five minutes later, Bettye walked out into the sunshine and sat next to me in the Ford.

"Well," she said, "we got through that, but she didn't get any less upset after you left. She could only eat half of her lunch. It was pretty tough for her to explain. She needed to use the girl's room before going back to work—had to tidy up her eye makeup."

"I'm not too good at deciphering young women's stories. I, like, don't, like, relate to their lingo. What did you make out of what she said? You think it was a legitimate rape?"

"I think she was terribly upset talking about that night. If I had to bet, yeah, I'd say he probably raped her. I think we need for those folks in Hamilton County to send us their case folder."

Bettye explained all the details of the conversation I missed. After Dallas evinced his kinky oral tendencies, Dorie told him she was not so inclined and made her preferences known. Then had Dallas, as Dorie suggested, played his cards right, they would have enjoyed a sexy evening and parted friends if not actual in-love lovers.

But perhaps, while discussing the birds and bees with his old man, Dallas may have been told that when a girl says no she really means yes. I needed to find out.

Dorie's mother, on the other hand, may never have taught her little girl the hard-to-get game. When young Ms. Asher said no, she, like, meant it.

Bettye said that at one point Dallas began getting a little rough. Dorie slapped him back, and it all went downhill from there.

Dorie reported the rape to the campus police who did the initial investigation before referring the case to the detectives from the Hamilton County Sheriff's Department.

A female campus police officer took Dorie to the local ER and had her examined. The attending physician used what we in the po-leece business—in Tennessee, New York, Alaska or anywhere else—call a rape kit, then turned it over to the detectives.

Our victim gave those detectives a statement, was released from the hospital, and the campus officer drove her back to the dormitory.

Dorie went on to tell Bettye how Dallas slapped, wrestled and manhandled her and how he spread her legs with brute force by punching her inner thighs. She alluded to his forcible entry and how he left her in the room, a disheveled mess, and walked away without so much as a thank-you-ma'am.

"Specifically, what did she say happened at the hospital?" I asked.

"It sounded like the ER people did what they were supposed to do," Bettye said. "She didn't know any of the terms, but I'd say they went through the normal routine with the rape kit. She got a thorough examination, and the campus officer, a woman named Sharla Hatfield, stayed with her for several hours until the county detectives came. Then Hatfield waited and took her back to the dorm when the detectives were finished."

"What did the county dicks tell her?"

"According to Dorie, they didn't tell her much of anything. They just asked more questions. She thinks it could have been as much as three hours before they showed up."

"And we assume the county dicks took the rape kit?"

"Dorie wouldn't know that."

"Did anyone ever get back to her?" I asked.

"The next day an investigator from the DA's office met with her, and it sounds like he did his best to discourage her from pursuing a persecution. You know the old routine about being a difficult thing to prove to a jury, how the defense will tear her apart on the stand, and all that."

I nodded. I knew what some detectives would tell a rape victim if they thought the charge might be difficult to prove.

"Sammy, she had to have been confused, shamed and left without someone to give her good advice about the legal system."

I nodded.

"After talking with the DA's investigator, she went to see Sharla Hatfield again looking for any help she could get. Hatfield gave her almost the same story—forget the incident and get on with her life. That's not something I'd want to hear, but coming from a woman, it may have had more influence than what the cops told her."

"And that was it?" I said.

"No, one of the county detectives waited another two days and phoned her again. He wanted to make sure she would drop her complaint before they closed out the case as a failure to prosecute."

"So, after all was said and done, Dorie felt violated, abandoned and more alone than she ever had before in her young life."

"Sounds about right," Bettye said.

"Did you get a release signed for us to obtain her medical records from the hospital?"

"Shoot, city boy, you think you're dealin' with an amateur?"

"Not me, Blondie. I have faith in you."

After Sergeant Lambert satisfied her obligation to smile at her boss, we wrapped up our business for the morning.

"Hey," I said, "how about we go to a real restaurant and get lunch?"

"You know, Sammy, I do believe y'all are a food snob."

"I am not. I just want to live to have another meal someday. That place makes Laddie Boy look like haute cuisine."

I took Bettye to El Jibarito in Maryville. She chose chicken enchiladas with salad and pico de gallo. I had the Burrito Supremo, rice, beans, salad and a Dos Equis draft. After that, I was a happy man again.

Chapter Five

I stood next to Bettye while she ran a couple of names through the computer. I sniffed and guessed she was wearing White Linen. At twenty-after-nine, John Gallagher walked through the front doors. He drew my attention, and I checked the wall clock. "Nice of you to join us today, Honorary Detective Gallagher." I made an exaggerated look at my watch.

"Oh, uh…hi, Boss. Hi, Sarge." He gave us his cat-that-ate-the-canary smile.

"Mornin', John." Bettye offered a quick, friendly smile.

At least she'd be sympathetic.

"I was, uh…running late this morning, and, uh…I left my car out last night, and the *crackles* got it."

Immediately, I knew that was worth exploiting.

"The crackles got it?" I said.

"Yeah, I had to wash it off. I couldn't see through the windshield, and that stuff's no good for your paintjob."

"Huh? Crackles?" I gave Bettye a sidelong glance and watched her try to stifle a laugh.

"Yeah, crackles—birds—a whole flock of them—hundreds maybe, maybe thousands."

"Grackles, John. They're called grackles," I said.

Bettye finally laughed.

"*Grapples*?" John said.

"Grackles." I tried again, exaggerating the pronunciation.

"I don't think it's grapples, Boss."

25

"I said grackles, damn it."

"*Crapples*? I never heard of crapples. Sounds like some kinda wild fruit. I don't think so, Boss."

Bettye giggled.

"Jesus Christ!" I walked away. *I can't win.*

* * * *

Later that day John Gallagher and I drove to Knoxville to meet Laura Hensley, Dorie's college roommate, for lunch. She worked for a law firm with offices downtown. We met in a restaurant called the Sun Spot on the section of Cumberland Avenue referred to as The Strip. It's the main east-west road running through the UT, Knoxville campus. If a restaurant opens up on The Strip and stays in business for more than six months, they're lucky and considered old timers. The Sun Spot had been around for years.

Like Dorie, Laura was an attractive girl in her mid-twenties. Understandably, she appeared a bit more effervescent. But Laura looked like a girl born fifty years too late. Her long blonde hair hung straight, parted in the middle like a college girl from the early 1970s. Her short sleeve, knitted top and worsted slacks were simple but expensive-looking. She needed and wore little makeup

We all sat in a booth on the right side of the restaurant. John and I ordered coffee and sipped it sparingly while we got to know our witness. Laura ate her oriental chicken salad special with much more enthusiasm than her ex-roommate had attacked her hamburger.

Laura's story picked up in the early morning hours not long after Dorie had been raped.

"I got back, oh, around two-thirty, three o'clock," she said. "Dorie was curled up on her bed, facing the wall, kinda fetal-like, ya know?"

Laura didn't wait for either John or me to acknowledge if we knew or not.

"I said something, and she, like, didn't respond. Not like she was sleeping, 'cause the light was on, ya know, but like something was wrong. So, I went over to her and saw she was crying." Laura stopped talking for a moment and shoveled a couple forks full of salad into her mouth. Still chewing, she continued. "So, I sat down on the edge of the bed and asked her what was wrong. And she, ya know, like, turned over. She'd been crying, like a lot, and she looked, like, beaten up, ya know?"

"I guess I do," I said, "but please explain what you saw."

"Well, she had almost a bruise on her cheek—the left one, I guess. And her blouse was, like, open—a couple top buttons. I looked and one, no, maybe two buttons were missing."

Compared to Dorie, Laura's language and delivery were almost the same. There must have been an elective course at UT, Chattanooga called: *How to, Like, Talk Like an Airhead, Ya Know, 101.*

Laura paused, took a big sip of her soda through the straw and just looked at me.

"Uh-huh?" I said.

John's always been good at keeping a straight face during interviews, no matter what the situation. He had to sip his coffee to hide a smile.

"Huh?" she said. "Oh, you're, like, waiting for me to keep going?"

"Sure. What happened next?"

John sat quietly next to me. He took another sip of coffee.

"Well, like, I noticed her eye makeup was all messed up, ya know? So, I asked her what happened. And she goes, 'I was raped.' So, I go, 'What?' I was, like, shocked.

And then she goes, 'Dallas raped me. We got back here, and he raped me.' She got, like, really loud then and started crying again, ya know?"

"Yeah, I can imagine. And then what did you do?"

"I called the police, and this woman policeman came."

"Uh-huh. And?"

"And? Oh. And she, like, took over, ya know?"

"Did you see any more than bruises on Dorie's cheek?"

"Sure. Like her hair was a mess, and like I said, her blouse was torn open. And when the woman cop got there, Dorie showed her her thighs. They were all red, like her cheek, and the next day Dorie showed me again. They had started turning black and blue, ya know? Like bruises."

Laura had a habit of touching the corner of her mouth with her pinkie in between eating salad and telling the story. She wore expensive-looking stick-on nails. I wondered how she could type.

27

"Did Dorie tell you, in detail, what happened?"

"Yeah, like, oh my God, it sounded grisly, ya know? She said…"

Laura's account sounded much the same as the story Dorie Asher told Bettye.

She finished her salad and soda and said, "I gotta go. I've got a good job and, like, don't want to piss them off by being late from lunch, ya know?"

"Yeah, I do. Bosses can be a pain in the ass. Just one last question. Is there any doubt in your mind that Dorie was at least beaten up when you saw her in the dorm room?"

"Like, yeah. I mean, no. She'd been tuned up alright. No doubt about it."

"Thanks, Laura. Please don't discuss this matter with anyone. We want to do the best job we can for Dorie, and this has to stay confidential for now."

"Sure, I won't say a thing. Man, it's been such a long time. Somebody shoulda, like, helped her then, ya know?"

I smiled. "Thanks for your time."

She left. I looked at John.

"You want to have lunch here, Boss?"

"I'm, like, not in a salad mood, John. There's an Indian buffet around the corner. You, like, up for that?"

"Sure, Boss. I love Hindu food."

Chapter Six

After two plates full of things like chicken tika masala, vegetable pakoras, sag paneer and basmati rice, John and I waddled out to the Crown Victoria and began the drive back to Prospect.

"Let's take a chance and stop at the sheriff's office," I said. "Maybe Charlie Dietzen is working, and we can talk to him about Dallas Finchum's test.

A few rays of sun peaked through a bank of puffy cumulus clouds. The temperature topped off in the mid-seventies, and the rippled surface of Fort Loudoun Lake shimmered in the gentle afternoon breeze as we crossed the Buck Karnes Bridge heading south on US 129.

"This guy Charlie doesn't like to be questioned, Boss," John said. "As I remember, he got kinda huffy when I asked him if he was sure the kid told the truth."

"Great. Like we need a temperamental specialist."

Fifteen minutes later, we pulled into the parking lot of the Blount County Justice Center. I tinned our way past reception and walked back to the sheriff's CID—the criminal investigation division.

Detective Charlie Dietzen was busy conducting a polygraph test on a subject of another investigation. John and I spent fifteen minutes speaking with a detective we both knew, Bo Stallins.

After Dietzen got rid of his subject and cleaned up his office, John and I sat down with him in an eight-by-ten cubbyhole that he shared with a desk, a few chairs and two file cabinets.

"Charlie, do you remember doing a pre-employment test on Dallas Finchum?" I asked. "He's the kid we hired last February."

"Not *pacifically*. That's a year-and-a-half ago, but I know the kid you mean. I remember him. I don't do many pre-employment tests. The sheriff don't care ta use 'em."

Of course he didn't. If the sheriff knew everything about the political hacks he hired, he'd be more responsible for their conduct.

Dietzen was over fifty, tall and thin with a gray-flecked mustache and a bad comb-over. He wore his dark gray suit over a pair of black, pointy-toe cowboy boots. A bolo tie with a silver and turquoise Navajo medallion decorated the neck of his light blue shirt.

"I received a phone call complaining about him being a rapist." I said. "This stems from an incident three years ago."

Dietzen began smiling and nodding his head.

I continued. "The mother of his ex-girlfriend is bringing up the matter again. Do you remember specifically questioning him about *that* incident?"

"I do now. The boy—nice kid, too—told me the whole story. Yep, I remember. Happened on the campus in Chattanooga. Fer as I'm concerned, the boy told me the truth. She said yes 'til it was all over, then she had second thoughts and claimed rape. She's the one needs ta be tested. I think she's y'ur liar."

"You have a file on your pre-test interview, a worksheet, maybe, for us to refer to?" John asked.

Dietzen smirked. "Don't need a file. I remember what the boy said. I remember his responses. He was truthful."

"Could you check the chart for me," I said, "and see if there's something that may look irregular. Maybe he skipped a beat when you asked that specific question or on the last catchall question of whether he lied about anything previously on the test."

"Told ya, I don't need ta look. Like I said, I remember. The boy told the truth. End of story. Now, if ya don't mind, I got another test comin' in I got ta prepare fer."

My eyes shifted over to John. He looked at me. Neither of us asked another question.

"Okay, then," I said to Dietzen, "thanks for your time."

* * * *

We cleared the front entrance and walked down the steps before John asked, "What do you make of that?"

"If you were questioned about an old case, what would you do first before discussing it?"

"Get the case folder."

"Exactly. At first he didn't remember the details, and then he was certain about everything."

"If he was a suspect, Boss, I'd say his story was bullshit."

"If this thing plays out like I think it may, somewhere down the line Detective Dietzen may be a suspect in a political corruption case."

"You hear what he said? He said he didn't *pacifically* remember. I can't believe people around here mispronounce words like that."

I looked at John—*speechlessly.*

Chapter Seven

I tossed my sport jacket at one of the armchairs in the lobby to the right of Bettye's desk. The jacket missed my target, and I swore silently as it hit the floor. After spinning an armless chair around, I sat next to her, shook my head and rested my chin on the chair back. Already feeling the stress of the Dallas Finchum business pressing atop my shoulders, I acted like a little boy with a monumental problem. Bettye looked at me and smiled. Then she stood, walked over to the chair, picked up my jacket, dusted it off and placed it on an empty hook on her coat rack. The woman shows great patience.

Bettye sat, and I began to report.

"Laura told us the same story you got from Dorie," I said. "Literally the same. Really, like the same, like, story, ya know? Do your daughters talk like that?"

"Well, like, no, I'd, like, kill them," she said.

I laughed.

"I wish someone down in Chattanooga had sent us something more detailed. This failure to prosecute noise ain't gonna git it," I said.

"Are you goin' down there?" she asked, probably assuming I'd leave her alone to run the department while I drove around acting like a detective.

"I'll send John. He knows what to get. Junior can go, too. It'll be good training for the kid."

"Junior likes to play detective."

"I'll wait until they get back before talking to Dallas. I don't want to shake him up if he's innocent, and I don't want him calling one of his dumbass uncles if he's not.

"Good idea," she said.

I noticed a copy of Robert Parker's new *Jesse Stone* novel lying on her desk; a plastic coated bookmark with a red tassel stuck out of the top.

"And I guess, somewhere along the line, I have to discuss this with the mayor."

"I guess that would be nice," she said, with a touch of good-natured sarcasm.

"Maybe you should do that for me," I suggested, followed by a smile designed to win friends and influence women.

"Do whot?" She gave me a look that could kill.

"God, you sound like such a local."

* * * *

"Okay, John, I want you to go to Chattanooga and scrounge up any paperwork anyone has on this. And interview anyone who worked on the case—anyone. You've got a few names already. See if you can get more."

"Okay, Boss."

"Take Junior with you. Teach him how to be a world-class detective. And his ID will get you through any door if someone questions your auxiliary police status."

"No sweat."

"You ever been to Chattanooga?" I asked.

"Didn't I pass *Shattanooga* coming up from Florida on I-75?"

"You did. It's about two hours south of here off the Interstate. Junior should know his way around pretty good. Drive me home tonight, and you can take my car. Start out early, and you can put in a voucher for meal money. I'll give you a credit card for gas."

"I can take your car? I didn't think you'd let anyone use your car."

"Well, you can use it, but if you eat lunch in my car and I find any crumbs, I'll kill you."

"Okay, Boss, don't get excited. You're not getting any younger, and you need to watch your blood pressure."

"My blood pressure has been the same for thirty years."

"How do you know, Boss? You never go to the doctor."

"You're pushing your luck, John."

The aging leprechaun grinned at me like an alligator eyeing up a tethered goat.

"Okay, Boss. I'll shut up now since you said I can put in for meal money. Wow, you're too good to me."

"Hey, don't even think about some super expensive meal. And teach Junior. Do not corrupt him. Understand?"

"Sure, Boss. Trust me."

Never trust someone who says, "Trust me."

* * * *

That afternoon I looked up to find Junior Huskey staring into my office with a sheepish, embarrassed expression.

"Hey, kid, what's up?"

"I talk with ya a minute, Sam?"

"Sure, what's wrong?"

He walked in and sat in front of my desk.

"John called me 'bout tomorra. I kindly like got a problem with that."

That surprised me. "What's the problem? You don't want to work with John?"

He took off his green PPD ball cap and ran a hand over his short dark hair.

"No, sir, I got me a problem investigatin' Dallas."

"Ah, the thin blue line rears its head," I said.

That expression didn't register with him.

"Do what?"

"One cop not wanting to look into another cop's possible illegalities."

"I guess."

"Age old story, kid. Look at it this way. Suppose Dallas went out with your sister—either before or after he got to be a cop. And suppose he raped her. How would that make you feel?"

34

"Not so good, I guess. I jest don't wanna be the guy who's known for havin' went behind his back lookin' into what a girl said he done."

Junior had just turned thirty but still looked about nineteen.

"I think it's time to grow up, Junior. All our lives would be simpler if we hadn't received this complaint about one of our own. No matter how it plays out, this stinks."

He nodded and raised his eyebrows.

"No one's going to be a winner in the end," I said. "But we have the reputation of Prospect PD to think about. If Dallas did rape someone and he got away with it and he stays employed here, then all of us—you, me, Bettye, Stanley and every other cop here will be looked at by people who don't know us as potentially guilty of something. Tell me that idea doesn't stink."

Junior wrinkled his brow and looked at me like I just told him we were investigating Santa Claus for pedophilia.

"Look at it this way," I continued. "Suppose Dallas didn't rape the girl? Suppose if we just dropped this and his innocence is never established with some amount of certainty? Don't you think he'd like someone to put out a little effort and clear his name so he can tell the world that he's not guilty of anything?"

Junior shrugged.

"Conversely," I said, "if he is a rapist, we didn't do anything wrong by establishing that, and then we let the chips fall where they may."

"Aw, shoot, Sam. I gotta go?" When Junior worked the street, he acted like an adult, a professional cop. When he kvetched about something he didn't like, he looked more like a little kid.

"You don't *gotta* do anything. I'd like you to go and help John. I'd like you guys to do a thorough, impartial investigation. I think you're honest and smart enough to do investigative work."

"Okay. If you want."

I hoped it was what he wanted.

"Thanks. I think John would like some help getting this squared away. I'm guessing he feels that some other cops may have snowed him when he did Dallas's background investigation, and he let this one get by unnoticed. He needs to resolve this one way or the other. It's kind of a reputation thing with detectives."

Junior nodded, but he didn't look very happy with his new assignment.

* * * *

I didn't see John or Junior the next day. That surprised me, so I prepared myself for their requests for overtime. The next morning, John strolled into my office with a dumber than usual look on his face, and Junior Huskey following him with a bottle of Mountain Dew in his hand. Before sitting down, Gallagher spent a moment with Mr. Coffee.

They both stood in front of my desk. Junior said nothing. John started off with a sip of coffee.

Then he said, "What a bag of worms we found in Shattanooga."

"Sit," I sighed, "I can't wait for my life to get more complicated."

"First, we went to see the campus police," John said and crossed his legs. "Nice little place they got there. All we got was a file card with Dorie's name on it, a date of the complaint and the names of the county dicks who picked up the squeal. It didn't say much, so we looked for this Sharla Hatfield. Not a bad lookin' girl if she lost twenty pounds. Right, Junior?"

Junior sat upright. He shrugged and then nodded, still not looking overly enthused over their trip to Chattanooga.

"Sharla's a sergeant now." John smiled. "Wonder how she got promoted?"

I could see where the gist of the conversation was heading.

"She was off duty, but the chief called her in to talk with us," John said.

I watched a ladybug start walking north across my desktop. When John began his story, she was about three inches from the left edge.

"I asked what she saw that night. She gave us the basic story that sounded copasetic with everything else we've heard. But then I asked her why she told Dorie not to stick with the prosecution. And she says she thought Dorie would have a problem with the trial because the defense might bring up the fact she slept around. So I asked how she knew Dorie slept around. And she bobbed and weaved and said something like, well, you know how these college girls are. That wasn't good enough for us. Right, Junior?"

36

Junior nodded again and drained his plastic Mountain Dew bottle.

"So," John continued, "I pressed her, and she admitted that a county dick, a guy named Arlis Hitson, called her and told her that if Dorie ever spoke to her again, she should recommend dropping the complaint." He sipped from his coffee cup and grinned like a weasel. "Whaddaya think, Boss?"

I asked John to spell *Hitson* and jotted down the name of a new player in our saga.

"I think," I said, "at the very least you've got a lazy-assed squad dick who didn't want to send time in a sex crime he didn't consider a slam-dunk."

"Maybe," John said.

Junior seemed content to listen. He played with the cap of his soda bottle, twisting it on and off.

"What did Sergeant Sharla think about Dorie's condition the night she made the complaint?" I asked.

"She danced around a little more, but when we pressed her," John said, "she admitted Dorie looked like she had gotten tuned up pretty good. You tell him the rest, Junior."

Junior blinked a couple times as if he just woke up. "Uh, I asked her if the victim just got hurt or if she looked like she'd been raped." Junior shifted in his chair and prepared to pick up the story. "Sharla said she stayed with Dorie all through the deal in the hospital, and she figgered Dorie looked like she'd been raped. The preliminary tests they took in the hospital showed semen on her."

"And Sharla stuck with her story about Dorie having a hard time with cross examination?" I asked.

"No, she backed off a little," John said. "She didn't admit being pressured into making the statement, just that this guy, *Hickson*, called her and gave her instructions."

"You mean Hitson?"

John looked at me like I had two heads. "Yeah, that's what I said."

Junior smiled.

"Did you get to see him? Hitson, I mean."

The ladybug had made almost two feet of progress.

"Yeah, well not exactly." Gallagher picked up the conversation again. "We went to the Hamilton County sheriff's place and got shuffled around some while we tried to explain what we were doing. Finally, we get to see one of the detectives who handled the case, not Hickson, but his partner, a guy named Bing Rigsby. Almost like Bing Crosby, huh, Boss?"

"Yeah, John, almost." I rolled my eyes and added Rigsby's name to my list.

The ladybug stopped at the edge of my phone. She wouldn't go right or left to get around it. She just stopped there.

"This guy," John said, "gets almost as defensive as our poly examiner, like he's annoyed we're asking. He tells us they didn't see any signs of force. He says the girl just changed her mind after it was all over. He said he wanted to charge her with falsely reporting an incident, but his partner, *Hickman*, didn't want to waste their time."

I didn't bother to question *Hickman*. I know better.

John continued. "Then we get something else I didn't know before." He set his empty cup on the edge of my desk. "And this is even stranger. Right, Junior?"

Junior nodded again, but didn't look any happier than when he walked in.

"This guy Rigsby says he wrote up the arrest papers and sent it to the DA. He showed me their case file. It had a detention log in it. Dallas was in custody for over four hours before he got ROR'ed." His weasel grin came back again. "Weird, huh?"

"What happened to the arrest?" I spread my hands out to the side. "Why didn't we get anything back on it?"

"I'm gettin' to that," he said. "Who gets ROR before arraignment on a violent felony?" He did the same thing with his hands. "There was no paperwork on the rape kit or info on the hospital visit of the girl either. Next, this guy Rigsby, he says he thinks the arrest was sealed because Dallas was a first-time offender and the complainant failed to prosecute. And that's why we never learned anything about an arrest."

"And this Detective Rigsby disagrees with Sergeant Sharla's opinion about Dorie being obviously beaten up?"

"So he says. But wait, there's more." John sounded a little excited.

"You sound like Billy Mays," I said.

"Willie Mays?" Now he looked confused.

"Never mind. Keep talking."

John continued. "Okay, so we get finished with the sheriff's guys, and we go to the DA's office in the new courts building. Finally," he drew out the word for effect, "we get to talk with a female investigator. Nice girl, but she's new and says she wasn't around when the rape got reported. But she goes to look for the file for us. More weird stuff now." John looked proud of himself; he was on a roll. "She's gone about twenty minutes and never comes back. But, an ADA does, and he tells us the case is sealed, and we can't see anything. So I give him the general release Dallas signed, and because I'm so sharp, the specific release I had him sign for records pertaining to the rape charge." John paused, waiting for me to comment.

"That was sharp, John. You've still got the old stuff, huh?"

He shot me a big grin.

"Are you learning from this old duff, Junior?"

"Yes, sir, I'm learnin' all kinds o' stuff here."

John continued, "So this ADA goes and looks for the case, and then he comes back looking a little nervous and jerky and kinda embarrassed. He says they can't find the case. Just an empty folder."

I closed my eyes and shook my head.

John kept talking. "He said he'd have to start some people looking around, but he couldn't guarantee they'd find anything—least not on that day. Whaddaya think, Boss?"

"I think this sucks, John. Son-of-a-bitch, huh?"

I slammed my hand down on my blotter. The ladybug jumped, took flight and landed on the window overlooking the reception area.

"You know, guys," I said, "Sometimes cops are our worst enemies."

John said, "I hear ya, Boss."

Junior remained quiet but nodded.

"What did they say at the hospital?"

"Oh, yeah, they were a lot better than the cops. Right, Junior?"

"They were." Junior nodded. "We found us an old head nurse whose nephew is a Chattanooga city cop. She was right he'pful."

"Tell me."

John picked up the narrative again. "She got us the file and then explained all the medical stuff we couldn't understand. They didn't have the lab results of the rape kit—which seems to have been lost by the county dicks between the hospital and their lab, but know what's the best stuff, Boss?"

"I couldn't even hazard a guess, John. Tell me."

"Besides doing the regular preliminary tests for a rape, they took a couple of pictures of Dorie. They show the messed up hair, the bright red cheek, and her thighs were red, too. And they probably did get black and blue in a day or so, like Laura said."

"Would they give you copies of anything?"

"Boss, that hurts. You think we'd leave without them?"

"What was I thinking, John? Shame on me."

John smiled, and his head bobbed back and forth. "This head nurse called another nurse who was on duty that night. I spoke to her on the phone. She remembered the incident and said she had no doubt that Dorie was raped. She witnessed the doctor taking the smear, too. That and the wipes on her thigh tested positive for semen."

"How about the doctor? Did you find him or her?"

"Him, yeah. He was a resident back then. But now he's working at a walk-in clinic on the other side of town. We went there. Right, Junior?"

"Yes, sir, we shore did."

"Are you two working up a vaudeville act? Are you going to tell me or wait for a drum roll?"

"You know, Boss, they must make millions each day in those walk-in clinics. There were dozens of people in the waiting room, and more walked in every minute."

"John, am I going to have to strangle you to get an answer?"

"Have patience, Boss. Ha, like a clinic, have patients."

I closed my eyes and let my chin hit my chest. I groaned.

"Okay, Boss, don't get excited. Between patients, we talked to the doctor. Young guy. He acted like he was in a hurry, but he remembered the incident and gave us a quick statement. As far as he was concerned, she was raped. But he made sure we knew he didn't know who did it. He sounded like he didn't want to get involved in court, but he'd swear that it looked like Dorie had been sexually assaulted."

"See, Junior, guys like John are never too old to do good detective work. We never forget. Right, John?"

"Right, Boss. It's like falling off a bicycle. You never forget how."

* * * *

After John walked out of my office, Junior remained sitting in the chair in front of my desk. He played with the empty soda bottle, still twisting the cap that didn't need tightening.

"That cap isn't going to get any tighter, kid."

"Oh yeah, I guess."

"Something wrong?"

"I guess I should apologize for not wanting to go with John."

"No need. You went. And you guys did a good job."

"Sam, after hearin' all we heard, I guess I'm thinkin' that Dallas really did rape that girl. I jest cain't believe that. Dallas is a pretty nice guy."

"Yes, he is. And I'm inclined to say you're right. He probably did what he's accused of doing."

"You ever have to do something like this before?"

"Similar, but not exactly the same."

"It's not easy for you either, is it?"

"That's why I get the big bucks, kid."

"What's gonna happen?"

"I'm not sure yet. I'm guessing nothing good."

Chapter Eight

"Sammy, I don't know if it's good news or bad news, but, darlin', this one's for you," Bettye said before forwarding a call to my line.

"Good mornin', Sam. You doin' all right today?"

I recognized the voice immediately. "Hello, Judge. Yeah, I'm fine. You doing well?"

"Yes, sir, I am, I am indeed. Sam, I called to see if you had any more news about this Dallas Finchum affair."

"Yes, sir. I'll take it from the top, so when I repeat something I've already told you, bear with me."

I told Judge Tipton what we had learned so far about the rape and Hamilton County's investigation...or lack thereof.

"I thought we were getting a run-around from the law enforcement people in Hamilton County who were involved with the case," I said. "And now, the polygraph examiner up here in Blount County is doing the same. I sent a couple of men down to Chattanooga to dig into this. Simply put, the people down there were pathetic. They're screwing around trying to cover this up and weren't competent enough to erase their tracks. We've got enough paperwork from the hospital and statements from the medical personnel to establish that she was probably raped, and then the cops not only dropped the ball, they hid it. It's hard not to smell fish when it rots."

"You're convinced that we're looking at an intentional cover-up, probably requested by someone acting on young Finchum's behalf?"

No one was watching me, but I shrugged. "It's hard to think

42

otherwise. If I looked at this as strictly a criminal matter, one that would move through the system in the usual way, I'd say there was certainly enough probable cause to sustain an indictment and go to trial. But, as my senior investigator so aptly put it, this is a bag of worms."

"I agree, Sam. I agree indeed. You have more than enough cause to consider the complaint against Finchum credible. What are you going to do?"

"I thought I should give the cops involved another chance to make things right on their end. I sent John Gallagher down to Chattanooga to investigate this. He's got enough experience to know the facts of life when he sees them."

The judge interrupted. "Gallagher is that feller you hired as a clerk-typist?"

"Correct. The ex-detective who needed a job."

"I'd like to meet him some day."

"I think he's a man you'll never forget."

"Sam, I interrupted you. Please continue."

"I thought that if John spoke with the detectives who handled the case, in a cop-to-cop situation, they may have given him a wink and told him the real story. Unfortunately, he got stonewalled. It also seems that those detectives influenced, at the very least, the female officer at the campus police, perhaps even her chief. So, they too have been compromised. Then all the cops handed everything off to the Hamilton County DA. And they conveniently lost the case file."

"You spoke of a polygraph examination right here in Blount County. What happened there?"

"We spoke to a Detective Dietzen just the other day. That conversation was much the same as the Chattanooga run-around. When John and I interviewed Dietzen, he got overly defensive. After a few more minutes of conversation, he turned downright obnoxious. I can understand him trying to protect his professional reputation, but his behavior was so over the top, I can only think, he protesteth too much."

"So what happens next, Sam?"

"I'll do what I always do. I'll keep on looking and keep on stirring a pot that other people obviously do not want me to mess with. I'll start with officially requesting the polygraph charts for a second opinion."

43

"I understand. If I were you, I'd do the same. But, Sam, be careful here. I'll not try to dissuade you from getting to the bottom of this. But, son, I will tell you to be careful. Plenty of people with real power will oppose you. And they don't play by the rules. Well, maybe they do, but they're rules made up as they go along. And they're rules you'll have trouble winning with."

I was beyond the beginning of a world-class tension headache. "I've been through things like this before. I understand dirty fighting."

"I know you do, Sam. I know what you're capable of. But there are a couple of people involved on the fringes that aren't part of the crowd I have influence over. Understand what I'm sayin'?"

Again, I thought, why me? "I do."

"I'll try and run interference for you, if I can, but these people are— what would you call them—loose cannons? Be careful, son. I mean that."

"I'm not at the point of asking a favor from you, Judge, but if you have occasion to speak with anyone on the roster of this game, you may want to remind them I've gotten very friendly with people in the Federal Bureau of Investigation. Those are the ones I can dump this whole thing on if I find my little police department overwhelmed, and we can't settle this thing in-house. The FBI loves to take over these local corruption cases. Small time politicians make tasty finger-food for assistant US attorneys who have their sights trained on bigger and better careers."

"Point taken, Sam. I understand indeed. I'll keep that in mind, and when you think you need that favor you call—any time."

Chapter Nine

"Sit down, Sam. Sit down," he said, pointing to one of the green leather chairs in front of his desk.

The mayor dropped into an oversized burgundy leather swivel chair behind a walnut topped workstation resembling a small aircraft carrier, in front of the big bay window overlooking the Prospect town square. He leaned back, sighed and almost touched his sprayed, immobile dark blond hair. Touching Ronnie's hair would have been a capital offense had it been entered in the book of city ordinances.

I hesitated and remained standing. I wanted a psychological advantage over him. I wanted Ronnie Shields to feel like a suspect and not my boss. I wanted him to feel pangs of guilt for insisting that I hire Dallas Finchum.

"As my assistant so correctly called it, Ron, this whole situation is a *bag of worms*. Actually, I think the more commonly defined term is a *can of worms*, but you know John and his problems with the English language."

Ronnie nodded and waited for me to continue.

"I'm guessing the one phone call Dallas was allowed after the Hamilton County detectives arrested him went to someone who started this dirty little political machine running at full speed."

"Sam, I'm embarrassed to remind you that we on the Council earmarked the PO's job for this Finchum boy. I can only apologize to you. I assure you, we're behind you a-hunnert pa-cent in resolving this situation."

45

I had planned on chewing him out, and he beat me to the punch by apologizing. He took half the fun out of what I had to say. I collapsed into the green chair.

"There's only one thing, Sam. I hope you can resolve this with as little adverse publicity as possible and with as little intrusion into other places, too."

"I assume you're referring to all the times that personnel at WNXX aired stories about the incidents in Prospect."

"Well, uh, I guess, uh, we'd all rather not see us look foolish at six or eleven o'clock." His bright blue eyes blinked more rapidly than a hooker closing in on a client. Ronnie was feeling the stress.

"I understand, and I can tell you the victim's mother has already called WNXX advising them about the original incident. It's only because I have a good relationship with people there that this hasn't already been on the news."

"And don't think we don't appreciate you asking her to hold off on the story."

Why would he assume I spoke to a 'her'?

"If Dallas persists in denying the rape allegations, I'll need some hefty horsepower to get the other jurisdictions to turn over the reports that are mysteriously missing. If you or whomever you call can convince Dallas to take responsibility for his past actions and just resign, I believe I can talk the victim and her mother into being satisfied with that."

Ronnie didn't look like he felt confident about having all the other politicos in the palm of his hand. I pressed him further.

"Without Dallas's cooperation," I said, "the complainant can demand he be prosecuted. The rape happened three years ago, and technically a prosecution was initiated, so even the five-year statute of limitations on a felony can be extended."

Ronnie closed his eyes, shook his head and looked terribly troubled.

"In any event, I believe the boy should be suspended. It will look more proper to anyone who sees this unfolding. It's your option whether it's a suspension with or without pay."

The mayor sighed, and his shoulders dropped three inches. "I'll call an emergency meetin' of the Council, and I'll have an answer for ya tomorrow about the pay. But, by all means, Sam, tell the boy he's under suspension. Make that effective immediately. Yes, sir, immediately."

Ronnie can be so forceful at times.

* * * *

Dallas Finchum was scheduled to work a midnight tour that day, so I called his home. His mother answered and told me she would bring her son to the phone.

A minute or two later I heard, "Who's this?" I didn't recognize the voice.

"I beg your pardon?"

"I said, who's this. This is Billy Ray Finchum, Dallas is my son. Who am I talkin' ta?"

"This is Chief Jenkins from the Prospect Police. May I speak to Dallas, please?"

"You may not! You have nothin' ta say ta my boy. Anythin' y'all have ta say, ya kin say it ta our lawyer."

That surprised me.

"Mr. Finchum, I'm your son's employer. Are you suggesting I communicate with him through an attorney? That's absurd."

"I happen ta know y'all are investigatin' some trumped-up charge ag'inst my boy. That's a charge already proved false by the po-leece, and it was made by a damn liar."

"Sounds like news travels fast, doesn't it?"

"Do what?"

"Mr. Finchum, I have police business to discuss with your son. Are you going to put him on the phone or not?"

"I done tol' ya ta speak with our attorney, Mr. Robbie J. Blanchard of Murr-vull."

"Okay, Mr. Finchum, have it your way. I have no interest in speaking with your lawyer at this time. Tell your son that as of right now he is suspended from duty. You can inform your lawyer whenever you want. Dallas can expect a registered letter notifying him of the official suspension. That will be in the mail today. I'll have a supervisor drive to your home this afternoon to pick up his badge, ID card and his issue handgun. Make sure he's there, or I'll have a court order served mandating him to return that city property forthwith. Thanks for your time." I slammed down the receiver.

* * * *

At 3:30 that afternoon, Sergeants Bettye Lambert, Stan Rose and I sat in my office discussing Dallas Finchum.

"Stan, take another man with you—around dinnertime would be good—and pick up Dallas's badge, gun and ID."

"You da boss, white man, but how come I gots ta do dis?"

"Because, my large brown friend, Old Man Finchum seems to hate me already. I can't understand why. I'm such a nice guy and all. Make sure you give him a receipt."

"Is there any chance this will just go away?" Bettye asked.

"Well," I said, "Ronnie and the City Council had good intentions. They'd be happy to let Dallas resign and fade into the background with as little adverse publicity as possible. But as I've learned, the news of our investigation got back here from Chattanooga before John and Junior could burn up the blacktop on I-75. I also wouldn't put it past Charlie Dietzen from the Sheriff's CID to have made a call as well. I'd bet he was on the phone as soon as John and I cleared his doorway."

Bettye shook her head and looked like she was waiting for the sky to fall. Stanley took it more stoically.

"If you ever meet Billy Ray Finchum, you'll see how enthused he is about bumping heads with me over this," I said. "Talk about an over-protective parent."

"It sounds like the kid should just cut his losses and hope he doesn't end up in court," Stan said.

"You spoke to the girl's mother, Sam," Bettye said. "Did she talk about wanting him rearrested?"

"Not yet. The mother is mad. She thinks Dallas is a rapist and shouldn't be a cop. It's tough to argue with that. You spoke to Dorie more than I did. Didn't she seem reluctant to rehash this business?"

"Sure she did. If her mother hadn't called, she never would have complained again."

"But who knows," I said, "what might happen if this goes public and some ambulance chaser smells a big contingency fee and suggests to the Ashers that civil court may offer the biggest pound of flesh."

"What's the kid thinking?" Stan asked. "Does he assume his uncles have enough horsepower to keep the whole world quiet about this?"

"As far as I can tell, Uncle Buck is a dead issue. He most often lives in Florida, and everyone would be happy to see him stay there. He was an embarrassment to everyone who supported him. Uncle Claude is another story. He's still on the County Commission and keeps getting reelected. And he's tight with Micah Blevins, the chairman of the Commission. Lord knows, I'm not one of his favorite people."

Stan laughed, and Bettye gave me a look mothers reserve for their problem children.

"Maybe Claude's got all the power," I said. "Personally, I don't see it, but somebody pulled the strings to get this squashed, and someone still has enough umpf to warrant a quick call from the Hamilton County DA's office."

Stanley shrugged, and Bettye continued to look like her tidy little world was crumbling down around us.

"Either of you know what Billy Ray Finchum does for a living?" I asked. "Maybe it's him or one of his relatives."

Stan shrugged again and shook his head.

"He's an Airport Authority fireman. A lieutenant, I think," Bettye said. "And I understand he hangs with all the politically correct people in the county."

"Great," I said, "a professional envelope stuffer. Well, someone's got a lot of juice. But power or not, I can't see how these people think they can keep the press from knowing."

"If we could make Billy Rae just go away, this might resolve itself," Bettye said.

I shook my head. "Dorie's mother already called WNXX. It's only because Rachel called me first that it's not been on TV. We've got a very small window of opportunity to convince Dallas to do the right thing—if his father and the family lawyer will allow us to speak with the kid. Otherwise, who's to stop Mrs. Asher from calling the other stations or the papers?"

"Only one way I can think of," Stan said.
Bettye opened her eyes as wide as they could go.
I rolled my eyes. Stan sipped his coffee.
"Don't even think that," I said.

Chapter Ten

The next morning, Ronnie Shields called to tell me about the Council voting to suspend Dallas Finchum with full pay until the matter got resolved.

At ten-after-ten, I was on the phone to the director's office at the Tennessee Bureau of Investigation. His secretary put my call through immediately.

"Dooley Barlow speakin'. How kin I he'p ya?"

"Mr. Barlow, my name is Sam Jenkins. I'm the chief at Prospect PD in Blount County. How are you this morning?"

"Well now, I'm real fine. Yes, sir, real fine. But look here, Sam, y'all kin call me Dooley, okay?"

"That's kind of you, Dooley. I wonder if I could ask a favor."

"Well, you surely can, Sam. Ya know, we've not met, but I've heard all about you and what you're doin' in Prospect. They were good things, Sam. Yes, sir, real good things."

Yeah, Dooley, old buddy. I'll bet you have.

"Well, thanks again, sir. It's nice to hear that I have at least one fan hiding in a woodpile who's not afraid to say they know me."

Dooley chuckled at my self-deprecating humor.

"The favor I have to ask deals with a rather delicate matter I'm investigating. It's sort of an internal affairs kind of thing, if you know what I'm saying."

"Well, yessir, yessir, I surely do. And how can the TBI he'p ya?"

I remembered someone telling me that Dooley Barlow had been a trooper sergeant with excellent political connections, but no one knew of

51

him ever doing any detective work.

"Since I'm investigating a local cop, I don't want to put another local officer on the spot and ask for their expertise on a subject of which I personally have little technical knowledge. I thought, perhaps, you could lend me one of your polygraph examiners to interpret the charts done by the Blount County examiner to see if somehow my subject may have beaten or cheated the machine. I'd hate to ask the local examiner to admit that maybe someone fooled his machine." I took a moment to sigh for a theatrical effect. "I wouldn't want to embarrass another detective, if you know what I mean."

If someone said that to me, I would have gagged and hung up on him.

"Sam, I understand what you're sayin'. I surely do. I've got a real fine polygraph man here, a senior agent who's got family right there in Blount County. I'll have him he'p ya out, and he can visit with his people all at the same time. How's that?"

"Dooley, you're a fine American. I don't know how to thank you. Just ask your agent to give me a call, and we can set up a meeting."

Dooley and I spent a few more minutes exchanging pleasantries. We spoke about fly-fishing for trout in my neck of the woods. To me you swat a fly, not cast it. I was always more of a saltwater bluefish and striped bass fisherman. Then we parted company, the best of friends.

* * * *

On the afternoon of the second day after my conversation with Dooley Barlow, I waited for TBI agent and polygraph examiner, D.L. "Butch" Cobbins to arrive in Prospect.

I sat in the lobby with Bettye and John Gallagher. Ronnie kept his calendar open and waited for us in his office.

At 1:30, a tall, balding man in his late-forties with a comb-over almost as bad as Charlie Dietzen's showed up. He wore a light tan blazer and black pants just a little too short for his long legs.

"Hey," he said "How y'all doin'?" He showed us his credentials.

"Hello," I said. "This is Sergeant Bettye Lambert, Detective John Gallagher, and I'm Sam Jenkins, the chief here. Thanks for coming to help."

We shook hands all around.

"The mayor would like to sit in on our conversation and learn some of the mysteries of the polygraph," I said. "So, let's take a walk upstairs, and I'll introduce you to His Excellency."

Butch smiled, and his shoulders moved up and down a little in a silent laugh. I suppose he thought I was comically irreverent.

As we ascended the marble staircase to the hallowed second floor, he asked, "Y'all want me to do a test for ya?"

"Not exactly. As soon as we let the mayor in on the discussion, I'll have him call the county sheriff, and we'll have a chart picked up. I'd like you to review it."

He gave me a confused look.

After Ms. Connor, the mayor's secretary, ushered us into Ronnie's office, more introductions were made, and Butch again heard more thanks for his help. I began with my full explanation.

"Butch, as I started to tell you on the way up, the mayor will call the sheriff and arrange for you to see a chart the sheriff's examiner generated on a pre-employment test. I believe that examiner may have missed an important point. And he most likely didn't catch a deception. New evidence now contradicts his findings."

"Do whot now?" Butch began the telltale fidgeting of an uncomfortable man.

I tried again, with a little less flourish. "I think the sheriff's man screwed up. We have incontrovertible evidence that the subject of that test lied. I want to give both the subject and the detective the benefit of the doubt and have you review the chart to see if, you know, he missed an obvious lie."

"You want me to second guess another examiner?"

His remark came out almost like a gasp. I didn't think I asked something unreasonable, but old Butch obviously felt exceedingly uncomfortable with my request.

I glanced at Ronnie, whose expression looked like someone who just heard that they cancelled Christmas this year.

"Yes, the detective acted very defensive when I asked if he could have made a mistake. He refused to even look at the chart. So I called your boss, and he called you."

That wasn't a very long or complicated explanation, but Butch squirmed in his chair more with every word. His face paled a bit, and he automatically grabbed for his pack of Marlboros.

"Gee, I'm sorry, Butch," I said before he could strike a flame from his plastic Bic. "But you can't smoke in the building."

That seemed to cause him even more distress.

I knew what he would say next.

Butch looked at the mayor, who had yet to speak on the subject, and then back at me, and once more back at Ronnie, who's much friendlier looking than I am.

"Uh…Mr. Mayor, uh…Mr…uh, Chief…I, uh, uh, have a problem passing judgment on another officer…uh, examiner, after they conducted a test and offered an opinion. That's kindly like actin' like Internal Affairs."

Ronnie was about to speak, but I interrupted.

"Agent Cobbins," I said, "experts look over other expert's findings all the time. Anyone can make a mistake. We're not asking you to testify in open court. We're just looking to see if a man who we hired lied to a polygraph examiner—and the examiner missed the lie. Something that could happen to anybody. That's all."

If I'm any good at reading facial expressions, I would say Ronnie yearned for me to fix a situation that appeared totally lost.

"Maybe the subject learned how to beat the box—alter his breathing, step on a tack at the right moment, anything." I said. "In that case, the examiner isn't at fault. But maybe the examiner just had a bad day. I'll say again, it can happen to anybody. I don't know. If the detective screwed up, okay, I'm not his supervisor, and I don't care. I do care that we may have been lied to."

I got a little impatient with Butch being so namby-pamby. He just looked at me like a deer caught in the headlights.

"Look, I'm not going to fire anyone," I said, "or discipline another man's cop based on what you say. I'll just take your information under advisement, and if you think there may have been deception involved, I'll continue to investigate."

"Like I said, Chief, I'm not comfortable with any o' this. No one told me I had ta review another man's work. I don't want to get a reputation for putting another man on the spot."

Ronnie was again about to speak. Again I interrupted.

"Is that your final answer?"

Jeez, I sounded like Regis Philbin.

"I guess, I . . ." He played with the knot of his tie, trying to loosen it a little.

"Fine," I said. "If you don't like the idea of finding the truth, I guess I couldn't trust what you might tell me. Thanks for your time. And thank your boss for sending you."

I stood up and opened the door to Ronnie's office. "Good to meet you. Remember your way to the parking lot?"

Butch Cobbins left with his head a bit lower than when he arrived. I sat down and looked at Ronnie.

"What a chicken-shit son-of-a-bitch," I said. "I've seen guys with no balls before, but he's right up in the top ten."

Ronnie looked like he was about to pass out. "Did you not explain what you needed to the TBI director?"

I took a deep breath and didn't scream. "Of course I explained. What happened after I hung up is anyone's guess."

Ronnie raised his shoulders back up to normal level. "What do we do now?"

He did not look like a happy mayor. Or one with an idea of his own.

"There's always the FBI, but they usually want to take over total jurisdiction when you ask for assistance. We'll hold them on the back burner for now, but they're always there if we end up against a stone wall."

"Oh, Lord have mercy, Sam."

"I feel my diplomatic skills quickly sliding downhill," I said. "Will you call Sheriff Hartung, explain the situation, and have one of his chief deputies—I'm assuming they'd be trustworthy—grab Finchum's file and polygraph chart before Detective Charlie Dietzen can lose that one like the boys in Hamilton County lost their case folder. As soon as Hartung has it in hand, I'll send someone over to pick it up."

"What will you do with the charts? You know how to read them?"

"No, I don't. It'll cost us a plane ticket, but I'll get a polygraph examiner here who knows what he's doing and has a pair of nuts between his legs."

"Not from the FBI? A civilian?"

"No, a cop. Oh, and, Ronnie, if Jo-Dee Hartung gives you any crap about borrowing his files, remind him that if our back goes up against the wall, I'll have no choice but to ask my good friends at the FBI to send us a polygraph expert from Quantico."

"You want me to threaten Joe Don Hartung with bringin' in the FBI? Lord have mercy, Sam."

"You're the diplomat, Ronnie, not me. I know Jo-Dee was never a cop before he got elected sheriff, but have him ask one of the old-timers in his office what happens when the Feds smell a police screw-up. They send a squad of agents, guys who just sharpened their fangs, out for local cop blood. He'll get the idea."

I didn't give Ronnie any more time to agree to what I asked. But since he didn't disagree, I figured we were on the same page.

* * * *

"I saw that TBI man walk out," Bettye said. "What happened?"

"Gutless bastard," I said. "He wasn't *comfortable* looking at another cop's work. I mean really."

When Bettye sees me upset she knows the best way to calm me down is to smile, bat her eyelashes and say nothing. It always works. I smiled back.

"Hey, John," I said. "Get me a phone number for the old job, will you?"

"Sure, Boss. Who ya callin'?"

"A couple of years ago when I got his Christmas card, Vinnie Falcone told me he transferred from our old office to the polygraph unit. I'll get him down here."

"No kiddin'? Vinnie's a polygraph examiner now?"

"No, John. That was an elaborate lie to see if I could fool you."

"See how mean he gets when he's mad, Sarge?" Gallagher said to Bettye.

"I know, John," she said, "but isn't he beautiful when he's angry?"

I laughed. "Okay, you guys got me. I apologize, John, but I still think you're an insufferable whittling."

"Gee thanks, Boss. Flattery will get you everywhere."

"And you," I said, looking at Bettye, "now I hate you as much as Gallagher."

"Oh, surely you don't mean that, Sammy, darlin'?" The eyelashes went back into action.

"No, surely not. Only an idiot would hate the beautiful woman he spends his days with."

"Well, aren't yew jest so sweet?"

* * * *

Ten minutes later, I sat in my office on the telephone.

"Polygraph Unit, Sergeant Murdoch."

A picture of the old main office building flashed through my mind. The polygraph unit was on the second floor a couple doors down from the Chief of Detectives' office.

"Hi, Sarge, my name's Sam Jenkins. I retired from the job in '92. I'm looking for Vinnie Falcone. Is he working today?"

"You were a dick lieutenant up here, weren't you?"

Perhaps I found an old fan.

"I was," I said.

"I remember you teaching something at the Academy. Right?"

I hoped he didn't remember failing one of my tests.

"Yeah, I used to do the guest lecture thing."

"Sure, some criminal law classes and something on use of informants. Right."

"Right again. You've got a good memory. When did you go through the Academy?"

"I started in April of '85."

He still sounded friendly.

"So, you've got your twenty plus. Good for you. Must be hell working with an old coot like Falcone. What's he doing, staying around for forty?"

"Who knows? Pretty soon I expect him to pay the county to let him come to work. Can you imagine the pension he could get to stay home?"

"Just thinking about it puts me into a higher tax bracket. Is he around today?"

"Yeah, I saw him bullshittin' with Tony Krecko in the Chief of Detectives' office."

"Jeez, I remember Anton. He's been on almost as long as Vinnie. Two ex-second precinct cops. Say hello to him for me, will ya?"

"Okay, Loo. Hang on, and I'll get Vinnie."

Three minutes later, I heard a familiar voice.

"Hey, boss, what's goin' on?"

"Hi ya, Vinnie." I told him the story I'd grown tired of repeating.

"Yeah," he said, "some of these polygraph guys are hot shit. They worry about getting' excommunicated from the examiner's association or somethin'."

"So, can you get a few days off and come down to beautiful downtown Prospect?"

"Sure, I'll take a few sick days. I've got more in the bank than they'll ever pay me for when I retire. How do I get my ticket?"

"I'll have John Gallagher make arrangements to have one waiting for you at the counter at MacArthur. He'll call you with the details."

"I heard old sausage belly was workin' for you again. It'll be like old home week, huh?"

"Yeah, we'll find a few good places to eat."

I remembered how Vinnie, a perpetually thin guy, never finished his meals. That drove me crazy. My mother always wanted me to clean my plate.

"Same old Sam. You gettin' fat yet?"

"Not yet, but I keep eating."

"I thought you would. Okay, this all sounds good. Want me to bring anything?"

"Can you get one of the spare machines?" I asked.

"I've got my own. I bought one, and I do pre-employment tests for a couple of the chain drug stores on my days off."

"You're going to be the richest guy on the job soon."

"Probably not, but I'm workin' on it."

"Okay, Vinnie, see ya."

Chapter Eleven

"What the hell you want now?" Billy Ray Finchum asked me.

"I'd like to speak to Dallas."

Again at my desk, I never got a chance to put my feet up and relax before Billy Ray pissed me off and had me on the edge of my seat.

"'Bout what?" he asked, bristling with bad attitude.

"Mr. Finchum, Dallas is an adult. He works for me. Stop treating him like a Cub Scout, and put him on the phone. If he tells me I should speak to him through his attorney, so be it. If he wants to hear what I have to say, let him tell me so."

"Think y'ur hot shit, don'tcha?"

I could only hope for a few minutes behind the diner with that guy.

"I think I'd like to speak with your son."

The phone dropped unceremoniously onto whatever surface the instrument stood upon.

A few moments later, I heard a sheepish, "Hello?"

"Dallas, this is Sam Jenkins. I'd like to speak with you."

"Yessir."

"Are you willing to hear me out, or do you want me to call your lawyer and tell him what I have in mind?"

"Nosir, I'll listen."

"Good. You know what's going on here. You know what Dorie's mother has called me about."

"Yessir, I do. I'm sorry this is happenin'. I'm just as sorry as I can be."

"Okay, kid, listen. When you got arrested, someone started making

59

phone calls, and a whole shitload of political stupidity fell on both Chattanooga and Blount County."

I paused for a moment, waiting for Dallas to reply. I heard nothing.

"Just tell me something," I said, "without your father's input, and I'll know how you feel. You once told me that the relationship between you and Dorie was just two kids consenting to sex in a dorm room. Is that right?"

Silence. I waited several long moments.

"Dallas?"

"Yessir?"

"Are we still working on your same story?"

Another few moments of silence.

"Yessir, that's right."

I had trouble believing him, but for the time being, I played along.

"Okay, here's an option. Right now it's she said—he said. How about taking another polygraph test? A test with a totally neutral examiner. If you're telling the truth and you take the test, and if you pass, you're forever vindicated." Well, maybe that was a stretch, but it sounded good at the time. "You could get your job back, and you can go on with your life. Would that work for you?"

Silence again. I had tired of those pauses in our conversation, but I understood the kid feeling like his head was in a vice.

"Sir, I'm so damn nervous, I don't know if I could take a polygraph test and not look like I was lyin' even if I just told the examiner my name. Can I get back with ya on this?"

"Yeah, sure you can. Take a little time. Talk with your lawyer, and call me before five o'clock tomorrow."

"Yessir, thank ya. I'll call."

Chapter Twelve

I called Vinnie Falcone on Tuesday. John Gallagher arranged for him to get an early flight from Islip-MacArthur Airport Thursday morning. Vinnie was scheduled to arrive, after a stop in Charlotte, at McGhee-Tyson Airport at 2 p.m. John drove fourteen miles to the airport to pick him up.

The back door to the PD opened, and a few seconds later something, a suitcase maybe, hit the floor. Then two sets of footsteps tapped down the hall toward my office and Bettye's reception area.

I walked to my doorway and saw John leading Vinnie Falcone into Prospect PD.

"Hey, boss, how's it goin'?" Vinnie said.

We hadn't seen each other in many years.

"Vinnie, paisan, how ya been?"

He grabbed my hand with both of his and shook it enthusiastically.

"Jeez, Vinnie, how long's it been? Seventeen, eighteen years now?"

"Yeah, I guess. I remember the day you retired and walked out. You dropped your car keys on Nancy's desk, and we all looked at each other. It felt like, I don't know, like they took somethin' away from us. We missed you, Sam. We were all happy for ya, but we wished ya never retired"

"I missed you guys, too. I missed the whole damn bunch of you."

After a moment of awkward silence, Bettye came to the rescue. She cleared her throat.

"Oh, Vinnie," I said, "I want you to meet somebody. We're not making a cop film here, but this movie star is my all-time favorite partner, Bettye Lambert. Betts, this is Vinnie Falcone, a still-employed detective from the old place where John and I used to work."

Vinnie, as usual, was dressed in a three-piece charcoal gray suit, white shirt and conservative striped tie. About sixty, he had mostly dark hair, not much of it, but with enough gray at his temples to make you think he worried a lot.

He shook Bettye's hand and offered a perfect greeting. "Nice to meet you, Sarge. I give you credit for workin' with these two guys and still lookin' sane and normal."

"Nice to meet you, too, Vinnie, but please call me Bettye. In Tennessee we're not very formal."

Vinnie activated his Italian smile. "Okay, Bettye. If you had seen us back on Long Island, you'd think we were anything but formal ourselves."

"You know, Sammy," Bettye said, "Vinnie is so well dressed, I'd have thought he worked for the FBI."

"Yeah, Betts, before he worked with us, Vinnie was a cop for Army CID. So, he's a Fed at heart. But don't pay much attention to him. He's just another Italian boy from Queens like Ralph Oliveri."

"Who's Ralph Oliveri?" Vinnie asked.

"A local FBI agent," I said. "We're all sort of friends."

"You're friends with a Fed? Jeez, what's next? You friends with a reporter, too? Where in Queens is he from?"

"South Ozone Park," I said.

"Hey, forgetaboutit," he said with an unmistakable city accent. Then he decided to give Bettye a brief Queens County civics lesson. "Bettye, Ozone Park and all those south shore places, that's strictly a swamp guinea location. I'm from Astoria on the north shore. The high-class part of Queens."

"Vinnie, I'll believe anything you tell me," she said and gave us all a smile capable of melting the frozen tundra.

"You've been on the road since early this morning," I said. "Have you eaten? You want coffee?"

"I ate somethin' before I left Charlotte. I'm okay. But if you've got a fresh pot, I could do a cuppa kawfee."

"Sure, Vinnie," John said, "we've always got coffee on. Let's go in the Boss's office and get a cup."

Those two disappeared into my office, and Bettye looked at me.

"He seems nice. I'm happy for you. I'm glad you and John have the opportunity to work with one of your friends again."

"Vinnie's a good man," I said. "He'll make a good polygraph examiner—an honest one."

"I'm almost afraid to hear what he says after he sees the polygraph reports."

"I guess it's time to find out." Bettye and I joined the other two in my office.

John and Vinnie sat in the guest chairs in front of my desk, each with a mug of coffee. Bettye took the side chair next to my desk.

I opened the evidence closet, took out the polygraph file and handed it to Vinnie. I moved away a few items and told him to spread out the chart on the wide surface of my desktop. He started by reading over the pre-test interview work sheet.

"This is an old Richard Arthur format worksheet," he said. "Probably hasn't changed much since right after World War Two. Just like the old-timers from our job did, lots of cops around the country went to his school. That was before the Army MP School opened up polygraph classes to civilian cops."

"Does it look like he asked the right questions?" I said.

"Yeah, these are pretty standard. He used the basic format to establish a rapport. You know, basic questions to warm up, and then more specifics. But I don't see anything pertainin' to a particular crime or sex act."

"Nothing on the pre-test? How about after the kid was hooked up to the box?"

"He roughed out seven questions for the machine. I think that's too many. I like to stick with five, six at the most—things requiring only yes or no answers. But these are general, nothing but catchalls. Let's look at the chart."

He took that document from the manila folder and spread it across the desk. Vinnie spent a couple of moments scanning the paper that spanned more than three feet. He shook his head several times."

"You've got one nervous subject here. This is his base-line," he said, pointing to one particular, wavy line stretching the length of the chart. "That's his heartbeat. It's way too high. Normal heartbeat is about seventy-two per. This guy's around a hundred. Way too high. He shouldn't have been tested. He's way too nervous and jerky.

"Look here," Vinnie continued. "This is a control question. You tell him to lie to see how he reacts on the machine. Like if I asked him, 'Are you ninety-five years old?' and tell him to say yes. I know that's false. It's gonna register a lie, but not like this. The needle almost went off the page. This was like asking Lee Harvey Oswald to lie about killing Kennedy."

He pulled the long sheet of paper to his left and pointed to another area.

"Now, look at this. Another simple control, maybe, 'Do you live in Tennessee?' That should be a no-reaction with a truthful answer. Not this guy. Every answer gets a wiggle. This boy was so nervous the test was invalid. The report should have said inconclusive.

"One last thing. The peak of tension question, maybe something like, 'did you lie to me even once today?' Another big wiggle. If he didn't lie, something was really bothering him."

"Any idea what?" I asked.

Vinnie shrugged and made a disgusted face. "His galvanic reaction is weird, too. This guy was lucky he didn't have a stroke while he was hooked up to the box."

"If he agrees to be tested again, do you think you can calm him down?" I asked.

Another shrug. "I can try. Not everyone can be tested. If this guy doesn't have faith in me and the machine, he may think he's getting' sandbagged and no matter what he says, the polygraph will tell me he's deceptive. But I won't know until I get him hooked up."

"Betts, can you track down Dallas and ask him for a yes or no. Try his cell phone, and maybe we can avoid his humpy father."

"I'll try, darlin'." She walked out to her desk.

Vinnie looked at me over his reading glasses. "Darlin'? Mannaggia! You still married?"

"Yeah, same woman—for many years. Bettye just likes me."

"Minga! Good-lookin' woman, this one."

"Yeah, she's a nice girl."

John sat there grinning like the village idiot.

Bettye walked back into the office after several minutes on the phone.

"I have Dallas on the line. He says his father told him not to take another test. He asked me if he would lose his job if he refused."

"You seem to be doing pretty well with him," I said. "You have that motherly influence over cops. There's no sense putting dad on the phone when he's being so nice to mommy." She gave me a dirty look over the tops of her granny glasses. "What shall I tell him, Daddy?"

"How about there's only one sure way to establish his innocence? Tell him I've got the number-one *pro from Dover* here who'll give him a fair shake. Also tell him the first test he took should have been thrown out. He was too nervous for that one to tell us anything. I can elaborate on that if he comes in here." I turned to Vinnie. "When do you want to test him?"

Vinnie looked at Bettye. "Tell him tomorrow at nine would be best. Have him get a good rest tonight. Eat breakfast tomorrow, but not too much kawfee. I'll give him a fair test."

"Okey dokey, not too much kawfee." She pronounced coffee just like Vinnie. "You northern boys sure do talk funny." She turned and left.

Vinnie looked at me and then John. "A beauty queen that says okey dokey? No wonder you love it here."

Chapter Thirteen

One of the reasons I liked Dallas Finchum was his promptness. At quarter-to-nine the next morning, he sat in the squad room, fifteen minutes early, waiting patiently.

Not in the mood for friendliness at that hour, I didn't say much, deferring instead to Vinnie Falcone to lead the way.

Dallas dressed comfortably in a red polo shirt and relaxed-fit jeans. As usual, the kid appeared well-groomed. His dark hair never looking like it needed cutting or combing.

Vinnie set up his polygraph in our combination juvenile offender/private interrogation room on a three-by-four metal table. He wanted to conduct the pre-test interview in my office without me present.

After being dispossessed from my own work abode, I decided to sit out front and bother Bettye and John.

But first I flexed my supervisory muscles by hanging a sign on the back door warning any rowdy POs who decided to stop at headquarters. The sign read: QUIET! above slightly smaller letters, POLYGRAPH EXAM IN PROGRESS.

Vinnie was about half an hour into the pre-test interview when Bettye's phone rang.

"Yes, sir," she said. "Yes, sir, he's right here with me. Yes, sir, he's been here for almost an hour. He's with the polygraph examiner that the Chief brought in from New York. No, sir, not yet. They're still doing the preliminary interview. Yes, sir, I'll tell him. You have a nice day, too. Bye now."

"Ronnie?"

"Uh-huh."

"What's up?"

"Dallas' father walked in up there. He's sittin' in Trudy's office. Ronnie wants to know what he should do."

"Jesus H. Christ. He's the God...forsaken mayor. He's supposed to run this city, and he asks *me* what to do. He should throw the arrogant bastard out on his ear. Right, John?"

"Whatever you say, Boss."

"What does he want from me?"

I started to feel my blood pressure rise.

"He'd like you to take a walk up there," Bettye said. "I think he's uncomfortable talkin' to the man himself."

I looked at her, almost in disbelief. "Yes, ma'am. I'll be upstairs protecting our fearless leader. Holding his...bloody hand."

I just knew the tips of my ears had turned red.

"Now, Sammy, you be nice."

"Nuts," I said.

John laughed. He knew me. Bettye shook her head. She did, too.

I had no intention of speaking with Billy Ray-Goddamn-Finchum. I took the marble steps two at a time, pushed open one of the two palace doors and looked at the man sitting in one of the six armchairs along the wall of the mayor's anteroom.

To Finchum's right sat Darnell Means, Ronnie's deputy mayor and a guy I wouldn't trust as far as I could throw a Cadillac Escalade.

Finchum didn't even have the courtesy to wear a jacket and tie. He looked much shorter than his son who stood almost six-feet-tall. If I were Billy Ray, a full-time professional fireman, I'd try to lose fifteen or twenty pounds of baby fat, but that's just me. He sat there wearing a dark blue Airport Authority Fire Department T-shirt with orange letters and matching, blue tactical pants.

"Hello, Trudy," I said and walked past her desk without acknowledging Finchum or speaking to Darnell.

Trudy Connor may never get used to me. Apparently, I don't behave like the other city department heads. I was about to breech protocol by not allowing her to announce me.

I'm also guilty of many other violations of her unwritten code of conduct for Prospect employees for which she may never forgive me.

I took hold of the knob on one of the mayor's massive oak doors, looked back at her and smiled. Her mouth hung open. She said nothing, and her big brown eyes popped open a little wider than usual. She sat there with her phone in hand while I breezed into Ronnie's office.

"What's this shit-bird want?" I asked the mayor.

"He wants you to stop giving his boy a polygraph test."

Ronnie looked stressed. His jacket hung on the back of his chair, and his tie, which he never loosens, had been undone and his collar opened. I should have looked closer. I may have even seen a hair out of place.

The door opened and closed again, and Darnell Means stepped up between Ronnie's desk and me. I looked at him, but didn't acknowledge his presence.

"We haven't started the actual test yet." I knew that sounded sarcastic.

"He says he told you not to speak to his boy except through his lawyer," Darnell said.

"So what?"

Ronnie's left eye began to twitch.

"The boy's entitled to legal representation." Means, a law school graduate who never passed a Bar exam, couldn't resist adding his opinion.

"The last time I looked," I said, "Dallas was twenty-five years old. He's an adult, a policeman, employed by us. We say he's old enough to take away a citizen's freedom or their life. He's old enough to make his own decisions. Yesterday he decided to take a lie detector test. His old man has no say in the matter."

"Y'ur sure about all that?" Ronnie asked. "Positive?"

"Finchum's son is an adult, for chrissakes. If this guy was a halfway decent individual, I'd talk to him. But if you haven't yet formed an opinion of him, let me tell you, he's a prick. I have nothing to say to him. Throw the bastard out."

"Lord have mercy, Sam! You want me to throw him out?"

"The man's entitled to speak," Darnell said.

I ignored Means and spoke at Ronnie. "You're the mayor. Just refuse to speak with him. If he doesn't leave in a reasonable amount of time, I'll have two cops escort him out of the building. I'd do it myself, but that wouldn't be my first choice since I may have further dealings with Dallas's lawyer. If I acted on my instincts, I'd toss him down the stairs and kick him in the head. But I'll behave in deference to you."

Ronnie blinked like a camera running through frames on motor drive. "Lord have mercy, Sam. Y'ur sure? Y'ur sure?"

"Trust me, Ronnie. I know what I'm doing."

"I'm opposed to these Gestapo tactics, Ronnie," Means said.

The mayor closed his eyes and shook his head. "Lord have mercy."

"Yeah, yeah, I know," I said, trying to calm down my boss and offer some sage advice. "This hump has enough political horsepower—from somewhere—to start the ball rolling on one of the most corrupt schemes I've seen in all the time I've been here. So, if you have *somebody* to call, do it. Have your people call his people, and get him to back off. I don't plan on losing this one. I don't plan on running a department that the people in this neighborhood see as corrupt." I took a step closer to his desk and scowled. "Take that one to the bank."

I shot a challenging look at Darnell who chose to remain silent.

"All right, Sam, all right," Ronnie said. "Jest please, make this happen."

"That's why you hired me, boss. Now, sit back, and watch it work."

Darnell had to stick in his two cents. "Ronnie, as your legal adviser, I recommend you speak to Mr. Finchum and see what he wants."

"Thanks for your opinion, Darnell. Now would you give the mayor and me a moment?"

"Do what?"

"If Ronnie wants you to know what happens here, he'll tell you. Personally, I think it's none of your business."

"Ronnie, I strongly suggest..."

I had heard enough. "Would you mind leaving?"

"Y'all can leave, Darnell," Ronnie said. "Sam and I will handle this."

Without a word, Means stormed out of the office.

I picked up Ronnie's phone and called John Gallagher's extension. "Hey, I want you to call in the meanest-looking guy on the road. Give him a 10-12 forthwith. As soon as he's here, call the mayor's extension. Then get your asses up here immediately. I'll give you two minutes from the time you hang up. When you see me walk out of the mayor's office, I want you to come in and escort this Finchum guy out of the building. When you're outside, whisper in his ear, and let him know that if he ever shows up here again he may leave with broken legs. Of course, no one else should hear that. We clear?"

"Sure, Boss. Harley Flatt's working. I'll get him."

"Sounds good, buddy."

I looked over at Ronnie. "In less than ten minutes, this part of the drama will be resolved."

"Good Lord, Sam! Y'all are goin' ta threaten the man?"

I scowled again. "You never heard me say anything of the sort. Look, Ronnie, if I took this guy behind a diner somewhere and had a conversation with him, I'd end it by kicking him in the balls and sending him home crying. Sometimes, that's the way things are done. In the end, he'd get the message."

Ronnie covered his eyes with his right hand. "Oh, Lord have mercy."

We didn't have to wait ten minutes. Ronnie's phone rang. I answered.

"Boss," John said, "Harley's here. We're on the way up."

"Good. Wait for me to show."

I looked at my watch and counted off the time. After two minutes, I opened the door and stepped into Ms. Connor's room. I looked at Billy Ray Finchum.

"Lieutenant Finchum, I'm Chief Jenkins. Nice to meet you." I looked to my right. John Gallagher and PO Harlan Flatt walked into the room. The timing was perfect.

"These gentlemen will escort you out to the parking lot. Have a nice day."

Finchum stood, began to speak, but Harley Flatt stepped in front of him. Harley stood at least four inches taller than Finchum with a pair of extremely wide shoulders. With his thumbs hooked on his gun belt, Harley, who never smiles, looked very intimidating.

John said, "Follow us out, sir. We'll make sure you get to your car safely."

After they left, I entered the mayor's office again and closed the door. "One more tidbit of advice, Ronnie. Do not trust your deputy. He's up to his ears in county politics, and I have a feeling he's one of the players in the background. Don't get caught with your pants down."

Ronnie shook his head. I turned and walked out.

Finchum, I later heard, had turned red before he hit the first floor. But by being conspicuously outnumbered, he capitulated. I won that battle, but as I'd soon learn, the war was far from over.

Chapter Fourteen

Vinnie Falcone walked into my office carrying a manila case folder. He stood in front of my desk, showed a face marked with distaste and tossed the folder onto my blotter.

"Well?" I said.

"If I didn't know better, I'd say that was a waste of time."

"You got the same results?"

"I asked better questions, and we had a good pre-test chat, but this guy gets so wound up, he could set the machine on fire."

Vinnie stood there with his vest unbuttoned, his tie undone, and his shirtsleeves turned up, his forearms thin and sinewy.

"Another inconclusive?"

"Not for nothin', boss, but this kid gets so stressed on that box, I wonder if he could function as a street cop during tough times."

"Everybody here seems to think he performs well enough." I found myself defending Dallas.

"Look," he said as he sat in a guest chair, "let's forget the polygraph. I spent almost an hour talkin' with him before I hooked him up. All you gotta do is watch his body language. He gets all nervous and jerky when I asked about the date rape. If I never put him on the machine, I'd think somethin' there wasn't kosher. But when the charts show the kid's on the brink of takin' the big one every time I ask him a simple question, it makes me think he may need some serious shrink time."

I nodded and kept listening. I noticed two buttons on my phone console glowing red. Both John and Bettye were on the phone.

"You know how we do that card trick to make them believe in the machine?" he asked.

"Sure, they pick a card and then you have them say none of the cards you show them is the one they saw."

"Right. When they lie to the card they actually did see, the machine blips, and I know which one. When I showed this kid the jack-o'-clubs and he said no, the needle almost tore the page in half. When he saw the machine react so radically, his heartbeat went up twenty beats per. He's nuts. Nobody gets that twisted outta shape for nothin'. He's scared to death of the machine."

"And he still won't go for the rape? Not even a little compromise?"

Vinnie has never been able to mask his feelings. The expression on his face said more than his words.

"He insists everything was cool. She said yes right up until he was finished."

"How does he explain people seeing her bruised up?"

"He's not comfortable talkin' about sex like most cops. He he-hawed around, but said they were both pretty excited and passionate so her thighs probably got all the wear and tear. Then he claimed after they were finished she got freaky and started slappin' him. He defended himself when he couldn't just block her punches. So, he clocked her once and left."

Vinnie got up, walked over to Mr. Coffee and poured himself a cup. A few moments later, he returned to his seat.

"Well, that's a new chapter I haven't heard before," I said. "If he had explained it that way from the beginning, I think most of us would have had a different take on this. That, at least, sounds possible. I wonder if he's been coached, or it's the truth."

"The one thing I can tell you for sure is, the only one who knows the truth—if she allows herself to admit it—is the girl."

Vinnie sipped his coffee and took a breather. Both lights on the phone console had gone out moments earlier.

"I'm not sure Dallas remembers what really happened that night," Vinnie said. "He may have run a fairy tale through his mind so often that he can't distinguish fact from fiction any more. And the machine will never be able to help you get the truth from him." He finished his assessment with a disappointing reality.

"What am I going to do with this kid, Vinnie?"

He shrugged like the answer was simple, like something written on the men's room wall.

"He's still on probation. Fire his ass. John told me you have enough evidence without a confession. You're not lookin' to put him in jail. You just don't want a sex offender wearin' a badge."

"I wish the kid was a hump no one cared about."

He gave me a look that said I should know better. "Hey, you're the guy who scored so high on the promotion tests, remember the old management principal of 'if in doubt, resolve the situation in favor of the organization?'"

I nodded. My decisions have never been scratched out for me on the outhouse wall. *Life should be so easy.*

"If he'd just resign and make it easy for us." I shook my head in frustration. "He could go about his business and get on with living. If I fire him, what's he going to do for the rest of his life? Take in money at an all-night gas station?"

"If his old man exerted as much pressure as you say to get him this job and to cover up the rape, you don't think he'd pull more strings to get him a job somewhere else? That's what political shitheads do."

I couldn't argue with logic like that.

"If only he didn't turn out to be a nice kid."

A compassionate smile broke across Vinnie's face. "I thought old guys like us are supposed to get eccentric, not soft."

"Yeah, I know. Where is he now? Maybe I'll give him a try now that you've got him all freaked out. Maybe he'll want the mental pain to stop so badly that he'll resign and fade into the sunset."

"He's in the men's room. I wouldn't be surprised if he shit in his pants."

* * * *

A few minutes later, Dallas stood in front of my desk looking worse than Ray Milland in a scene from *Lost Weekend.* "Detective Falcone said you wanted to see me, sir?"

"Close the door, and sit down."

I gave him a few seconds to get comfortable and me time to decide on my opening line.

"Your father came here looking for you," I said.

"Sir?" He looked surprised.

"Your father walked up to the mayor's office and demanded we stop the polygraph test."

"Sir, I'm sorry. I didn't know."

The kid must have spent his time in the men's room splashing water on his face. Dark sprinkles showed on his light shirt.

"I'm sure you didn't. I threw your old man out. You're an adult. He's got no business dictating what you will or won't do on your own behalf."

"Yes, sir."

"Dallas, why did you take that test?"

"Sir?" He wrinkled his brow and reminded me of a confused Shar-pei.

"Simple question, son."

"I wanted to prove I've done nothin' wrong." His face opened up. He looked sincere.

"Dallas, I'm watching you here and the more you say, the more you throw me for a loop."

"Sir, I don't understand." His voice sounded strained, and I could almost feel his pain.

If frustration could be bottled, Dallas would have had gallons on hand.

"Okay, listen carefully. You want me to believe your story. I understand that. If you're telling the truth and no one believes you, the frustration must be unbearable. But look at things from my prospective. You've been a cop for a couple months now. You should be thinking like one."

I saw more wrinkles, more confusion, accompanied by fidgets—the look of mental anguish on Dallas's face as he listened to my every word became pitiable.

"I get a complaint about you," I said. "You've already told me a little about the incident a long time ago. I speak to the so-called victim. I speak with a witness. A competent investigator speaks with hospital personnel. Everything tends to corroborate the victim's story. It's become obvious that the sheriff's polygraph examiner dummied up your test results. The cops in Chattanooga were at least damn lazy in the way they kissed off that case and more probably influenced by someone wanting a favor. The campus cop sounds like she was either coerced or bribed to forget things. And the Hamilton County DA conveniently lost all your paperwork."

Halfway through that thought he closed his eyes. When he opened them, a tear rolled from the corner of his right eye.

I continued. "I couple that with what I know about your Uncle Claude and his political shenanigans and how much of a pain in the ass your father has been, and it's difficult for me not to think cover-up for a damn good reason. The people all around you have gone to such great lengths to commit criminal conduct and political corruption, what can I think?"

The kid just sat there, immobile, looking like a small child I just threatened with suspension from school. Dallas's world was literally crumbling around him.

"Since you don't have much to say, keep listening. If I fire you, there will be an open file on the reason why. If you look for another decent job and those people contact us for a reference, they're entitled to know all about this. And I'm under no obligation to color you as other than what I see."

He remained quiet, occasionally nodding. I suppose his way of letting me know he understood.

"If, on the other hand, you resign, saying no more than you wish to leave for personal reasons, you walk out of here on your terms. You are officially rejecting us. You go about your business. I wish you a good life, and we all part company without hard feelings."

As he nodded, I saw another tear run from the outside corner of his right eye down his cheek. Both his eyes appeared red and glassy.

"When we first spoke many months ago, I told you that if you lied to me and took this job under other than honorable conditions, I'd not only see you fired, but I'd kick you down the stairs from the second floor and step on your neck when you hit bottom. That was before I got to know you, before I got to like you. You're a nice kid. Everyone says so."

I turned my palms up and spread my arms. "Okay, I retract my earlier statement. I do not want to hurt you. If you leave here voluntarily, I promise what happened will remain confidential."

He began blinking. "Thank you, sir." His voice sounded thick and congested.

"I'll make it real simple, Dallas. If you don't complicate my life, I won't try to ruin yours."

"You'd let me just resign?" he asked, sounding like a child I offered to take to the zoo.

"Yes." It wasn't the first time in my life I've felt like a bastard, but that episode ranked up there as a real doozie. Then I remembered how Dorie Asher might feel.

"I like this job, sir. I think I'd be a good police officer. I really have to think about that. Do I have to make a decision right now?"

He took my bait, but did his best to muster up the dignity he had in reserve and fired his guns at me. Two points for Dallas.

"You can think about it, but don't take too long. If all this becomes so complicated that we spend too much time investigating this can of worms, I doubt I'd have a problem convincing the mayor to let me dump the whole thing on the FBI. Then I could just sit back and watch all the players fall by the wayside."

He swallowed a couple of times with difficulty, nodded thoughtfully, but said nothing.

"It's your choice, Dallas. Call me back in the next day or so."

"All I ever wanted to do was be a good policeman." Again, a tear rolled down his right cheek, joined by others on the left.

Chapter Fifteen

That afternoon, I met one of the most revolting characters I've ever set eyes upon.

After lunch, Vinnie hung out with John. They both wasted time telling Bettye old New York war stories.

I felt restless and stood looking out the back door—for what, I didn't know.

I saw parked in one of the PD visitor's spots, a black H2 Hummer with Alabama plates. Six fog lights mounted on a bar spanned the roofline. Big push bars and brush grills protected the radiator and headlights. Shiny Armor-All coated tires were mounted on twenty-inch, hip-hop wheels. All these aftermarket extras and many of the factory components were bright and shiny chrome. That Hummer would have made a '55 Buick Roadmaster jealous.

I laughed inwardly, shook my head at what I thought garish and absurd and walked back up front.

Rather than return to my office, I chose to look at a man who walked into the lobby. He reminded me of a gory traffic accident—something you really shouldn't look at, but a thing you're drawn to anyway.

He stood in front of Bettye's desk looking down at her. I put him at about six-one and in his late-forties. He wasn't fat, but was definitely pear shaped, with narrow sloping shoulders and wide hips atop long legs. He wore a black double-breasted suit with pegged, baggy trousers. His gold silk shirt was buttoned up to the top, but he wore no tie. Below his pants cuffs, champagne-colored, lizard skin cowboy boots showed conspicuously. He wore a 21st century, country-and-western zoot suit.

If his outfit didn't cause a person to stare, his mug surely would. He possessed the longest face I'd ever seen. A protracted, undefined chin seemed to blend into his soft neck. His small mouth looked almost lost. A forehead that spread upward for five or six inches above pale blond eyebrows stopped where his almost white hair began. The hair appeared fine and shiny, ethereal almost, and pulled back tight against his head, terminating with a ponytail longer than Bettye's. The only facial hair showing was a small triangle of fur beneath his bottom lip.

I stood about ten feet from him and smelled the medicinal odor of old-fashioned Listerine.

He looked directly at Bettye, ignoring me and the two men who sat close-by. His smile would have made a Komodo dragon back off.

"Howdy, ma'am," he said. "Name's Telford Bone. I'm a private investigator from Huntsville, Alabama."

No doubt the owner of a customized H2.

"I'm sorta payin' y'all a courtesy call, lettin' ya know I'll be workin' in y'all's area for a bit."

I watched Bettye jot down his name. Both John and Vinnie had their eyes glued on him.

"What sort of business do you have here, Mr. Bone?" she asked.

He gave her a reptilian smile while his hands moved restlessly inside his pockets.

"I been hired by the Finchum family. I'm sure y'all know young Dallas Finchum. I'm gonna do what I can ta prove the boy innocent of any false accusations made against him."

Vinnie had instinctively brushed his jacket slightly to the right leaving his gun closer at hand. John sat upright, his fist resting on his thigh, only inches from the butt of his Detective Special. It's funny how some people set cops on edge.

I decided to rescue Bettye from any more of the distasteful conversation.

"Hello, Mr. Bone. I'm Chief Jenkins."

Neither of us made a move to step close enough to shake hands.

"Chief." He nodded, and another distasteful smile changed his face. He pursed his lips, and his eyes narrowed. Then his tiny mouth opened to show long straight teeth, something you'd expect to see on an exaggerated cartoon caricature. Everything about him was repulsive.

"The crime Dallas was accused of allegedly took place in Chattanooga three years ago," I said. "There's nothing in Prospect in the way of evidence."

"Well, sir, I unnerstand that, but there's a complainant here. And someone who claims ta be a witness—a witness after the fact, so ta speak."

He pointed at me with his right index finger, punctuating his last thought. My first impulse was to bite off the finger and spit it back at him.

"I certainly can't speak for those people," I said, "but I can protect their privacy. If either person you mentioned refuses to be interviewed, I hope you take no for an answer."

"Yes, sir, absolutely. Ab-so-lutely," he said with yet another obsequious grin.

A blast of Listerine swept over Bettye's desk. I almost took a step backward.

"I don't mean no one no harm," he said. "If I's goin' ta cause trouble, I'da not come here ta introduce m'se'f."

Vinnie kept staring at Bone. I saw John glance several times toward the lobby as if he were checking for an accomplice. They made a good team for two old guys.

"That's good, Mr. Bone. I'm glad to hear that. Would you have a business card to leave with Sergeant Lambert?"

"Well, o' course I do." He took a wallet from the inside top pocket of his suit jacket and placed a card on Bettye's desk. "Ma'am, if you're ever in Alabama needin' any assistance or even jus' need some local directions, I'd be honored if ya called."

Bettye and everyone else ignored his offer.

"You wouldn't be carrying a firearm, would you, Mr. Bone?" I asked.

"No, sir. I didn't think I'd be needin' ta shoot nobody." He laughed, looking like a grotesque jack-o-lantern and more Listerine polluted our atmosphere. "'Sides, I believe that'd be a violation o' your laws, wouldn't it?"

"Oh, yes, I believe it would," I said. "Hey, is that your Hummer parked outside? The one with the Alabama plates."

"Why, yes, sir, yes it is. That's my baby. Some rig, ain't she?"

"You bet. I've not seen another one like it."

A few seconds went by without another word.

"Well, sir," he said, "I guess that concludes my bidness here. Nice meetin' ya, Chief." He put his hands in his pockets again and addressed Bettye with a leer that could have removed the varnish from her desk. "And, ma'am, it's been my pleasure meetin' you, too. Yes, ma'am, a real pleasure." He jingled his loose change with one hand and made it obvious he was playing pocket pool with the other.

When Bettye didn't return a comment, Telford Bone let his smile fade, did an about face and swaggered out through the main doors.

I turned quickly, went to the back door and wrote his plate number on my palm.

Back in the lobby, we all looked at each other.

Bettye stood abruptly. She looked first at John and Vinnie and then at me and shuddered before she spoke. "If you gentlemen will excuse me, I believe I need a Lysol shower."

When Bettye stepped out of range Vinnie said, "Man, what a fuckin' creep. He stunk, too."

"Yeah," John said "What was that smell?"

"I think it was Listerine," I said. "Either that or he fumigates himself instead of bathing."

"That bastard probably uses mouthwash as cologne," Vinnie added.

John stood up, stepped over to Bettye's desk and picked up the business card.

"Telford Bone, investigations and a phone number. That's it. No address."

"Just investigations," I said. "Doesn't say *houses haunted, women violated* or *I bet I can make your skin crawl*?"

"Did you get his plate number, Boss?" John asked.

"Of course, you Irish weasel. You think you're dealing with an amateur?"

"Not me, Boss. Gimme what you got, and I'll run it while the Sarge is trying to get that mook outta her mind."

81

Chapter Sixteen

"Judge, I think it might be time for you to call someone with influence over one or two of those loose cannons you spoke of." I sat in my office with a cup of coffee Bettye had just made, the second pot of the morning.

"Are things going downhill on us, Sam?" Minas Tipton asked.

"Perhaps quicker than I thought. Correct me if I'm wrong, but is Claude Webbster the man who asked Ronnie Shields to hire Dallas Finchum?"

"No doubt about that one, Sam. Brother Buck may have instigated the idea, but Claude's the one with the current power to influence most of Prospect's councilmen."

I thought about dropping a hydrogen bomb on an assembled multitude of Blount County politicians.

"But am I still on the right track when I call Billy Ray Finchum the loosest of those cannons?" I asked.

"Right again, son. He's unpredictable, and that wouldn't surprise you if you had known his daddy, God rest his soul. Delmer Finchum had been a deputy sheriff for some years before he got into politics and county government," the old man said. "Billy Ray idolized the man. And Delmer was, how can I put this, Sam? He was a pretty rough and dirty politician. Yes, sir, rough indeed."

"It sounds like Billy Ray learned his ways from Daddy, but takes advantage of his brother-in-law's power. Is it possible that he derives power from anyone other than Claude?"

"I have no idea on that, Sam, but I'll ask someone who may know."

"It would be my guess that he does," I said. "If not actual local power, then perhaps he's found inside knowledge or influence or just a brand of worldliness not usually found in the halls of Blount County government. I believe he's got the help of someone a lot craftier than Claude Webbster."

I told Minas Tipton the story of Telford Bone.

"So, if this guy is a legitimate PI," I said, "he may just be here doing a job. If he's a hired thug, here to intimidate the victim or a witness, I'll lock him up and go after his license. One look at this guy and you'd know he shouldn't post a picture on his ad in the Yellow Pages."

"Ha, ha, ha, ha," the judge laughed. "I can see, Sam, this rascal has made a bad impression on you. Well, I guess it's his misfortune. And Claude's too, if you catch him with his pants down far enough for him not to run off on ya."

The judge laughed again. He seemed to be enjoying himself. I hoped he'd get his kicks watching Beverly Hillbillies reruns and consider this serious business.

"Judge, I wish Claude and his cohorts would crawl back under their respective rocks and leave me to conduct business as usual. I never thought he was a man with far-reaching powers."

"I agree with ya, Sam," he said. "I've never known Claude as someone with influence outside the state. He's too much of a country bumpkin to orchestrate a complicated operation of witness tampering and not get caught. But, I'll admit, I don't know much of what Billy Ray is capable of. I'll try to find out for ya."

"I'd appreciate that, sir. Will you call Claude and get him to back off in any further involvement if in fact he's still pulling strings?"

"I won't call him myself, Sam. That wouldn't have the impact I want ta generate. I'll get Jimmy Dillworth ta call him. One of these local politicos will respond to a suggestion from Washington like nothing else. If they don't toe the mark for DC, the National Committee could cut their political lives mighty short if you know what I mean."

"Yes, sir, I understand. Say hello to Congressman Dillworth for me." I hoped he didn't sense any irony in my sarcasm.

"I'll do that, Sam. I'll surely do that. And you keep me informed about this private eye you'll be watchin'. If you need me to shake up any of those Alabama boys for help in gettin' information on him, you just whistle."

"Thanks, Judge, I'll do that."

* * * *

The next morning a Knoxville lawyer named Mitch Callow called as I read some of the reports having nothing to do with the Finchums and Telford Bone. My desk had turned into a place where I might get to hear all the new bad information in the world.

"Chief, I'm calling because I thought you and I can have an intelligent, unemotional conversation about something that happened to an employee of mine," he said.

"Don't stop now, Mr. Callow. You've captured my interest."

"I know you've just spoken with Laura Hensley about a crime of which she had information you needed."

Well, so much for Laura not discussing Prospect Police business with anyone.

"This morning she came to work more upset than I've ever seen her before," he said.

Two weeks earlier, I hung three framed eight-by-ten photos I took on a trip to Custer State Park in South Dakota on the wall in my office—a herd of buffalo, a pair of pronghorn antelope, and a mule deer with a twelve-point rack. All stared at me while I listened.

"Don't tell me, Counselor. I'm activating my psychic abilities. A guy named Telford Bone paid her a visit last night. Am I right?"

"Correct. You must be a whiz at cocktail parties. This man claimed to be a private investigator working for Dallas Finchum, the person who supposedly raped Laura's former college roommate."

"I met Mr. Bone yesterday. I can understand Laura's, ah…discomfort with him. Even a brief and impersonal encounter with Telford Bone would upset the most robust of women."

"So I understand."

"I actually don't think Dallas Finchum hired this guy Bone. I put this on young Finchum's father," I said. "I wouldn't be surprised if Dallas has never met Mr. Bone himself. Dallas's father is, in my opinion, one of Life's less savory characters and would seem to fit in nicely with this private cop. Did Bone threaten Laura?"

"The way I heard it, no. Not in so many words. Laura is actually smarter than she sometimes sounds, if you understand what I'm saying."

I chuckled.

"I believe she gave me a credible account of the conversation she had with Bone. He was careful," Callow said. "He skirted any actual threats by using hypothetical possibilities. None the less, the threat was implicit. And it worked. She's very upset—and frightened."

"Having Telford Bone say good morning would upset me, Mr. Callow. I sympathize with her. Perhaps it's time for me to have another chat with Mr. Bone and skirt a few subjects myself. But I'd like to speak with Laura first. I'd like to hear exactly what she remembers."

"Certainly. She's upset, but totally functional and can give you as good an accounting as she gave me."

"Right now on the phone would be best for me," I said, "but if she would rather, I can drive to Knoxville."

"I think the phone would be fine. Hold the line please, and I'll get her. She can use my office for privacy."

A few moments later, Laura Jean Hensley picked up the telephone.

"Okay, Laura," I said, "let's start with you telling me exactly what happened, and I'll ask questions when I need something clarified."

"Well, yeah, sure, like, that's okay," she said. And then it sounded like she sipped soda or some other liquid through a straw after she spoke. "This guy, Telford Bone, he, like, got me totally freaked out. I mean, like, what kind of a name is Telford Bone?"

I laughed silently.

"Anyways," she continued, "have you, like, seen him? He's, like, amazing looking. Like totally creepy."

"I couldn't have said it better myself. Everyone in my office mentioned the same thing. When and where did he confront you?"

"He, like, came to my home. Is that like gross or what? Last night, maybe around seven. We had just finished dinner, and he knocked on the door."

Liquid gurgled through the straw again.

"Did you invite him into your home?"

"Well, yeah, we, like, sat in the living room. When I told him I really didn't want to talk about anything, he said he'd, like, have the lawyer he worked for subpoena me for a deposition."

"Did he name this lawyer?"

"No."

"Okay, what happened after you invited him in?"

"Well, ya know, he, like, started off asking what I saw. So I, like, told him—just basically."

"You said that you saw Dorie had been beaten?"

"Well, yeah, ya know, that's all I saw."

"Good. What happened next?"

I heard another slurp before she answered.

"He wanted to know if I saw Dallas that night, and ya know, I, like, really didn't."

"Okay, and what else?"

"Well, like, I guess that's all he asked. Then he started talking himself, and obviously I, like, got totally freaked."

"Obviously. Try and tell me what he said, using his exact words."

"Well, ya know, he didn't say anything specific, but he, like, warned me in not so many words."

"How so?"

"He said, like, if I told my story, I really couldn't say I saw Dallas do anything. Which is, like, true, ya know. I only saw Dorie the way I described it to you—like after the rape. Then he said that if I believed Dorie and told her story to a jury, it would only be hearsay, which I kinda, like, know is true. And if I said these things I could ruin Dallas's life."

As I looked at one of the photos, I'd swear I saw the mule deer roll his eyes as Laura did her rendition of a Tennessee valley girl.

"Did he ever tell you that you had better not say *anything* about Dallas?" I asked.

"Not specifically. What's he mean about me testifying in court?"

"I don't know. No one has said anything about court yet that I know of. What else did he say?"

"He said it's possible that if Dallas's lawyer proved my statement hurt Dallas's character he could, like, counter-sue me. Mr. Callow says that's not entirely true, right?"

"Mr. Callow knows what he's talking about. This man, Telford Bone, just wanted to frighten you."

"Well, yeah, ya know, he, like, did a good job. I'm, like, totally freaked out."

"Did Bone say anymore?"

"Yeah, like, just before my father told him to get out. Dad had been in the kitchen listening, and when that guy said if Dallas thought I was lying about him or adding to my story to hurt him, he wouldn't be surprised if a guy in that position might not do something really serious. I guess he stopped there because my father came in and told him to go, or he would call the sheriff."

"Did he give your father an argument?"

"No, he just, like, kept smiling that creepy smile. God, he was, like, totally repulsive. I told my mother we should get the house fumigated."

"Did he show you any identification? Credentials, business card, anything?"

"He left a business card on the coffee table."

"While he was in your home did you see him carrying a gun?"

"He has a gun? Oh, man, if I knew that…"

"Laura, I don't know that he has a gun. I asked him if he did, and he said no. But sometimes when a guy like Bone tries to intimidate someone, he may casually let his subject see a gun to frighten them even more."

"No, I didn't see one. Do you think he'll try and do anything to me or my family?"

"I'd be very surprised if he tries to contact you again. I think you've seen the last of Telford Bone. But if he ever comes anywhere near you, call 9-1-1 immediately. Then call me."

"Okay. Has he tried to see Dorie, too?"

"I don't know, but I'll call her mother and find out. Remember, if you need anything or if your parents need anything, call 9-1-1. A local officer will get to you quickly, and then call me."

"Okay, thanks."

"Don't worry, Laura, we'll take care of you. Will you put Mr. Callow back on the phone?"

I finished up by having a short conversation with Mitch Callow, asking him to give Laura a little free legal advice and assure her she wouldn't be held liable for telling the police the truth about what she had seen or what she'd been told. He seemed to have her best interests at heart.

* * * *

People like Laura Hensley tend to give me a headache. I was only an inch away from taking the bottle of Glenfiddich out of my desk drawer and pouring a stiff drink. Instead, I poured another cup of black coffee, which is no doubt destroying my stomach lining, and used it to wash down four Advil.

I stretched, tried to loosen my shoulders and walked out to see what the team could do about getting more information on Telford Bone.

"John," I said, "call the phone company, and see what they can tell you about the number on Bone's business card."

"Okay, Boss."

"Betts, call Huntsville PD, and see who we have to speak with to find out if Bone is a licensed PI working out of that town. If they don't know him, try the Alabama Attorney General."

"Okey dokey, darlin'."

"Whaddaya want me ta do, boss?" Vinnie asked, sitting next to John with his feet up on the edge of the desk.

"I thought you were flying home."

"That's not 'til noon. I can cancel if ya need me."

"You check out of the motel yet?"

"Yeah, but corn beef and cabbage here has a guest room. He invited me down to play golf with him. I'll just invite myself there now. He only wants me to play golf because he can beat me. You need some help?"

"Sure, but I can't pay you."

"Hey, come on, I'm not lookin' for money. You picked up the plane fare and motel bill. I've got time comin' ta me. I'll make a phone call. I can't leave now. This is gettin' interesting as all hell."

"Okay, sounds good. The people around here won't know one badge from another if you need to tin someone."

"Do I have to work for John?"

"No, you can work for Bettye."

"Good, 'cause if John were my boss, you'd really owe me."

"I know. There's only so much a man can pay back."

He grinned, and I knew Vinnie was hooked.

I saw the main office line light up on Bettye's phone console. She was busy with Huntsville PD, so I took the call in my office.

"Chief, this is Jodelle Asher. You know anythin' about a private detective goin' around sayin' he's workin' for the Finchums?"

"Yes, Mrs. Asher, I met him yesterday. I assume he's already stopped to see Dorie."

"Well, he tried—last night. I run him off. Threatened ta call the sheriff."

"What did he say to you?"

"Tried ta tell me that if Dorie stuck with her complaint, the Finchum's lawyer might sue her."

I shook my head, amazed at Bone's nerve. "That's absurd. Did he threaten you or her in any way?"

"Didn't give that hairy-faced fool the chance. I wasn't about ta listen ta him talk about no lawyers or nothin'. My li'l girl was raped, Chief, and I don't plan on worryin' about no damn lawyers."

"Good for you, Mrs. Asher. Stick to your guns. If he comes onto your property again or tries to talk to either of you or he confronts Dorie somewhere else, call 9-1-1 immediately. If you have to start screaming your head off to draw attention to yourself, do it. Just don't talk to the man. After you call 9-1-1, call me."

"Chief, I got no in-tention o' talkin' with that ugly devil."

I laughed to myself, liking her description.

"And I don't mind tellin' ya," she said, "this bidness got Dorie all wore out and tore up. She's re-grettin' I ever called ya."

"Try to make her feel better, Mrs. Asher. I know it's not easy for her or you, but hang in there. We're doing the best we can. Please don't mention this to anyone, but Dallas has been suspended, and we're doing a lot of investigating."

"Well, thank ya, Chief. I shore do thank ya."

"Thanks for calling, Mrs. Asher. I'll keep you informed about what we learn."

Before going back out to the lobby, I stared at the pair of antelope.

They both shook their heads.

* * * *

My crew of two plus Vinnie waited for me when I hung up.

"Okay, guys. What's up?" I asked.

Bettye started. "Neither Huntsville PD nor the Attorney General have any record of a licensed PI named Telford Bone. He could be working under someone else's license as an employee, but no one with his name is licensed, bonded or recorded in the state business files."

I spun her side chair around and sat. "Isn't that interesting?"

Bettye nodded. "I ran his motor vehicle records. Yesterday, John found out the Hummer is registered to him using a PO Box in Tuscaloosa. Today, I learned his driver's license was renewed three years ago—before he bought the Hummer—with a PO Box in Alabaster, Alabama."

"Alabaster is just south of Birmingham," I said.

"It is," she said.

"John, what do you know about the phone?" I asked.

"It's a pre-paid cell phone, Boss, purchased at Walmart. He registered it using a PO Box in Bessemer, Alabama. Bessemer and Alabaster are *both* part of metro-Birmingham."

"Either of you know if you need a permit to buy a handgun in Alabama?"

John laughed. I couldn't blame him.

Bettye looked at me as if I were a foolish child. "I doubt it. Probably need one for concealed carry, but how often does that stop someone?"

"I know. Silly me," I said.

I saw Vinnie smile. New York handgun laws are a little more stringent.

"Somebody call the Alabama troopers," I said, "and ask if they have something equal to our TBI instant background checks for gun sales. Run him through that. Somebody else do a package on him with NCIC, AFIS and whomever else you can think of who'd care. Betts, call FBI Knoxville, and do an official check with them. I don't want to call Ralph for a favor yet. If I have to explain all this corruption crap to him, I might put him on the spot with his boss later on. The less they know right now the better.

"I'm going over to the Foothills View Motel and see if Bone is registered there."

* * * *

The motel was only a short drive from the municipal building. I could have walked, but I was in no mood to stroll around while time was a'wastin'.

The summer of '09 broke the back of a drought that had devastated East Tennessee for six years. We already had over seven inches of surplus rain for the year. The vegetation appeared lush and healthy. The big old tulip poplar trees on the town square looked better than I'd ever seen. The grass below them could rival a golf course. Three squirrels zig-zagged across the grass with no apparent purpose, changing directions on a whim.

I turned into the driveway of the motel and drove up the long blacktop road to the parking lot.

I opened the office door and felt a blast of cold air.

"Howdy, Chief." Clay Plemmons, the motel manager, sat behind the tall registration counter in the lobby.

"Hello, Clay. Got time to do me a favor?"

"Shore. Whatcha need?"

"Check the cards for the last two days. Did you register a guy from Alabama named Telford Bone?"

"Don't need ta check that. He was here last night. Checked out this mornin' 'bout ten-thirty. Hard ta fergit a body like him. Strange lookin' feller, ain't he? But even if he weren't so odd lookin' himse'f, I'd still remember that big ol' Hummer he drives, one with all that chrome."

"What address did he use?"

"Hang on, I got it rot here. Bookkeepin' ain't seen it yet."

He thumbed through a short stack of cards sitting in a little vertical file box. Clay Plemmons chewed on the tip of his tongue while he worked.

"Here ya go, yessir. Telford Bone used a PO Box address in Alabaster, Alabama. Never heard o' Alabaster m'se'f."

"Any other information on the card except the license plate

number?" I asked.

"Nosir, nothin' but the PO Box an' his tag."

One of the housekeepers, dressed in a pair of khakis and a Best Western polo shirt, walked behind the desk, heading who knows where.

"He didn't happen to say where he was going next, did he?"

"Not ta me."

"How did he pay?"

"Cash."

"Why am I not surprised?"

Clay shrugged.

"Mind if I take a look at the room he used?"

"Course not." He turned and called to the woman who just walked past. "Alma, you clean up 214 yet?"

"Becky pulled the sheets and towels out, but we ain't had a chance to do any more," she said.

Clay handed me a key card, and I walked outside to the nearest stairway and climbed to the second floor. The Foothills View is an impeccably clean, old-fashioned motel with each room having an individual outside entrance. 214 took me twelve doors from the staircase. I didn't need the key. The door stood open.

The motel always seemed pretty upscale to me. They decorated with rustic log furniture and Scottish plaid carpets. Forest green drapes and framed Lee Roberson prints, depicting various Smoky Mountain scenes, hung on knotty pine, tongue-and-groove paneling in each room.

I started looking in the closet. Nothing there but empty hangers. Nothing on the shelf either. I checked the chest of drawers. More nothing.

I pulled a pair of latex gloves from my pocket and moved to the trashcan. Telford had purchased enough junk food from the Git 'N Go Market in town to sicken one of those South Dakota buffalo pictured on my wall. A thirty-two-ounce drink cup with the melted ice and straw still intact, wrappers from three microwave burgers, a cardboard container from a large order of Tater Puffs and a half dozen empty ketchup envelopes lay in there along with a few used tissues and two feet of dental floss. Yuck. That's an example of the distasteful part of detective work.

I checked the mini-fridge and the microwave. Nothing, except on the top of the microwave, I found a takeout menu from El Jibarito, the Mexican restaurant a few miles down the road in Maryville.

After I found nothing behind the furniture or under the bed, I walked back to the office where Clay Plemmons showed me that Bone could have found the menu on the rack of tourist information in the lobby. I wondered why he ate Mr. Patel's Git 'N Go garbage rather than good Mexican food.

I filed the menu in my pocket and started the drive back to the PD through a Tennessee town as green as something in the suburbs of Seattle.

* * * *

"Confound it." I said, trying to sound like a famous three-hundred-pound pompous detective, "Make sense out of this flummery."

"Sam Jenkins, what are you talkin' about?" Bettye asked.

"Huh?" John said.

Vinnie smiled. "He's doing his Nero Wolfe act."

"Who?" Bettye asked.

"What?" John said.

Vinnie picked up the ball again. "I'm surprised he doesn't call us all into his office and sit at his desk with two bottles of beer in front of him and bellow, "Report!'"

"Oh, Vincent, you're so literate," I said. "And you've got such a good memory."

"We're like Archie, Saul and Fred?" Vinnie said.

"Which one am I?" Bettye asked.

Describing the look she gave me would be superfluous.

"Uh, well, I guess you'd be Archie," I said. "Figuratively speaking, of course. Wolfe's right-hand-man, most trusted partner…you know."

"No, I don't know. And don't even think about callin' me Archie or a man, city boy."

Bettye holds on dearly to her feminine side.

I smiled, trying to keep Mrs. Lambert unruffled. "Vinnie's right about the Nero Wolfe thing," I said. "Wolfe and I have a lot in common. We're both geniuses, but I'm much more modest. And, Betts, Wolfe

93

didn't have a female companion. I could call you Lilly. She's the only recurring female character, but Lilly Rowen was Archie's girlfriend, not one of Wolfe's operatives." I smiled again and shrugged.

"Sammy, do you want to hear about what we know or talk about detective stories?" She sounded impatient.

"Sure, I'm ready." I grabbed Bettye's side chair, spun it around and sat with my chin resting on the chair back.

"Okay," she started off, "I called the FBI. One of the girls there will run that handsome devil, your Mr. Telford Bone, through their local files and call their Birmingham office, too. She'll call me back. We'll listen to John next 'cause Vinnie did most of the work."

"Okay, Boss," John said, "the Alabama troopers ran their Brady Law gun records and came up with nothing. He hasn't bought a gun legally in Alabama. If he's got a gun, it came from out of state or from a gun show or some other private sale.

"They checked their criminal and non-criminal records, too," he said. "Nothing but the DMV stuff the Sarge already had."

"Okay. Vinnie?" I turned in Detective Falcone's direction.

"Wait, wait," John said. "I've got more." He looked down at the yellow pad sitting on his desktop.

"Vinnie, standby," I said. "Detective Gallagher, please continue. I'm overwhelmed with anticipation."

"Thanks, Boss. I looked up numbers for PDs in Alabaster, Bessemer, and Tusca, uh… *Tuscaloga* and got nothing there either."

"You found a Tuscaloga PD?" I was more than willing to play along.

"Sure."

"If you can't spell Tuscaloosa, how can you find a number for them?"

"Tuscaloosa?"

Bettye had gotten used to John. She just smiled. Vinnie was out of practice. He shook his head and closed his eyes.

"Yeah, Tuscaloosa," I said.

"It was right in that big book we've got."

"Uh-huh, okay. Vinnie, you're up."

"I still got more." John interrupted.

94

"Sorry, Vinnie, you're next."

Bettye stifled a laugh. Vinnie smiled. John persevered.

"I called for credit checks," he said.

"Very good. I'm so damned proud of you, John, I could just wet my pants."

John smiled like a little kid reading his book report in class. "He's got three cards—Visa, MasterCard and American Express."

"No Diner's Club?" I asked.

"I didn't see one. They still make them?"

"I don't know."

"Well, anyways," John said, "he never applied for those. Well, he applied, but the records show that those three places offered him a pre-approved card first. You know what I mean?"

"Sure, I get offers like that all the time."

"You do? Hmm, you must have good credit. But," John continued, "he hasn't used the MasterCard or the Amex in over a year. And when he does use the Visa, they said it's only from places around Alabama, like zip codes that sound like they're near Birmingham. And, this is strange, Boss, so listen, never at gas stations anywhere else. And if he does run up a bill, he pays it in full the next month. There's not much activity on the card, and there are records of his non-use, too."

"Interesting."

"Who pays off a credit card every month?" John asked, incredulously.

"Me," I said.

"Yeah, no kiddin'?"

"Yeah. No kiddin'. Can Vinnie speak now?"

"Sure, Boss, I'm done."

"Thank you, John," Vinnie said, "Okay, I've got some decent info. A couple of dead ends, but some interesting stuff, too. Let's get rid of AFIS first. They say there's no recent fingerprint activity. That's a check by name only, using the DOB Bettye got from motor vehicles in Alabama.

"NCIC is better because they were doing prints long before AFIS was in business. They have him printed for his application to join the Marines in 1979 when he was nineteen. I'll get back to his military

95

record later. Okay?"

"Sure, I'm enraptured watching you work," I said.

Vinnie smiled. "Yeah, right. So, in early1984 he applies for a job with US Customs, then again a few months later, for the Border Patrol. NCIC has no dispositions for those applications, so I assumed he didn't get the jobs. I called both their personnel—sorry, human resources— departments, and thank goodness for computers. I learned that in both cases he never got investigated. He passed the written tests, the medicals, but failed the psych exams. No surprise there, huh?"

"Hardly," I said.

"Now, back to the Marines. I called a guy I know at the personnel records center in St. Louis, and he looked up Bone's 201 file or whatever the jarheads call them."

Vinnie was an ex-soldier, and he knew I remembered a 201 file as an Army personnel folder. Since he was on a roll, I didn't mention that the Marines call their enlisted personnel files SRBs or service record books.

"He spent almost four years in the Corps, the whole time in their aviation branch. He started as a mechanic and went into the cargo business. Actually, he didn't do too badly as a Marine. He got to be a corporal. His final duty MOS was cargo handler. The guy I talked to said he was probably looking to be a loadmaster on C-130s or whatever the hell they use now."

I was going to interrupt, but Vinnie waved me off. "But wait, there's more. Our man Bone does not remain a corporal forever. He gets busted down to E-3. That was after a company level Article 15 hearing. So there's no record of a judicial proceeding. We just assume that for something, and we're not sure what yet, he was considered a bad boy."

I raised my eyebrows and shifted in the chair.

"Then lo and behold, he comes up for another Article 15, and he does not finish his whole four-year commitment. He gets a general discharge and a five-month early-out. The wording on the discharge reads: 'for the good of the Corps'."

"Sounds like a real winner," I said.

"Yeah, but I didn't stop there. Knowin' he spent time at both Coronado and more recently at the USMC Aviation Support Facility in

Beaufort, South Carolina, I had a reason to talk with NCIS. You know who they are, don't you?"

"Sure, I watch them on TV—every Tuesday night."

"Yeah, same guys. So these Navy cops... He paused a little too long, smiled and said slowly "from Naval Criminal Investigative Service."

"I said I know who they are."

"Yeah, I know. I wanted to make sure John knew."

"Will you get on with it? We've been listening to you for hours."

"Yeah, right. So, these Navy cops at Beaufort tell me Bone was on their radar for a while as an unconfirmed sex offender. He was a good suspect for stuff we would recognize as sexual abuse, sexual misconduct, rape third and even a possible sodomy or two."

Bettye tossed a pen across her blotter a little too forcefully. "Ugly *and* perverted."

"You bet," Vinnie said. "Back then, DNA wasn't a very popular factor, and he was seen as a tough nut to crack during interrogation."

"They get anything to hang on him?" John asked.

"Simply put," Vinnie said, "he wouldn't go for spit when they questioned him. No victim could identify him because the subject they were after always wore a ski mask or stocking over his face, and they never had enough to sustain an arrest."

"So, how did he get his general discharge from a lousy Article 15 offense?" I asked.

"The agent looked that up for me," Vinnie said." They tried to make a sex crime case against him, but they came up short. His CO believed the agents had the right guy, and he was fed up with Bone, so he convened an Article 15 hearing at battalion level—adding some horsepower. They charged Bone with striking another NCO. Specifically, a female sergeant. He grabbed her inappropriately. Under the UCMJ, that's the uniform code of military justice, John, that's enough to constitute a simple assault."

Vinnie continued. "Rather than pursue a vigorous defense he couldn't afford and because a JAG lawyer wouldn't represent him on an Article 15 and the company grade officer they assigned to defend him looked about as smart as a carrot, Bone didn't want to chance more serious problems, and in essence copped a plea. So, Bone accepts a general discharge with no confinement, no loss of back pay, and he keeps his lance corporal rank."

"Bone got a sweetheart deal, and the Corps got rid of a potentially constant headache," I said.

"Yup," Vinnie said.

"Anything else?"

"Sure, boss, I'm just gettin' warmed up. The agent I spoke with is going to get us whatever he can from Beaufort PD and South Carolina State on Bone. But there was a note in the case folder that the local cops said the reports of sex crimes seemed to drop way down as soon as Bone got outta Dodge."

"So what didn't happen, says more than what they tried to prove against him," I offered.

"Exactly. Now, the last thing I checked—Social Security—can, as you know, be a real pain in the ass with all the government's privacy crap. You know how they want a case number with the subject of the investigation as the actual suspect?"

"Yeah, I know."

"Well, I called another guy I know, and he's getting us a printout. It'll take a few days, but we don't need a release or nothin'. What he could tell me was that Bone got his Social Security number in Mississippi when he was fifteen. Cool, huh?"

"You did all that while I was gone?"

"Yeah, well." He shrugged. "You know how it is."

"You're showing off, Vincent."

"Hey, I don't care about you or John. I wanted to impress Bettye."

"She's impressed. Right, Betts?"

"Vinnie, darlin', I haven't been this impressed since Sam got here."

"Hey, Sarge, what about me?" John sounded neglected.

"I'm sorry, Johnny. You're impressive, too."

"Hey, Sam, she called me darlin'." Vinnie raised his eyebrows twice, showing the appropriate amount of excitement.

"Betts," I said, "don't ever kiss him. He'll never wash again."

Chapter Seventeen

After learning all that good stuff about the dastardly Telford Bone, I had the enchanting Lady Lambert inform all the knights of Prospect to search the length and breadth of the land for Bone and his garish Hummer. She also requested assistance from the sheriff of Blount and all his mobile minions.

At eight that night, Stanley Rose called me at home. A county sergeant named Hugh Bledsoe spotted Bone's Hummer parked outside Jodelle and Dorie Asher's home.

Stan and POs Bobby Crockett and Junior Huskey responded to the Maryville neighborhood and confronted our private eye. Stan convinced him to drive to Prospect PD for a chat with yours truly. I never asked how Stanley was so persuasive.

"What do you say, Telford?" I asked as I walked into the squad room. "Still working around beautiful downtown Prospect?"

Bone turned his pale gray eyes on me and smiled in a way that made me want to caress him with a Louisville Slugger.

He said, "Well, hello, Chief. Long time no see."

Looking at Telford Bone felt something like being forced to spend time in the serpent cage of the Knoxville Zoo. My three cops didn't seem any more pleased with his company than I did.

Bone wore his nighttime work clothes. He left the zoot suit at home, but kept the gold silk shirt, by then sporting extensive underarm perspiration stains and tucked into black hip-hugger jeans that made his wide ass look even more ridiculous. A black tooled belt with a large silver trophy buckle, half the size of a manhole cover, kept the jeans from falling.

"Why were you sitting outside Dorie Asher's house?" I asked.

"Just thinkin'." He showed us an insipid, lingering smile. "I do my best thinkin' when I'm near the person I'd like ta interview."

"This is the second time you've shown up at the Asher's home. The first time you were told not to come back. Under normal circumstances if you were foolish enough to try for three, we'd lock you up for harassment. I'd even check into the stalking statutes and see if there was a spot in there for you."

He retained the smirk and shook his head. "I ain't had no intention o' harassin' or stalkin' no-body. I'm just doin' my job."

I took a turn smiling. "But some of us think you came here to intimidate a victim and a witness. And we take that personally and contemplate doing things that might make your lawyer shiver in his three-piece suit. Are we clear on that?"

While I spoke, Bone sat there picking at his cuticles, not looking at me. His version of cool.

"I surely can't understand why y'all are gettin' upset over me doin' a simple job I been paid to do," he said.

"In both Alabama and Tennessee you have to be licensed and bonded to hang out a PI's shingle. You are not so endowed in either place," I said, offering him enlightenment.

"No law against doing some work for a friend who needs the he'p I can provide, is there?"

He bit off a snip of hangnail and spit it into hyperspace. I wanted to smack him. Slob.

"Telford, you can split all those hairs with a judge if you'd like. You're here voluntarily, and I appreciate that. So tonight, you've used your get-out-of-jail-free card. Listen closely, and when I'm finished you can leave—this time."

He tilted his head and lost the grin.

"I'm revoking your right to investigate in Tennessee. If you go anywhere near the Ashers or Laura Hensley, I'll charge you with tampering with a witness and hindering prosecution. Since the underlying crime we're interested in is a felony, each of those charges are also felonies. Capishe?"

My short criminal law lesson didn't seem to impress him. He dropped his eyes and continued tearing his fingers to shreds.

I glanced at Bobby Crockett. If the look on his face reflected his true feelings, he stood within a few seconds of placing a strangle hold on our detainee.

"And since the closest thing we can find as a home for you is a couple of PO Boxes south of Birmingham," I said, "I don't doubt my request for a remand to our county jail will be approved. And, as you know, things move slowly here in the South. The term *speedy trial* may be a very subjective thing."

Bone looked up in to my eyes. He squinted and scowled. His version of trying to intimidate a police chief. I glared back before speaking. He lowered his eyes.

"Look, Telford," I said in conclusion, "you gave this your best shot. It won't work. Call Billy Ray Finchum. Tell him you're heading back to Alabama."

He first moved his upper body in my direction, then pivoted his whole head like an owl, lowered his platinum blond eyebrows and looked at me through reptilian slits.

"Well, well, well," he said, "I guess I'm not wanted hereabouts."

"That's a good guess, Telford." I said that in the nicest possible way.

"Lord have mercy, but I'd get me a complex if I had ta deal with y'all very often."

The same odor of Listerine I smelled at our first meeting permeated his body, fainter but still unmistakable.

"Let's not fart around, Mr. Bone. You were sent here to scare off the people who can tell me about Dallas Finchum's past deeds. I'm not going to allow that. Go back, and tell Billy Ray his tough-guy act is ineffectual. I'll dig out my law books and see what's the most I can do to hurt him and especially you, if you two persist in sticking your noses into this business. I ask you again, are we clear on this?"

He closed his eyes and nodded his long head. He reminded me of an odd-looking puppet, manipulated by an unseen master.

"Oh, Chief, we are indeed." His smile came back momentarily. Then he pursed his lips, looking like he just sucked on a lemon. He turned his moods on and off like a light bulb.

101

"May I go now, or are you chargin' me with somethin' t'night?"

Arrogantly, he looked at my three uniformed cops. Stanley gave him an evil eye in return. Junior and Bobby stared back at him, unfazed by his act. Once he finished with them, he turned his eyes on me.

"I planned on watching a few Law & Order reruns," I said. "I don't have time for you tonight. And these gentlemen have real people to deal with."

He got up slowly, hiked up his low-cut pants, moved his narrow shoulders around a little and said, "Gennlemen, I bid y'all a good evenin'. Oh, and Chief, do say hello to Sergeant Lambert for me. She's a lovely woman."

His eyes looked like those of a piranha watching a small animal swimming through brackish water.

After he walked out of the building, all four of us looked at each other.

Bobby Crockett said, "Where the hell'd you find that one, boss?"

"Turned over a rock, be my guess," Junior said.

"I've seen some major league assholes in my life," Stanley said, "but that one is right up on top of the list."

"My, how perceptive you lads are tonight," I said. "Mr. Bone reminds me of something out of an old-fashioned horror flick. If I were ten-years-old again, I'd have nightmares."

"I can't say he did anything to improve my appetite, but I'm on my way home for dinner," Stan said. "I'll try not to think about Telford Bone while I'm eating. My wife would get upset if I threw up."

"Then, for the next hour, you two brave young men can keep the streets of Prospect safe for democracy. See you guys tomorrow." I gave Junior and Bobby each a pat on the back.

As I turned and walked toward the back door, I heard Junior say, "That's one mighty weird-lookin' booger."

"Yeah, bud," Bobby said. "I wouldn't mind wrappin' a night stick 'round his head."

Chapter Eighteen

Standing in the large doorway of the city garage, I scanned the municipal parking lot. Nothing unusual there. I switched my look to the Hardee's burger joint across North Main Street. Three-quarters of the parking spaces were full, and vehicles in the drive-up lane wrapped around the building and spilled out into a side street. Someone must have broadcast a public service warning, "Calorie and fat levels thought to be dangerously low—stock up now."

At 10:15, Earl Biggins, the city mechanic, and his helper, young Logan Mapes, looked about half-finished changing the oil on my Crown Victoria. With a little time on my hands, I stepped outside into the September sunshine and made a phone call.

"Hi, did I wake you?" I asked.

"It's after ten o'clock. I've been up for a little while," Rachel said, but still sounded sleepy.

She usually gets home sometime after midnight, not long after her half-hour eleven o'clock news program ends.

"Are you still in your nighties?"

"Wouldn't you like to know?"

"Yes, I would."

We had lots of conversations like that. Rachel and I like each other. But we're very careful not to use the other L word.

"You are such a phony," she said. "If I invited you here and met you at the door in a sexy negligee, you'd probably leave."

"I probably wouldn't leave, but I'd force myself to behave."

"I own some very sexy lingerie. Don't bet your next paycheck on that one, mister," she said.

"I have a will of iron."

"Okay, big tough guy, be here in an hour and see what my nighties look like."

I let out a guttural growl before speaking. "I refuse to be taken for granted."

"Ha. Coward."

The woman can be perceptive at times.

"That may be true, but the last time I looked, we were married, and not to each other."

"Pooh. You're such a chicken. I can spot one a mile away," she said.

"Yeah, what makes you so smart?"

"I'm a reporter. I know everything."

"Who'd you learn that line from?"

"Some tall, dark and handsome guy who lives in the Smokies. Oh, wait, he's not so dark anymore. There's lots of snow on those mountains."

"Well, I was going to be nice to you, invite you to lunch and give you an update on all the excitement in Prospect. But now I'm not sure I want to hang out with a short woman who's over forty."

"You can be such a snot, and it comes off effortlessly."

"Yeah, I know. A doctor's trying to help me, but the medication isn't working."

"I think he gave you stupid pills."

I often wonder why I let the women in my life get away with saying things like that.

"In spite of your nastiness," I said, "I invite you to lunch. Do you know where the Crown and Goose is?"

"No, never heard of it."

"It's on Central between Summit Hill and Jackson. They have a free parking lot across the street. I'll be there at high noon. If you get there before me tell the host, his name is Geoffrey, who you're meeting. I'll reserve a table in the tap room."

"Wow, the host knows you personally?"

"Sort of."

"What's this place like?"

"Like a London pub. They have oodles of English beers on tap, super pub-grub and a posh atmosphere."

My mind began wandering. I started thinking about her nighties again.

"What's pub-grub?" she asked.

"Shepherd's pie, fish and chips, ploughman's lunches, all kinds of stuff."

"Can I get a salad?"

She would order a salad in an ice cream parlor.

"Sure, they have plenty of rabbit food for you skinny little girls."

"Hey, I'm not skinny."

"I've noticed, baby. Va va voom."

"What's that mean?"

"It means I'm getting hot just thinking about that body in a night gown."

"You can be such a pig without even trying."

"Surely you don't mean that." I tried sounding hurt.

"Well, maybe only a little. You always say complimentary things…sometimes in a very *personal* way. How did you find this place?"

She can change a subject as quickly as I can.

"Ralph told me about it. The FBI guys go there."

"He isn't going to be there today, is he?"

"Who knows? Who cares? I'm getting a table for two. Ralph and the other Feds can go pound salt"

"I love it when you talk tough."

I thought I should interject a little Humphrey Bogart into the conversation. "That's me, sweetheart, a hardboiled gumshoe. An old school tough guy. Every girl's dreamboat."

"Oh, please!"

"See you at noon, doll-face. And put on some clothes."

"Creep-o."

"Here's lookin' at you, kid."

"Oh, good-bye."

* * * *

The sign on the restaurant, a Kelly green shield with yellow letters and a big white goose under a king's crown, would have looked appropriate in any English city. A similar sign marked the parking lot on the opposite side of South Central Avenue in Knoxville. After parking my Crown Victoria and using the side window as a mirror, like a good soldier, I insured that my shirt, belt buckle and pants lined up in a perfect 'gig-line'. Satisfied with that, I straightened the Windsor knot of my necktie and walked across the street to the Crown and Goose Pub.

Geoffrey, the owner's son, a tall young man with brown hair, dressed in a light gray suit, took me to a round table across from the long, dark wood bar. As usual, Rachel was running late.

At ten-after-twelve, I watched her enter and stop at the host's station. Geoff looked about a foot taller than her. Rachel took off her large oval shades and dropped them into a black leather purse. She spoke to Geoffrey. He smiled and led her to the table.

She wore a white and black wrap-around dress that almost caused me to have an optical illusion. If it hadn't fit so well, I would have thought it a bit too loud. But she could easily get away with it.

Geoffrey pulled back a chair for her. She smiled at him and sat.

"Can I get you something to drink?" he asked. I had already gotten a pint of their house bitters.

"Chardonnay, please," she said and settled into the chair.

"We have several available by the glass—California or Australia?"

"Oh, you choose. I'd like something more fruity than dry and oaky."

"Okay," he said. "I'll be right back with something nice and fruity." He grinned and tried to look suave.

The young man actually tried to flirt with my date. I'd show him how to act suave.

As he walked away, Bogey helped me say, "Hi ya, Shorty. You look swell today."

Mrs. Williamson wrinkled her brow and gave me one of those looks women use when they're not sure if you're crazy or cute.

"Thanks, It's good to see you," she wiggled her chair closer to the table. "This is a nice place. Are the pubs in England all like this?"

"You've not been?"

"No, I never thought of England as a place to vacation with kids."

106

Rachel has two sons, one sixteen and one thirteen.

"Yeah, I guess it's no Disney World."

"So, is this a typical English pub?"

"It's like a classy London pub. The country pubs seem to be darker, older-looking, maybe more cozy. This is nice in a city sort of way. Good service and good food."

It's a habit with me. I always steal a few looks beyond the person I'm talking with. A few people sat at the bar—two couples and three single men, all with drinks. By quarter-after-twelve, most of the tables were occupied, and the conversational noise steadily increased.

Rachel opened her menu and looked at the salad selections on the left side page. I already knew I'd have the shepherd's pie.

"These salads sound interesting," she said and kept looking. "Oooh, this one sounds delicious." She pointed to one of the descriptions.

"Good, I'm glad you're easy to please. Most good-looking girls are a pain in the keister."

She looked up at me, smiled and placed her hand over mine. "I'm just happy to see you," she said.

Geoff came back to drop off Rachel's chardonnay. He tried to sound cool by telling her he chose a William Hill '07. He was spending my money, what did he care? Rachel gave him her million-dollar smile and a sexy thank you. Then he just stood there, the young putz. I reminded him we needed to order. He left and sent a waitress to handle that.

I noticed a little guy in a chocolate brown suit sitting at the bar talking on his cell phone. Then he held it at arm's length looking at it. Maybe he needed reading glasses.

"I'm glad to be with you, too," I said, wanting to sound sincere.

She held up her glass. I picked up my pint and touched the rim of her wineglass.

"Of all the cockamamie places in the world, sweetheart, we'll always have Knoxville."

"Oh, Bogey, you're such a smoothie," she said.

"That's me, sister. A dame like you brings out the gentleman in me."

She laughed and shook her head. "So, tell me, what's exciting in Prospect?"

I gave Rachel the whole story, including a detailed description of

Telford Bone.

"Yuck. Where did you find that guy? He sounds repulsive."

"Ask Bettye about him sometime. He gave her the creeps, too."

"What are you going to do next?"

"I think Dallas Finchum is a soon-to-be-unemployed policeman. Other than that, who knows?"

"Will he be arrested for the rape?"

"Probably not. Hamilton County would have to do that. I don't think our victim is up for the trip and all the crap she'd have to face in court. And all the mishandled evidence and other problems with the case would make it a waste of time."

"Will he be punished at all for what he did to her?"

"Not in the conventional way. He'll lose his job. He'll have to live with what the Prospect cops think of him, and I don't know what else. Dallas isn't a criminal type, and he won't be pleased with what the next few months bring."

A waitress came with my shepherd's pie and Rachel's meal, something called a Kensington Garden salad, probably named for all the vegetation somebody once saw growing there—roasted eggplant, tomatoes, mushrooms, artichokes and a dozen other things on a bed of lettuce, topped with balsamic vinaigrette.

"Would you like anything else to drink?" the waitress asked.

"Sure, two more, please." I said.

Rachel smiled and shook her head again. "Do you always drink this much at lunch?"

"Only when I'm with you, baby. I need the alcohol to curb my lust."

"Oh, oink, you're so easy to hate."

"Quite the contrary, my dear woman. I believe you're smitten by my boyish charm." I let the pub atmosphere influence my London accent.

She flipped a switch and showed me a 500-watt smile. "I know."

I must have looked exceptionally charming and irresistible at that moment. Rachel leaned closer and kissed my cheek.

I noticed the little guy at the bar played with his cell phone again. To our right, four yuppies wearing white shirts and ties drank beer and looked at their menus. I watched Geoffrey running around helping the waitresses and seating more guests.

"Do you think I can do a story soon?" Rachel asked.

"Probably soon, but I don't know when. I have to wait for the mayor to tell me they're terminating Dallas."

"What's he waiting for?"

"He has to discuss everything from hiring and firing to from whom we buy the toilet paper with the City Council. And I guess he still hopes the kid will act like a stand-up guy and resign."

"Do you think Dallas will?"

"I gave him a pep talk. It's to his advantage to leave voluntarily. If he does resign, I'll probably have to make a deal to keep my end confidential. If that happens, you'll have to get your story from Jodelle Asher and maybe her daughter."

"No comment from my favorite police chief?"

"Not if I make a deal with the kid. I can point you in the right direction, but I can't give you anything from my office. All the internal paperwork will be made confidential."

"I could get a court order."

I made a face and then smiled. "No, you can't."

"Can't fool you, can I?"

"Hardly."

"You can be so honest it's disgusting. Speaking as a reporter, that is."

"It's what you like most about me."

"And I thought it was your old Austin-Healey."

"Not my boyish smile?"

"Well, that, too. But if you can't tell me anything, will you take me to lunch again?"

"A man's got to eat. And I hate to eat alone."

Chapter Nineteen

At 9:30 the next morning, my cell phone rang. Weeks before, Junior Huskey showed me how to download a ring-tone. Now the thing vibrated and played an instrumental version of *Paint it Black*. I answered.

"Hello, Mr. Jenkins, this is Sara Wiston in Maryland. Do you remember me?"

"Of course, Ms. Wiston. How are you?"

Maryland meant Fort George G. Meade, an interesting little place just outside the hamlets of Odenton and Columbia. I certainly remembered Ms. Wiston.

"I'm well, thanks. I have a call for you from Mr. Irving."

I couldn't let her get away with something like that. "Mr. Irving? I don't know a . . . Oh, yes, of course, that Mr. Irving."

My old friend Irv Kauffmann, currently seconded from the CIA to the NSA, suffered from terminal spookisytis and enjoyed using numerous sobriquets.

She laughed. "Please hold one. As long as you remember him, I'll connect you."

"Thanks ever so much. I'm ashamed of myself for not remembering sooner."

She laughed again. "You're very welcome, and please don't be ashamed."

The transfer went through with a click.

"Sam?"

"Sam who?"

"For God's sake, Sam. It's me."

"Me who?"

"Sam!"

"That's Mr. Samuel, if you please."

"May we stop this?"

Like many high level Federal civil servants, Irving has very little sense of humor.

"Hi, Irv. What's the haps?"

"You normally don't speak like this."

"I know, but our usual conversations are so littered with spook-speak that I've grown tired of them."

"Be serious, please."

"Only if you insist."

I hoped we were being recorded by one of Irving's big satellites in the sky. I love to embarrass him.

"Sam, do you have a Detective Falcone working for you?"

"Why do you ask?"

I wanted to hum *Telstar,* but I didn't know the words—if there were any words.

"A red-flagged item was just brought to my attention. Something based on a telephone inquiry from a Detective Falcone of the Prospect, Tennessee Police Department."

"He sort of works for me."

"Sort of?"

"He's still on the payroll of my old department, but he's currently *assisting* me with a problem I have."

"Is he authorized to make inquiries?"

"Of course he is."

"He called NCIC and other Federal resources for information on one Telford Bone. Are you investigating this man?"

"Aha!"

"Aha?"

Irving Kauffmann is someone I met many years ago during the Vietnam War. Currently, he's one of the many deputy directors of the Central Intelligence Agency. His present assignment deals with all the computer operations at the National Security Agency at Fort Meade, Maryland. More importantly, Irv still owes me a big favor.

"Do you or your cronies know something about Telford Bone?" I asked.

"My cronies? Oh, come now. I remember that term often used in conjunction with the infamous Madam Mao and her followers," Irving said.

"So, what's your interest in Bone?"

"It's a long story."

I sat up and waited for an interesting saga.

"It's your dime." I prompted him again.

"Yes, well…"

"You know him personally?" I asked.

"You're interrogating me."

"I'm a cop. It's what I do."

"I don't know him personally."

"I'm listening."

"Telford Bone came to our attention back in the eighties." Irv spoke with his usual professorial delivery. "After his severance from the Marine Corps, he found his way into the employ of Southern Air Transport. I'm confident you know SAT was part of the Agency's civilian air augmentation."

"Sure, the Air America equivalent for Central and South America."

"Basically, yes."

Air America and Southern Air could well have been called Air CIA by travel agents worldwide.

"And you want me to leave Bone alone? Sorry, I didn't mean to sound poetic."

"Quite the opposite. Mr. Bone represents an embarrassment to my employers."

Why couldn't he just say the CIA?

"I can hardly wait to hear this."

"I'm sure. Well, as you may know, SAT was a main supply conduit into places like El Salvador, Guatemala and Honduras during those Reagan years. Telford Bone, as an employee of SAT, found his way there on many occasions. But he wasn't using the name Telford Bone then."

"I'd change that one myself. What did he call himself—Oliver

North?"

"Hardly. May I continue?"

"I'm beginning to palpitate. Please do."

"Between his USMC time and his 1986 hiring by SAT, Bone seems to have served in the Foreign Legion."

"French?" That *was* interesting.

"Yes, not Spanish."

"He got out of the Marines in '83 and was hired by Southern Air in '86," I said. "Why such a short stay in the Legion?"

"Officially, we know they terminated his contract. Conjecture is, his conduct was sub-standard."

"Sub-standard behavior for a legionnaire? Good Lord. I didn't know that was possible."

"We've heard the French suspected him of things we also hold against him."

"Conduct below the norm of both CIA and the French? He must be a vampire."

"That's not humorous."

I thought it was damned clever.

"Then I guess he's as bad as he looks," I said. "Have you seen a recent photo?"

"I've seen several, but nothing very recent."

"Take it from me, pal, you're lucky."

"Explain."

"I may be speaking subjectively, but the man's repulsive."

"Really?"

"Really."

"Our agent's notes on the man and the reports obtained from various police agencies around the globe tend to indicate that his conduct may be equally repulsive."

"Your delivery is flawless," I said. "Now I'm ready to pay you to finish your story."

"Not necessary, since I may be importuning you to assist us."

"Importuning me?"

"Yes, it means…"

"Stop. I know what it means. Finish your story, and tell me what you want."

"Right. Well, to make this story short, several jurisdictions—none within the confines of the continental United States—wish to question or arrest Mr. Bone for assorted sexually related crimes and the odd murder or two."

"Son-of-a-gun."

"In addition to these criminal acts that we are somewhat interested in," he said, "DEA believes that once Bone became familiar with the Latin American turf, he built up a list of acquaintances there for private enterprise. Mr. Bone has recorded no wages for many years, yet he seems to always fly first class, so to speak."

"And what is Latin America's most important product?" I asked. "Certainly not salsa music."

"Certainly not."

"Do you like him for gun running as well?" That seemed logical to me.

"That wouldn't surprise us."

"Great. I had him in custody the other night and released him after a few healthy threats to get outta Dodge."

"He's gone? You're joking?"

Irving always generates sarcasm within me. "Sure, he's right here, and we're both laughing our asses off 'cause we gotcha."

"Not humorous. Where is he now?"

"I hope close by, but if not—I haven't a clue."

"That's not good." Irving sounded upset.

Not my fault he called late. "As someone once told me, Irving," I said, "'Your problem, old friend, not mine.'"

"Sam, I admit no one has been beating the bushes relentlessly, but this is the first we've come close to Bone in a long time. Can you find him?"

"Maybe. I usually accomplish the impossible. Why not do it once more? Oh, modest me, I'm hogging the floor. Continue telling me more about our mutual friend."

"Yes, I may have facts that would be of help to you. It seems Mr. Telford Bone, originally of Mississippi, signed into the Foreign Legion as one Calhoun Grant. He used that name and a new Social Security number when he accepted employment with SAT."

"Wait a minute. You said Calhoun Grant?"

"Correct, Calhoun Grant."

"Calhoun spelled the Scottish way or like Rory Calhoun?"

"Calhoun spelled the conventional way, C-A-L-H-O-U-N."

"Close enough. This bastard has a sense of humor. Do you know who Calhoun Grant was?"

"Not a clue."

"Tisk, tisk, Irving," I said. "Colquhoun, spelled C-O-L-Q-U-H-O-U-N and pronounced Cahoon Grant, was a famous intelligence rider of the British Army, working for the Duke of Wellington in Spain during the peninsula campaign of the early 1800s."

"Your knowledge of military history is second to none," he said with a note of sarcasm.

"No need to get caustic."

"Of course, back to my story," he said. "This fellow Bone or Grant or whomever he is, while working for SAT—our company, so to speak—is suspected of what you and I would consider heinous crimes against women."

"And that embarrasses your employers."

"Exactly."

"After twenty years?" I let my surprise show.

"There is no statute of limitations on murder. And these countries are still our allies. Besides, we have been lead to believe that Bone has been doing business in these same countries up to and including the very recent past. He is suspect in similar occurrences, some of which are quite recent."

"So everything has yet to be proven, but most of the cops with whom you're in contact believe Bone is a serial rapist and killer."

"Yes."

"Are there any warrants lodged against him?"

"No."

"You want him detained and held for questioning? I suppose asking under what authority would be a silly question."

"You're a most creative person. I have every confidence you'll think of something."

"Lucky me."

The things I've been called to do for my country. Jeez!

"Why didn't you call yesterday?" I asked.

"Another silly question."

"Not to me."

"Don't be melodramatic."

"May I assume that the information you're giving me is not for publication or sharing with other law enforcement agencies at this time?"

"I'm telling you because I'm confident you *will not* pass this intelligence on to anyone. You understand, better than most, how my employers feel about internal embarrassment. Your track record with me is beyond reproach."

"I'm flattered."

"So you should be."

Pfui.

"The FBI often overlooks the Constitution interfering with them depriving citizens of their civil rights," I said, "but they may want more than my request to hold Bone in custody while I find some spook willing to take a drive down to Knoxville."

"Here's a simple solution, my friend," Irv offered with some relish. "Tell the agent with whom you speak to access their liaison link with the Agency. Then simply use code word *Mandrake*."

"*Mandrake*? As in the Magician? That's the magic word?"

"It will open doors for you and the local Bureau people."

"Fascinating."

"We have our moments."

Chapter Twenty

I spent fifteen minutes going over my copy of the Villa Napoli's menu, preparing myself to go out to lunch with the guys.

"Look at the menu in the restaurant, Boss." John sounded impatient.

Vinnie Falcone waited patiently.

"Shut up, John. I'm reading," I said.

John stood in my office, jingling the change in his pocket.

"I like to know what I want before I get to a restaurant," I said. "I hate surprises."

Early that morning, John Gallagher appropriated an extra ten dollars in lunch money from his wife. He looked more than eager to get on the road, fidgeting like an expectant father.

"Relax, John. We got all day," Vinnie said.

I decided on Chef Tommy Cutrone's homemade ravioli with the stuffing di giorno and a house salad. I knew Vinnie would get a kick out of meeting Nick Cutrone, the restaurant owner and old gangster wannabe from Hoboken. And Nicky would like to meet another goombah from the metro area.

Then my phone rang.

"Chief, there are two gentlemen from the sheriff's office here to see you."

Bettye never calls me Chief unless she thinks there's important business afoot.

"Okay, Sarge, send them in."

John and Vinnie left to wait in the lobby.

"Detective Bo Stallins walked into my office with an older man I'd

117

never met before.

Stallins wore a white, short-sleeved shirt, black slacks and a red and blue striped tie. Bo was in his forties, about six-two and in reasonably good shape. His badge, cell phone and a holstered .40 caliber Glock automatic all hung on his pants belt.

The other man looked ten years older and twenty pounds heavier. All the same, gear hung on his belt. He wore a blue dress shirt, black knitted tie and gray slacks.

"Bo," I said, "how's it goin'?" We shook hands.

"Sam, you doin' aw right today?"

That's a local greeting, not a real question. As it is in most areas, no one ever waits for an answer.

"This here's Captain Barkens from our In-ternal Affairs section."

Barkens stuck out his hand. "Clifford Barkens, Chief. Good ta meet ya."

"Sam Jenkins. Same here." We shook hands. "Sit down gentlemen. What can I do for you?"

Barkens began. "Bo had standby last night—midnight to eight. He got a call to meet an assault victim at Blount Memorial."

I sat there not knowing why I should be interested in an assault victim in another jurisdiction. But I exercised restraint and tried not to think *ravioli*.

"The victim claims two uniformed Prospect officers beat him up around twelve, twelve-thirty last night."

That didn't sound kosher to me. "Where did this victim say it happened?"

"On Merritt Road in Maryville." The location rang a bell.

"I know nothing about this," I said, "but let me guess the owners of the nearest home."

Both Barkens and Stallins looked surprised.

I grinned. "After I use my psychic abilities to guess the exact location, I'll amaze you with the name of your complainant."

"I don't understand." Barkens shifted on his chair.

"I'll explain. First, how about house number 1869, the home of one Laura Jean Hensley and her parents?"

Stallins tilted his head, and Barkens nodded slowly.

"And," I said, with more than adequate theatrics, "the complainant is…a rather odd-looking chap…an unlicensed PI from Alabama named Telford Bone. Am I right?"

"That house is right close to where he said he got picked up. How'd you know that?" Bo asked.

I explained our relationship with Bone, stressing the fact that he seemed determined to intimidate both a witness and a complainant of mine.

Barkens added that, according to Bone, after confronting him on Merritt Road, the cops allegedly made him follow them to a non-residential stretch of road where they forced him to stop. Then they pulled him out of the car and took turns beating him.

I shook my head, having trouble believing anyone would entertain a complaint from titillating Telford. "Let me ask you this," I said. "Does Bone name the Prospect cops or just give a general description?"

"No names, good descriptions and two car numbers—501 and 507."

"Very clever," I said. "I wasn't at Merritt Road last night, but I'd bet a two week paycheck that this is one-hundred-and-ten-percent bullshit. Bone is a goddamn liar."

Bo looked apologetic and said, "I had ta take his complaint, Sam."

I nodded, trying not to make a friend and a good cop feel bad. "I'll also bet the descriptions will fit two cops who worked a four-to-twelve shift yesterday. These two cops and their supervisor, Sergeant Rose, picked up Bone sitting outside the Asher home. Dorie Asher is a complainant of mine Bone wants to interview. She refuses to speak with him."

I gave the two sheriff's men a brief account of the whole Dallas Finchum case so things would make sense to them.

"Those three officers brought Bone here, and I questioned him," I said. "The cops are Davis Huskey Jr. and Bobby John Crockett. They drive 501 and 507 respectively."

"You understand that I'm…we're obligated to investigate Mr. Bone's complaint," Barkens said. "I need ta interview Officers…Crockett and Huskey, you said?"

"That's right. They're off now, and they're doing another four-to-twelve today. Is tomorrow morning okay for you?"

"How about nine o'clock in my office?" Barkens asked.

"I'll have them there. But I've got to tell you ahead of time, I'm sending a lawyer with them. And for the record, I'm reiterating my thought that Bone's story is unadulterated bullshit."

"I understand."

Barkens looked agreeable to that—no faces or body language to make me think he resented the idea Junior and Bobby would be legally represented.

"I know you're just doing your job," I said, "but I repeat, we'll soon learn this story is fabricated, and if I obtain evidence of that, I'll prosecute Bone."

"Sam," Bo said, "Weren't no doubt this guy, Bone, was beat bad. He had a swollen cheek, and they had ta tape his ribs. He took it bad ta the body."

"Bo, I don't give a shit if he shot himself in the foot to make it look good. There's more to this than meets the eye. I'll...we'll sort all this out."

"I hope so, Chief," Barkens said. "I'm sure willin' to hear what your men have ta say."

"Bone says he's a private detective," Stallins said. "I ain't had time ta check him out. You think that's not true?"

"Gentlemen, if Bone is a private cop, I'm a Franciscan monk. We had time to check and found no trace of him being licensed in Alabama, and certainly not in Tennessee. Far as I'm concerned, he's an all-around liar."

"I'll be damned," Bo said.

"Do you have a local address for Bone?" I asked. "He had been at the Foothills View Motel. I've since learned he checked out. I need to see him again."

"Chief, I think it would be best if y'all didn't contact him while these charges are pendin'," Barkens said.

"Captain, I'll let you do your thing, but if I find Bone anywhere near my victim or the witness, I'll lock him up and charge him."

"I understand that, too."

* * * *

"John, Vinnie, you guys go to lunch without me. The shit just hit the fan, and I've got to start cleaning up."

"What happened, Boss?" John asked.

I told those two and Bettye the story.

"You don't believe either Junior or Bobby John had anything to do with that do you, Sam?" Bettye asked.

"No, of course I don't. I hope everybody involved sees this for what it really is. But the boys will have to account for their time."

She nodded and looked concerned for two of our boys.

"You want us to hang around and give you a hand with something?" Vinnie asked.

"No, thanks. You guys go to lunch. Just ask Nicky to make me a doggie bag—whatever ravioli Tommy made for today, a half loaf of bread and a bottle of appropriate wine. I'll trust his judgment."

"Sam," Bettye expressed a note of displeasure. I understood.

"Okay, forget the wine," I said.

She smiled. My work spouse had spoken.

I tried to look offended. "Now that I've just given up half my lunch, Miss Bettye, will you help me track down our two suspects?"

"Of course, I will, darling. What do you want me to do?"

"Find Bobby, and have him come in. I'll look for Junior."

* * * *

Neither Junior Huskey nor Bobby John Crockett proved difficult to find. When Bettye left for lunch at one o'clock, both were on their way to the office.

Junior arrived first. He waited while I took a phone call from a complainant and dispatched a car to handle her problem. By the time I finished that, Crockett walked in.

"Bobby," I said, "do me a favor, and answer the phones." He nodded and sat in Bettye's chair. "Come inside, Junior, and I'll tell you what's up."

"You gonna tell me, too, boss?" Bobby asked.

"Yeah, but give us a few minutes. I'll be right back."

Junior and I sat in my guest chairs facing each other.

"A captain from the sheriff's Internal Affairs section showed up here at noon," I said.

Junior looked at me like a kid sitting in the principal's office, waiting for an ax to fall.

"He told me that shithead Telford Bone accused you and Bobby of beating him up last night."

"Do what?" Junior looked at me as if I had just accused him of bestiality.

"He claims you two, both in Prospect PD cars, found him near Laura Hensley's house on Merritt Road in Maryville. He said you made him follow you to an isolated stretch of road, and then you two took turns beating him badly enough to put him in the hospital."

"Now that's a gat-dag lie!" Junior said, raising his voice.

"That's what I told the captain."

"Well, it is. You believe me, don't ya?" He searched my face for encouragement.

"I do. Sure. Tell me what you did last night from eleven o'clock on."

"I didn't do nothin' from 11:00 till 11:30 when I gassed my car. Then I brought in some paperwork. Joey Gillespie relieved me. He had the central sector last night. And then I left around quarter-ta-twelve."

"Where'd you go after you left?"

"They gotta know that?"

I hate when people answer a question with a question.

"Yeah, *I* gotta know that. Bone claims you two confronted him between midnight and 12:30."

"Aw, shoot, Sam, I gotta say exactly what I done? Cain't I jest say I went home?"

He really had me interested.

"Kid, I'm going to send you to see this Captain Barkens tomorrow morning with a lawyer. Today you're going to tell me exactly where you went and what you did."

Frustrated didn't adequately describe how Junior looked.

"Aw, man, can I jest tell ya where I went?"

"Okay, good start. Tell me."

"I changed clothes and went ta see Stephanie."

"Joe Costello's Stephanie?" I sounded surprised to myself.

122

"Yes, sir."

"Stephanie Garner?"

"Yes, sir."

Stephanie Garner works for the lawyer I wanted to represent my two cops.

"Stephanie lives with her parents," I said. "You got there after midnight?"

"They're away for a week."

"You two were alone?"

I guess I couldn't help smiling. I'm bad like that.

"Yes, sir."

"Are you two, uh…you know…uh…?

"I guess."

Junior squirmed in his chair.

I showed him a lecherous grin. "You bum. She's a movie star."

"Aw, man. I guess. I mean…uh-huh."

"And you two are…?

I must have sounded like a father proud of his son.

"Yeah, I guess. I gotta tell somebody else all this?"

"Maybe not," I said. "But remember who suggested that you invite Stephanie out to dinner."

"Yes, sir, I remember."

I suppose I was proud of myself.

"You bum. She likes you, huh?"

"Why're you callin' me that, Sam?"

"Hey, kid, good for you."

"I guess."

"Okay, sit tight. I'll take care of this. And don't be embarrassed."

It took him a long moment, but he answered. "Okay."

Easy for me to say. He looked embarrassed.

"But never tell John," I advised.

"Do what?"

"John can act like he's mentally twelve. He'd tease you to death."

"Aw, shoot."

Junior may not have seen his life getting any easier.

"Go tell Bobby to come in here, and you listen for the phones for a few minutes."

He nodded, still looking unhappy. "Okay."

Junior trudged out of my office and switched places with his coworker.

I asked Bobby Crockett the same questions.

"I was sittin' in here with Stanley till about 11:30 when Vern Hobbs came in. He had the northeast sector last night. Then I went home."

"Any stops? Any girlfriends? Any anything?"

"Yeah, I made a traffic stop down at South Main and McTeer Pike. Ol' boy ran the red light. I spent fifteen minutes or so with him 'cause he didn't have his license or reg-staration with him."

"So, you had the dispatcher check motor vehicle files?"

"Nope."

"Why not?"

"Man gave me a sob-story 'bout havin' a fight with his wife and takin' off without his wallet. Said he knew Harley Flatt and asked me fer a break. Since I already had my ten summonses fer the month and bein' off duty and all, I let him go with a warnin'."

"Remember his name?"

"Not exactly. Dewey somethin'. Said he's from down near Cold Springs."

"You check with Harley Flatt?"

"Uh-huh. T'day."

"And?"

"I'm guessin' the ol' boy hoo-dooed me. Harley didn't know who I's talkin' about."

"So, basically, you've got no solid alibi for your time after midnight."

"Guess not. 'Less we kin find that feller I gave a break."

"You might want to work on that."

* * * *

Both Junior and Bobby offered me alibis to prove Telford Bone had fabricated his accusations. But to substantiate their claims, I'd have to embarrass Junior and Stephanie Garner and find a, perhaps, unlicensed motorist who passed a red light and received a break from Officer

Crockett.

Bone engineered an elaborate scam to embarrass Prospect PD and stick it to me. Not being one to forgive or forget, I needed to get moving on a plan to bring all the appropriate miscreants to justice. I wanted to feel good about things again, but unfortunately, that good feeling might be a long way off.

John and Vinnie were taking an extra long lunch, but that presented no problem because they would come back with a tray full of ravioli for me.

Bettye had been gone almost fifty minutes. She'd come back soon, and the afternoon would return to something close to normal. I could visit Ronnie Shields, tell him we needed a lawyer to represent my two cops, and, with luck, he'd move his ass to get approval from the Council to fire Dallas Finchum.

The phones were quiet. The cars didn't need anything, and I didn't have to send the sector car operators anywhere to save humanity from itself. I decided to lean back, put my feet up and decide how to ruin a few lives.

Then I heard the back door slam shut—much louder than usual. Someone just didn't let it close on its own; they pulled it closed with great effort.

I heard the movement of an agitated body walking up the hall toward the reception room. Only a cop would have the code to get through the back door. I'd know who it was in a few seconds.

I spun around in Bettye's swivel chair. Bettye came in. She didn't look happy.

"Hi," I said.

The best I got was, "Hello."

She opened the large bottom drawer of her desk and literally threw in a purse the size of a small briefcase.

"Is something wrong?"

"Yeah, somethin's wrong," she growled.

She picked up her coffee cup, turned and walked toward my office.

I'd never seen Bettye that angry or upset before. She once told me she was mad at me, but after that, she just became quiet. I think she really meant I had hurt her feelings. This looked much different.

125

I followed her. She poured herself a cup of coffee from the maker sitting on a counter at the side of my room. She added a packet of Splenda and then took the pint container of fat free half-and-half from the mini-fridge next to Mr. Coffee.

I watched her stir the coffee and heard the spoon strike the sides of the cup more times than necessary.

"I don't know why I poured this damn coffee. I don't want it," she said, dropping the spoon onto a folded paper towel.

"It's no big deal. I'll wash the cup for you." I waited.

She put the cup down and turned to face me. Stress showed on her face.

"Sam, if you don't keep that…that *thing* away from me…I'll kill him."

I had a good idea who the subject of our conversation might be.

"What happened?"

At times like this, I feel at a loss for a place to put my hands. I didn't want to put them in my pockets and seem too casual. I asked her to sit. She didn't.

"I drove over to Ross's," she began. "I wanted to pick up a couple pair of jeans for Li'l Donnie. When I came out, I got into my car and opened the window, just until the air cooled it off a bit. And then, from where I don't know, he showed up standing next to my car, smilin' at me. He's the last person I'd want to meet in a parkin' lot—day or night. He makes my skin crawl, Sam."

Her usually sparkling hazel eyes had gone almost flat.

She continued. "He said, 'Hello, Sergeant. Buy yourse'f somethin' pretty in there?' I asked him what he wanted, and do you know what he told me?"

"No."

"He said he'd like to buy me lunch. Can you believe that?"

"I can't wait to hear your answer."

"Well, maybe you'll be proud of me. Maybe not. I said, 'Mr. Bone, I will not have lunch with you, and I'll thank you not to come anywhere near me unless you have business in my police department.'"

"That was very polite and businesslike."

"I won't look so polite or businesslike if I shoot that son-of-a-bitch."

Her whole body shivered. Tears had welled up in the corner of her eyes. I took hold of both her hands, wanting to tell her everything was okay, but she shook her hands free, put her arms around me and held tight.

"Sam, that man frightens me."

I whispered into her ear. "I know, Betts. He's that kind of guy. Listen now, I won't let him come near you again. I promise."

She squeezed a little tighter. I hoped I could keep my promise.

Again the sound of the back door opening floated into my office. She let go, and her hand automatically went up to push a few strands of blond hair behind her ear. A single tear ran over her right cheek. She brushed it away with the back of her hand.

John walked in. "Hi, Boss. Hi, Sarge." He canned his usual adolescent grin when he realized Bettye looked upset. "Am I interrupting somethin'?"

"No," I said. "We were just talking about our friend Telford Bone. He's causing more trouble."

"The guy's a real skell."

"Yeah, John."

Bettye shook her head.

"Here's your ravioli, Boss." John set a Styrofoam box on my blotter. "What's the story with T-Bone? What did those two sheriff's guys want?"

"I'll tell you about it."

Vinnie walked in and, after sensing the mood, didn't say anything.

Bettye said, "I'm going to wash out my cup. Excuse me," and left the office.

She stayed in the washroom long enough for me to tell John and Vinnie what Barkens and Stallins had to say. I'd let Bettye mention her encounter with Bone if she wanted to.

"John, call Bo Stallins and ask him for the local address Bone gave him. His captain didn't want me to have it, but I need to have another talk with Mr. Bone. Tell Bo not to mention this to Barkens, and we'll never say where we got the address. When you're finished with him, call Junior and Bobby John. I want Vinnie to give them a polygraph test."

"That's a violation of contract," Vinnie said, jumping in. "These guys aren't on probation like Dallas. They can't take a poly."

"We're not in New York, Vinnie. We don't have a contract."

He got a shocked look on his face. My statement would constitute blasphemy to any New York cop.

"Besides," I said. "I believe them both. Junior is in a sort of unique situation, and Bobby doesn't exactly have an ironclad alibi. A test can only help them with the sheriff's rat-squad. I want something to show Barkens and convince him Bone's lying."

"Okay, I'll do something very short and specific. Is your name this? Do you live here? Did you meet Bone that night? Did you ever beat him up? End of story. Nothing else that could get them jammed up in the future."

Vinnie, like many New York cops, is a real union man.

"Sure, whatever you think is best. Junior's going to tell you he was with a girl. Leave her name out of print. Bobby made a traffic stop, but didn't write up the guy. He'll explain."

"No problem."

"I've got to see the mayor now."

Bettye walked back to her desk. I stepped out of my office and moved closer to her.

"You okay?"

"I'm better now. Thanks." She looked more composed. "I'm not okay."

"Mind if I tell these guys what happened?"

"No, I don't care if you do."

I told them and made it brief. "That's an important reason why I need to find Bone and discuss his future."

"That hump needs a good beatin'," John said. "I wish I still had my blackjack."

"Don't waste your time. A beatin' wouldn't do no good," Vinnie said. "That mook needs ta swim with the fishes."

"There's an idea," I said.

"Gentlemen," Bettye said, "I shouldn't be hearin' this."

"I'll get you an address, Boss." John had a determined look on his face. "Don't worry."

When necessary, male cops act like big brothers around their female counterparts. Mess with a female officer and every man on the department wants a piece of your ass. As far as I was concerned, Telford Bone had committed a hanging offense.

"Did you get a chance to eat?" I asked Bettye.

"No." She shook her head. "I'll just have a container of yogurt. I've got some in the fridge."

"That's silly. How about some ravioli?"

"That's okay. It's your lunch."

"I want to share. Hang on a minute."

I went into my room, picked up the tray of ravioli and then got two napkins and two plastic forks from the cabinet under the coffee pot.

I opened the box on Bettye's desk, sat in her side chair and handed her a fork.

"Go ahead. Try one. What are they today, John?"

"Lobster, Vinnie had them, too."

"They're good." Vinnie said.

Bettye tried one. "Umm, they are good."

"Better than yogurt?" I asked.

"Oh, yeah."

"Want some more?"

"I guess. You think they're terribly fattening?"

"That looks like vodka sauce. Yeah, they're fattening."

"Here, you have one," she said. "No sense sinnin' alone."

She speared a ravioli and held the fork for me. I took a bite.

I nodded. "Oh, yeah, quite fattening, but excellent. I'll bet you're sorry they didn't bring back that bottle of wine."

"After the time I had, darlin', I'm sorry they didn't bring back two."

Chapter Twenty-One

I sat in the green chair, again staring at Ronnie Shields. He tried not to lock eyes with me. He looked at the deer head hanging on the wall, the dead stuffed fish displayed on a plaque at a right angle to the deer and anything else he could think of to keep from feeling my evil eye. Darnell Means had again weaseled his way into the room and sat less than three feet from me in another green chair.

"I know you dislike it when I cast aspersions on the local politicians," I said, "but it's my opinion that we have that fat bastard Claude Webbster to thank for the mudslide that's going to cover Prospect and surrounding areas of Blount County."

"Now, Sam, that's a pretty inflammatory statement. You think Claude's responsible for this man Bone you described ta me?"

"I think Claude started all the shit rolling downhill. I think Claude's brother-in-law, Billy Ray, asked him to make the calls and pull the strings. Then, when things didn't go according to plan, Billy Ray picked up the ball and ran toward some friends with more eclectic abilities and a more diverse sphere of influence. In effect, Billy Ray caused Bone to come here."

He winced after hearing my theory.

Means decided to act like he knew something about the law. "We have ta be careful what we say, Mr. Mayor. It's essential we tread carefully or be liable and find ourselves taken to court for unsubstantial aspersions against a private citizen."

"I've been told by someone well acquainted with this business that Billy Ray should be considered a loose cannon," I added. "And I can

130

substantiate every word I'll say about the man. I also plan on locking his ass up as soon as I see the probable cause necessary."

"Sam, you're makin' serious accusations."

"This is very serious business, Ronnie. Guys like Telford Bone seem to know just how far to go with their words. They get to within a hair of an actual threat. They leave nothing to their victim's imagination, but even if we recorded what they say, we'd have bupkis."

"Bupkis?"

Few people in Tennessee understand even the simplest forms of Yiddish.

"Personally, I don't care if Jodelle Asher ever gets Dallas Finchum into criminal court or beats his ass in a civil suit," I said. "Dallas's life is officially over. After he leaves here, he'll be lucky to get a job as a mall security guard."

"I suppose we'll have to fire him."

"You think?"

"Fire Dallas Finchum without cause or giving him due process and we could end up in court again."

Both Ronnie and I ignored Darnell's comment.

"Are you blamin' me for this, too, Sam?"

"I'm not the guy who's going to say I told you so. You're already saying it yourself. What I'm telling you—loudly and clearly—is that no one is going to stalk Bettye Lambert and keep all his teeth for very long. If you ever repeat what you've just heard me say, Ronnie, you and I will encounter a serious problem."

"Sam, Sam, hold on now. I agree with ya. I agree one-hunnert-p'cent. We cain't have this Bone feller going after Bettye, nosir."

"I'm glad we're in agreement on that. My other beef with friend Telford is the false accusations he's made against Junior and Bobby John. We'll work on explaining away that one to Blount County. But if Bone isn't stopped, and if Billy Ray isn't stopped, where else will they go as they try to discredit us and stress us out until we say uncle?"

"Lord have mercy, Sam. What's happenin' here?"

"Look, I'll take care of this—as quickly as possible. But I've got to have your word that if and when the phone calls come in, you hang up on all the local hacks who call you, and you back *me*. I may end up stretching the rules a little, but I won't embarrass you, and I won't violate the law."

He thought about that for a long moment.

"Oh, Lord have mercy, Sam. Alright."

"Ronnie," Darnell said, "I recommend that we all hand this to the city attorney and get his advice."

I ignored that remark, too. "The next thing is going to cost you money, but it can't be helped. I won't send two cops to the county Internal Affairs man without a lawyer."

"Of course, Sam. Like Darnell said, I'll call the city attorney and arrange for him to send someone."

I shook my head. "That's not good enough. We're not talking about some civil action against our men. This is criminal. I want to hire Joe Costello to represent them. It should only take one meeting to put this to rest—not a lot of cash."

"Sam, this is why we have a city attorney on retainer."

"With respect to our pool of on-call lawyers, I wouldn't trust them with my freedom. And they have no business hearing the operational planning of this case. If you want someone to appear before another emergency meeting of the Council, I have no problem being the bad-guy and reminding them that their own good ol' boy system has gotten us into this bucket of shit."

Darnell was about to speak when Ronnie began. "Alright, alright, Sam. I'll find the money some place. Y'all know he'll take the case?"

"I'm confident he'll want to see our people properly represented."

Ronnie didn't need to know that Junior and Costello's secretary were playing house while Bone got someone to tune him up.

"Is there anything else I need ta know?" he asked.

"I think you've heard enough for one day."

"Lord have mercy, but I shoulda stayed with my daddy's in-surance company."

* * * *

"Sam, if I find out Claude's continuin' to cause trouble here, I'll have that son-of-a-bitch's head on a pike. Now, I know Jimmy Dillworth spoke directly to him." Minas Tipton sounded angry as we discussed

County Commissioner Claude Webbster.

I lounged in my usual telephone position: tilted back in my swivel chair, feet crossed and resting on the edge of my desk.

"Judge, I may be wrong, but Claude Webbster and all the little Webbsters are out of their league when it comes to finding guys like Telford Bone. I think it's our loose cannon, Billy Ray Finchum, who's got to be stopped."

He paused for a moment. "I agree, Sam. I agree indeed. But Claude's sure not going to stop him. Billy Ray, from what I've heard about him, will run right over Claude."

"I doubt Billy Ray will respect a gentle hint given by the right person. He fancies himself a tough guy. And I don't know if there's anything we can threaten to take away from him to get compliance. I suppose I'll just have to build a case against him and lock him up. I'll take care of that, but I could use a little help finding out how he's tied up with Telford Bone."

"That I don't know, Sam, but I'll sure attempt to find out. Billy Elam is back from his vacation now, and we'll work on that for you. You have my word."

Sergeant Billy Joe Elam is a sheriff's man assigned as the retired judge's administrative assistant. Talk about having political horsepower.

"You also need to know that our junior politician and young deputy mayor, Darnell Means, seems to be taking an inordinate interest in this affair."

I imagined that Judge Tipton raised his white eyebrows two inches. I heard him sigh.

"He won't keep his nose out of the conversations Ronnie Shields and I have unless I chase him away. I may be asking for something that can't be delivered, but if, at all possible, can someone keep an eye on his uncle, Micah Blevins? Between that pair, I've got two enemies who'd like to see me and Prospect PD slide down the tubes."

"Ha, ha, ha, ha, Sam. I'll bet those two rascals would like to see you fail with this one. Yes, sir. They are a pair. I'll see what I can do. Leave this with me, but, son, keep watchin' your back. I wouldn't put anything past ol' Micah. He can be one nasty piece o' work."

"Thanks, Judge. You know I'm not looking for a full-scale scandal here. I just want the forward progress stopped and then let damage control and education for the future take its course. If this doesn't teach the Prospect City Council something, nothing will."

"I hear ya, Sam, and I'll do what I can."

* * * *

"Sam, I've got depositions all day tomorrow," Joe Costello said. "I can't be available to meet with this Captain Barkens."

With a cell phone to my ear, I stood at the back door of the PD looking out at a rainy parking lot. Earlier that morning the Ford's windshield wipers couldn't keep up with the pounding sheets of rain. More recently, the deluge calmed to a gentle but intense soaking. Our world had become so damp I didn't want to stand still too long for fear of turning green with mold.

"Joe, I really need you to rearrange your schedule. It's certainly in my best interest that you do, and after you hear my explanation, you'll agree you also have good reason to be there."

He sighed, "Go ahead. I'm listenin'."

Joe Costello is my idea of a good criminal attorney. I'll rephrase. He's a great criminal attorney, undoubtedly the finest in Blount County, and right up there as one of the five best in the state. I wanted him to back up Junior Huskey and Bobby John Crockett.

"Okay, Joe, here's your vested interest in the matter. Forget about Bobby Crockett for the moment. He stopped a driver for a red light during the time Bone said Bobby was beating him. He didn't write a ticket or even record the driver's name, but I believe Crockett. I'll do what I can to find the offender and get a statement confirming the time frame. We'll talk about him later. Junior Huskey is another story. After work, he went to see his girlfriend. She's unmarried so that's not a problem, but I doubt if her parents want their daughter's name to become part of a public record and Junior's alibi. They wouldn't like to have the rest of East Tennessee hear that PO Davis Huskey, Jr. couldn't be guilty of beating Telford Bone because he was having sex with Stephanie."

"Stephanie? Who Stephanie? My Stephanie?"

"Uh-huh."

"Junior is going out with Stephanie Garner?"

"Actually, I think they stayed in to have sex."

"Lord have mercy, Sam. Something like that would embarrass Mr. and Mrs. Garner ta death."

Costello rarely shows much emotion. That was an exception.

"I thought you might think so."

"All right, Sam. I'll cancel my morning appointments. Who's this captain I'll have to see?"

"Clifford Barkens, Internal Affairs."

* * * *

Somewhere along the line, someone must have heard me say, "There's no rest for the weary." My office chair turned out to be a very unlucky spot. Every time my phone rang, I began to think I should walk the other way.

"Sam, I have a major problem."

"What's wrong?" I asked Rachel Williamson.

"It's more like *we* have a major problem."

"We?"

"Yes, you and I."

"Rachel, we've never done anything more than have lunch together. You can't get pregnant from balsamic vinegar."

"For God's sake, Sam. Be serious."

The uncharacteristic bite in her voice sounded serious enough.

"Okay, tell me exactly what happened."

I wasn't prepared for what I heard, but all things considered, I should have been.

"Yesterday a messenger showed up at Boyd's office with a package of six eight-by-ten photos of us in that restaurant. One showed me holding your hand, and two had me kissing you."

Boyd is Rachel's investment broker husband. He's a real yuppie. I'm not overly fond of Boyd.

"Oh, no, not hand holding in the first degree," I said with a little exaggeration. "And you kissed my cheek. We didn't play tonsil hockey in public."

"Goddamnit, Sam, stop being stupid! I've got a real problem here. I wouldn't be surprised if the same pictures haven't been mailed to

Katherine, too."

"Okay, I'm sorry. No more humor. Boyd is really upset over this?"

"Upset? I guess so. I listened to him screaming at me for an hour last night."

"I'm sorry you've been subjected to a problem because of me. I know exactly what happened and who's responsible. I can't undo what happened, but I can get the guy responsible."

"That's great, Sam. I'm sure he'll regret the day he ever met Sam Jenkins after you get finished with him, but that doesn't help me. I won't say my life is ruined, but I've just had a major collision in my marriage."

"I'm not trying to blow this off as something unimportant, but don't you think Boyd will cool off after he thinks this over? If you think it would do any good, I'll speak with him."

"I don't think he'd want to speak with you. I'm afraid you're not one of his favorite people."

As previously mentioned, the feeling is mutual. He wears suspenders. Who can like a man with suspenders?

"I don't know if I'd react the same way or not," I said. "I tend to think not, but maybe I give myself too much credit."

"This is a complicated issue with him. Ever since you did something he and the FBI couldn't, something you did all by yourself, he's had a problem with you. You saved his wife from a kidnapper, and I've been stupid enough to mention you affectionately—more than once."

Six months after I took the job in Prospect, a disturbed man decided he couldn't live without the woman of his dreams and abducted Rachel. He whisked her away and left cameraman John Leckmanski lying unconscious in the parking lot of a Prospect auto repair shop. The FBI came into the picture because of the kidnapping, but I tracked the bad guy to a mountain cabin in a community called Top O' the World. Several of the Prospect cops and I rescued Rachel. I didn't do everything alone.

"I certainly won't apologize for that," I said.

"I don't expect you to. I wouldn't ask you to apologize. The problem here isn't really Boyd. It's the photographer. He wrote, 'If your wife doesn't get her friend to back off, I'll send these pictures to the papers and the other networks.'"

A Can of Worms

I sat in my office feeling victim of a major collision myself. Luckily, I lived in a gated community, and a messenger couldn't blithely show up at my door with a packet of photos for my wife. But he could call her from the gate and say, "Avon calling" or "This is Publisher's Clearing House with a million-dollar check." Or maybe just, "Hey, lady, I got a delivery."

Obviously, if the envelope was delivered to our PO box, Kate would be none the wiser; I always pick up the mail. At dinner, I'd tell her all about this little glitch in my investigation.

Honesty sometimes sucks, but you don't stay married as long as I have without encountering a few occasions where you have to adhere to the so-called best policy.

Just as I sat there feeling sorry for myself, Vinnie Falcone walked into my office and tossed another folder onto my desk.

"You got two good kids there, Sam," he said, referring to Junior and Bobby. "I ran two perfect tests. I'll write up a couple of reports for you, and I'll swear to them anywhere. Those guys are a-hundred-percent. This guy, Bone, is lying."

"Well, thanks for one good thing. I got them a top-notch lawyer earlier this morning. Tomorrow I'll take your reports along with the other things that will exonerate them to the sheriff's man, and with a little more luck, we'll close up this bogus assault business."

"Good for you," he said.

"Yeah, thanks."

* * * *

I took the last inch-long snip of asparagus off my plate and offered it to Bitsey. She sniffed it, shifted her eyes up at me and turned her head. I dropped the vegetable back onto my plate, wiped my fingers and scratched the old dog's head. She then turned and hobbled off toward the living room.

"She's not eating much lately," Kate said.

"Yeah, I've noticed. Poor old thing is having more trouble walking, too."

"And she has trouble seeing, and I doubt she hears much anymore either."

"She'll be seventeen soon. She's an old dog."

"I've read that Scotties can live for twenty years," she said, trying to convince herself as much as me.

I nodded, but expected the worst. "She's had a good life."

"Uh-huh." Tears began to well up in Kate's eyes. She sniffed and dabbed the tears away with her napkin.

I poured the last splash of pinot grigio into her glass. "The damnedest thing happened today," I said.

"What's that?"

"Someone's trying to blackmail me into backing off the Dallas Finchum thing."

Her dark brown eyes looked at me with an intensity they lacked just moments ago.

"Tell me that again. You said blackmail?"

"Yeah, here's the deal. You remember I said I ate lunch with Rachel Williamson the other day?"

"And what's that got to do with blackmail?" I could tell she expected a story she didn't want to hear.

Glad I had a reasonably soft story to tell, I began my explanation. "Someone took photos of us sitting in the Crown and Goose and mailed them to her husband."

Kate sat still, but visibly tensed up.

"Just photos in the pub?" she asked.

"In one she had her hand over mine. Sometimes she does that when she talks."

Kate paused for a moment. "She needs to hold hands with you while she talks?"

"We weren't holding hands. She put her hand over mine. That's all."

I tried to keep a sharp edge from my comments.

"And someone's trying to blackmail the two of you, I suppose? With one photo?" It didn't sound like she believed the simple version.

"There are six photos. One's in the parking lot. The others in the pub. They caught her kissing my cheek."

"She kissed you, too? Are we leading up to something else?"

Kate didn't try to dull the edges of her comments.

"No, and it was just a platonic kiss on the cheek. A thank-you for lunch."

"How do you think this makes me feel?"

"She's like you. When you see people, you kiss them. Your whole family does that. Obviously, so does she. Hey, you even kiss your shitbag cousin, and you hate him."

"I'm not talking about the social amenity of kissing someone hello," she said, getting a little hot under the collar. "I'm talking about you and that woman."

Everyone's heard the old cliché, she's beautiful when she's angry. That's true about Kate. Actually, she's beautiful all the time. She has been all her life. She's pretty enough to get away with not coloring the gray out of her hair and not wearing a ton of makeup to cover up a roadmap of age lines she doesn't have.

"*That* woman has a name, by the way," I said. "You've met her." I tossed my cloth napkin onto the table. "God, you're just like your mother that way. Have you forgotten her name?"

"No." she folded her arms across her chest and sat back in her chair, getting as much distance between us as circumstances allowed.

"*That woman* is my friend and someone I deal with professionally. There's nothing more. You won't ever hear me tell you that some asshole kicked in a motel door and photographed us in bed. It's never happened, and it won't happen." I heard myself getting louder. I took a breath, paused and started over. "I'm sorry I yelled."

She nodded, but didn't come close to smiling.

"This premise is silly," I said. "I've had coffee with junkies, hookers, gamblers, burglars and even an occasional killer. I didn't think a TV reporter was much of a stretch."

"My point is," Kate said, "the woman loves you. Surely even you can see that."

"That may have been partially true because of prior circumstances beyond her control. She and I talked about that, and as far as I'm concerned, we all, you included, put that behind us."

"You really think that's possible?"

"Yes. Look, Kats, I need favors from other people to do my job effectively. Rachel happens to be someone who can make my professional life easier at times. Our lunches are not much different from those I have with Ralph Oliveri or when I go fishing with Jackie Shuman. Rachel can feel safe with me. She knows I'm not going to try and seduce her or lie about a relationship that can never be."

Kate rolled her eyes and gave her head an almost imperceptible shake.

"Okay, believe that or not, but I'll admit that at times I exploit friendships to get what I want. Simply put, I'm a user. I use Rachel. I use Ralph. I use other people. Sue me."

"I just wish one of your friends wasn't a beautiful woman twenty years younger than me."

I bit my lip to keep from yelling.

"We've had this conversation before," I said. "You have nothing to worry about. You're a beautiful woman. You know how I feel, and it's inevitable that when I'm working, I'll meet people. It wasn't my idea to go out and find a new police job. You were the one who went out looking for all your volunteer work and left me alone."

"Please, let's not go through that again."

"Why can you broach the subject of me being friends with a woman and I can't mention how I felt abandoned when you'd work sixty or more hours a week for people who don't pay you a dime?"

"What I do isn't about money."

"I don't care about the money. I don't need money. I have two pensions and a good job. I wanted and needed more than you were offering."

"That's different. I don't have someone else."

"It made no difference to me. You had *something* else, and you spent more time with it than with me."

"Please."

"Please my ass. When I come home, I'm home and here for you. When you come home, it's better than a fifty-fifty chance you'll be on the phone or the computer for hours. I'll throw the same question at you. How do you think I feel?"

"I'm sorry." She didn't sound very convincing.

"I'm sorry I'm not enough stimulation for your intellect," I said. "You know when we take the time to be together, we're fine. When you're off on a crusade, we just share a house."

"I'm not a crusader."

"More than once you've used the word *passionate* about what you do. I can honestly say Rachel and I have never been in a passionate situation."

Neither of us said anything for a long moment. Kate broke the ice.

"So where does that leave us?"

"I don't know. If I asked you to stop what you do, you'd say no."

"Don't you think you've formed some kind of emotional connection with her?"

"Maybe I have. But you are my wife, and you are the only one I sleep with."

"Maybe you should ask someone else if your point of view is a valid one."

Chapter Twenty-Two

Standing in the reception room of the sheriff's office, I handed Joe Costello my memo to Clifford Barkens detailing the interviews I conducted with Junior and Bobby. He scanned over it the way lawyers read everything. When he finished and looked up, I handed him the two reports from Vinnie Falcone.

"Not admissible in court," I said, "but the tests confirm what the lads say is true."

He continued to scan, turned a page and nodded.

"Your man writes a good report," he said. "No doubt he covered all the important points—and nothing else. That's good.

"And what about my report?" I asked, trying to sound hurt. "People have said I've got a literary flare."

I heard Junior giggle. He does that a lot. Sometimes I could smack him.

"Uh-huh," Joe said. "And how do you know Vincent Falcone?"

He breezed right by my plea for recognition.

I explained Vinnie's history with me.

"Bobby could use corroboration for his time. Junior has it. I doubt Barkens will controvert any of this," he said. "It's pretty thorough and clear-cut. Bone claims two officers beat him, not just Bobby. Junior couldn't be in two places at one time."

He looked at Junior as if he were Stephanie's uncle and not exactly pleased with her new boyfriend. Junior hung his head and looked embarrassed. Bobby Crockett, the guy who didn't take time to record the name of an offending motorist he stopped, didn't appear any less so.

"Look, Joe," I said, "I received what I know to be competent information that Telford Bone is a genuine head-case. The people in my office did the basic checking, and with a few people Falcone knows, we learned quite a bit about Bone. I'm not sure Barkens would be able to get as much. Here's an outline of what we know."

I handed him another report. He read over the two and a half pages of notes.

"This makes me sure I won't invite Bone for Sunday dinner, but it doesn't mean he can't complain about an assault. There are no warrants out for the man."

"I have other information, too, but it's extremely confidential. It's all credible, and believe me, it casts doubt on Bone's sanity. I need some trust on this one. I shouldn't have said this much."

"I trust ya, Sam, but I'm not the one ya have to convince. Where did ya get this additional information?"

I looked around to be sure no county employees were close enough to hear our conversation.

"I can't tell you right now, and I don't want to try and explain it to the sheriff's people why I can't."

He sighed. "Then what am I gonna do except use what I have here?"

Typical lawyer logic, I thought. His expensive-looking suit was also typical for the breed. I'd never spend that much on clothes.

"I understand. And you said it should be enough," I reminded him.

"I believe what we've got here is sufficient to get the complaint marked unfounded. I can't guarantee they'll go after Bone for falsely reporting an incident, but I can't worry about that."

"I'll take care of Telford Bone myself."

He gave me a parental look, something designed to keep a wayward child from going after another kid who shot shaving cream into his hall locker.

"I'll give you a little free legal advice, Sam, and tell you to let it go. I'll get the boys off the hook, but you should let Bone slither back under his rock."

"I may not be able to do that, old buddy."

Costello shrugged. "Then I'd prefer not to hear any more of your future plans."

"I'll wait for you outside Barkens' office," I said. "But first I've got to see the sheriff."

* * * *

"Hello, Sam, you doin' aw right today?" Joe Don Hartung asked.

We stood inside his paneled corner office on the second floor of the Justice Center.

"Pretty good, Jo-Dee. How about you?"

"Jest fine, yessir, jest fine. What kin I do fer ya?"

I met Joe Don just after we first moved to Tennessee. He was a good-looking man then. Now, in his mid-forties, he still was, but getting soft around the edges. His slight paunch and gray-flecked hair let everyone know he wasn't the young, pretty-boy sheriff any longer.

"I need to speak to you about a polygraph exam Charlie Dietzen did for me a ways back."

I explained the whole shebang to Hartung. He listened attentively, made numerous facial gestures indicating his interest and surprise, and when I finished, he asked, "Do ya have real proof Charlie falsified the report?"

"Only as I mentioned. The coincidences are startling. Do I have a smoking gun? No. Do I have proof he didn't do as I requested? Yes. Did he lie to me and John Gallagher? Yes."

U.S. and Tennessee flags hung on walnut poles standing behind his large desk. His own picture hung on the wall behind his chair. Few cops would do such a thing. Most politicians would.

"I'm not looking to arrest him for malfeasance and get him into court," I said. "But just consider your personal credibility if somehow word of a bogus test gets out. Who would believe anything Charlie has said or written? Any half-way decent lawyer would make you look like a horse's ass."

"Y'all believe that's possible?"

"Anything's possible. Defense attorneys could question the integrity of any test he's given. It sounds like Charlie can be bought. And you know what happens if the Feds get a corruption complaint from someone. A team of agents would camp out here for as long as they want. Would you like to see that on the six o'clock news?"

"No, no, course not," he said. "What would you do in my place?"

That's what you'd expect to hear from a guy who never spent time in the trenches with other cops, slugging it out with bad guys.

"Charlie has what, twenty-nine, thirty years on the job? All he needs to retire is twenty-five." I hoped Hartung could grasp my implication.

"Hmm, I see yer point."

Lucky me.

"You may also want to take a personal look at this complaint a man made against two of my cops," I suggested. "Joe Costello is with your Captain Barkens right now disproving every one of the allegations. The complainant was hired by the same person who got to Dietzen. It's all about the same reason. This complainant, Telford Bone, is a genuine character. Look into his background, and you'll see for yourself."

"All right, Sam. I'll get personally involved with this one. I surely will. And thank ya fer bringin' this ta my attention. There anythin' else ya need?"

"No, sir, I'm good. Thanks for your time."

* * * *

I left the sheriff and walked downstairs to wait for Joe Costello. Five minutes after sitting on a chair in the hallway, Stan Rose walked in dressed in a suit.

"What are you doing here?" I asked.

"That captain from their rat-squad wants to see me."

"About what?"

"He wants my opinion of Junior and Bobby. Wants to know if I believe their story. Wants to know where I was at the time. Told me his complainant seems to be missing and if I think you may have gone looking for Bone and did something drastic."

"That son-of-a-bitch. He thinks I may have offed Bone to settle this bullshit complaint?"

Irving, Irving, Irving, why didn't you call a day earlier?

"Don't worry about me, boss, but let's make sure we never turn our backs on this guy Barkens."

Fifteen minutes later, Junior, Bobby and Costello walked out of Barkens' office. They were followed by Bo Stallins who began to walk away.

"Bo," I said, "Can I see you before I leave?" he nodded. "Give me five or ten minutes. Will you be in the squad room?"

"Yeah, I'll wait fer ya."

"We're good here," Costello said. "He believes what he heard, appreciates all the paperwork you sent, and he says he'll wrap this up in a day or so."

"Good, thanks for the help." I turned to Junior and Bobby. "I'm glad this went away quick and easy, guys. Stop at the PD, and hang out with Bettye and John until I get back."

They left, and Costello summarized for me. "This guy Barkens bought their stories quick enough, even divulging Junior's girlfriend's name was unnecessary, but he sounded very interested in why you had to import your own polygraph man. I gave him a brief story as I knew it, but don't be surprised if you hear from him again."

"I just covered the same subject with Jo-Dee Hartung. I hope they compare notes first."

"That's nothing either you or I can control."

"Yeah, right," I said, showing lots of attitude. "Just to let you know, Barkens is questioning Stan Rose about your two clients. He wants to know if Stan believes their stories. And he wants to know if Stan thinks I may be so inclined to kill Telford Bone because of his involvement here."

"Lord have mercy. You let me know if I can help *you* out in any way, hear?"

"Oh, yeah, if I need representation, there's only one man I'll call. Anyway, Joe, thanks for sticking up for my two guys. I owe you one."

"Well, glad to be of help."

"Thanks. Send Ronnie your bill."

"I'll have Junior's girl do that today."

* * * *

"You okay with all of this?" I asked Bo Stallins.

He sat at his desk in the CID squad room, and I on a rickety side chair next to him.

"Yeah, I'm good. I never took much stock in Bone's story. It

146

sounded plausible. I had ta entertain it, but I never believed what he said."

"Where's Bone now? Some motel?"

"I don't know."

"Wanna explain that for me?"

"We can't find him," Stallins said. "He checked outta that Fairfield in Alcoa near the airport, and we ain't heard from him since."

"You find that odd?"

"O' course."

"Think he's pulling some new trick?" I asked.

"Beats me."

I looked around the squad room. Four or five cops, detectives and uniformed deputies, bustled around, doing whatever they had to do. I lowered my voice and spoke again to Stallins.

"Keep listening. You're going to hear more about Telford Bone and some of his associates in the days to come."

"Care ta give me a hint?"

"I don't have much more to say than something you've already heard."

"From what I seen so far, I cain't think he's anythin' but big problems," Bo said.

"He's pond scum in a pair of cowboy boots. Take that as an understatement. Your buddy Barkens thinks I may have killed him." Stallins eyes widened. "Not yet," I said, "but if Bone keeps up the way he's going, we're going to get into it real soon—big time."

"Y'all be careful out there."

"Yeah, you, too, Bo. See ya."

* * * *

I walked in the door of the PD and started shouting orders. I wasn't mad at anyone, and no one looked like a malingerer, but I felt frustrated, and I wanted some action.

"John, you and Vinnie start calling all the motels in Blount County to find Telford Bone. He may be using another name like Calhoun Grant or something else. The name doesn't matter, but it's hard to disguise his unique looks or that Hummer he drives.

"Junior and Bobby, call all the small departments anywhere near us, and put out an official alarm for this guy or his vehicle. Bobby, when you're finished, see me.

"Betts, call all the on-and off-duty guys, and get them to call *all* the cops from surrounding departments that they know personally to get on the trail of this guy. When you're finished, come inside."

As all that took place, I received a cell phone call with the kind of news that made me think I should have taken a job selling vinyl siding.

Chapter Twenty-Three

"Sam, can you talk?"

"Yeah, Rachel, I'm alone."

I sank into my swivel chair with thoughts of anything but getting comfortable.

"My problems aren't going away." She sounded exceptionally upset.

"What does that mean?"

"It means Boyd won't let this go."

"I'm sure he just needs more time. He's a reasonable man. Would it help of I spoke with him? I'll apologize if you think…"

She interrupted, "I think you are the last person he'd want to see."

"That bad?"

I spun around, my back now to the door. I looked up at the wall behind my desk and the things I'd hung there.

"Yes, you apologizing would only rub his nose in it more."

"I don't understand."

"The pictures were only the straw that broke the camel's back. Your apology would only make this worse."

"I'm still unclear about that. Do I need to understand something I can't see?"

"Oh, God, Sam, it's so simple. How can you not see?"

"Humor me. Explain."

"An apology is the right thing to do. He doesn't need to see you do another right thing."

"Huh?"

"Please try and see this. He's jealous of you. He thinks he has to share me with you. He can't do what you can do. Even the kids think you're cool, like some kind of super hero when I tell them about something you've done. It's all my fault."

I stared at the wall as she spoke. A replica of an early Tennessee flintlock rifle hung above a shadow box with the medals and badges I received in the Army.

"I'm not arguing with you," I said, "and I'm not saying that's not true. But I think it's foolish. Of course, he can't do what I do. And I can't do what he does. He's a successful man. He makes all kinds of people all kinds of money because he knows his business, and he's smart. I couldn't do that."

"You still don't see, do you?"

I shook my head and sighed. "Obviously not."

"When I needed someone badly, he was helpless. You were not. You saved me. I never will forget that, and I guess it shows—all too much. Now someone threatens to embarrass him in public after he's lived with being embarrassed in front of himself."

"And what has he said or done recently that's a more serious problem?" I asked. "He hasn't gotten physically abusive, has he?"

"No, no, of course not." She paused, a little too long, before continuing. "He says we have to leave Knoxville if we have any hope of staying together."

Jesus Christ, I thought. I'm dealing with all kinds of loose cannons while trying to sort out a real can of worms, and this guy has to throw another monkey wrench into my gears. *Why me?*

"That's rather drastic, isn't it? What about your job? His job?"

"He can do business anywhere. All he really needs is a phone and a computer. I've been offered a job elsewhere. It's sort of a standing offer I've never taken advantage of."

"I said the other thing seemed foolish. This is plain stupid."

"I guess he thinks this is his only opportunity to beat you at something."

"I think he could use a few sessions with a therapist."

A Bronze Star and Purple Heart hung within the shadow box, both with a couple of oak leaf clusters attached to the ribbons. My tourist souvenirs from Southeast Asia. Several silver badges and other personal awards along with a handful of campaign ribbons made a colorful display.

"Probably so," she said, "but do you think I could convince him to go?"

I took that as a rhetorical question.

"Where is this job you've been offered?"

"Chicago. Years ago, the owner of an affiliate station up there offered me the job—whenever I want it. I've never considered leaving here, especially not recently."

I read between the lines of her last statement and really didn't want to hear the answer to my next question.

"Would this be a smart career move for you?"

"Yes. There's more money, a bigger station, more prestige, more all around."

"Hmm."

"Is that all you have to say?"

"No... Are you sure you couldn't convince him to agree to some sort of counseling? If he's got a problem with you, a marriage counselor. If he can admit the problem about me he's creating is within himself, he should spend some time in personal counseling."

"You're thinking like a cop again, Sam. You're solving problems. All you say makes sense, of course, but he's stubborn—and everything else that goes with being a man."

"How does this work out in your mind?"

"I have two boys to consider. They need a father, not a broken home and a mother who works weird hours. I don't think I really have a choice."

I shrugged. "I guess." I'm sure I didn't sound either encouraging or understanding.

Above the medal ribbons, I had pinned a silver and blue Combat Infantryman's Badge and a pair of silver jump wings with a small wreath and a star attached to the parachute canopy. More souvenirs from years of playing full and part-time soldier. They paid me to play little boy games.

"Sam, you sound terrible. I feel bad myself. But we both know there is no future for you and me. Where do we go from here?"

"You're right, I just—"

"Hold on, please."

"Sure."

She disappeared for a few moments.

"Sam, I'm sorry. I have to go. They're waiting to tape me. I'm so sorry. I'll call you again...soon."

"Okay, kiddo, go, and give them hell. Smile a lot."

I've spent more than twenty years as a cop. I had all kinds of fun doing that, almost like having my own TV show. And twenty-one years of soldering. Sure, I got hurt a few times. I was young then. I healed. And when I should be retired sitting at home growing eggplant and tomatoes, I get smacked with something like this. Back to my question: Why me?

* * * *

I swiveled around, hung up the phone and thought I'd have a few minutes to feel sorry for myself.

"Sammy, what's wrong?" Bettye asked as she stepped through my office doorway. "You look so sad. Did something happen?"

"Nothing." I shook my head. "What's up?"

She looked at me as if she thought someone must have stolen my Austin-Healey.

"You asked me to come in after I made those phone calls."

"Yeah, I did."

She sat down. I circled from behind my desk and took the chair next to her, sitting close. She waited for me to speak. I decided to violate my confidentiality agreement with Irv Kaufmann.

"Do you remember how I obtained the information that helped us learn who murdered Typewriter Murray?" I spoke quietly, recalling an old case Bettye was sure to remember.

"How could I forget that? But I never spoke with whoever gave you the information."

"No, I know you wouldn't have. And I never gave you a detailed explanation. The truth is, that man is now a fairly high-ranking government employee whom I met years ago when he had very little status. When I needed information to help us find Murray's killer I called him. He owed me a favor."

She nodded.

"Now he's called me to do him a favor. He knows Telford Bone. Bone is considered an embarrassment to his employers, a sensitive government agency, and is supposedly suspected of a number of sex crimes and possibly murders in a few Latin American countries."

Bettye closed her eyes and shook her head. When she opened them, she said, "Lord have mercy. How do you get involved in these things?"

I shrugged. "It's a curse."

More head shaking. "I'm sure."

"All the evidence is sketchy," I said. "Nevertheless, this friend wants me to put the arm on Bone and turn him over to the FBI. That may not be entirely above board, but I believe they'll get around the usual Constitutional rights of a suspected criminal because they'll claim Bone has some logistical ties to terrorists. We'll see our Patriot Act in action again."

"With a disgustin' snake like your Mr. Bone, who cares how they take him off the street?"

"Not my Mr. Bone, love. I'm just the one asked to whisk him away into the arms of a waiting Federal agent. I needed you to know what I'm doing."

"Who else knows about this?"

"Only you, me and a guy named Irving."

She nodded and then did something I swear only she has a knack for. She looked me straight in the eyes. I believe she sees within me and knows if I'm telling her the whole truth. If she can't do that, she certainly had me convinced.

"Thank you, darlin'. I'm glad you told me. Now you do somethin' for me. Promise you'll take a partner or two any time you go after that creature."

I didn't answer immediately. Instead, I looked back into her hazel eyes, noticing the brown and gold flecks.

"Damn it, Sammy. You have ta promise." She made her point again. That wasn't a question.

Her statement broke my concentration. I nodded first and then said, "Yes, ma'am, I promise. You're really feeling your oats this morning, acting like a tough guy."

"And don't you forget it, Sam Jenkins."

I smiled. Why argue?

"Did you watch the news this mornin'?" she asked.

"I didn't pay attention. What happened?"

"Terrible thing. After what you just told me, I'm wondering if it's a coincidence or has Telford Bone struck again."

She took a breath. I let her proceed at her own pace.

"A Mexican girl from the restaurant you like in Maryville—you know the one...we've eaten there before—was raped and stabbed to death last night. They found her body behind the stores this mornin'."

* * * *

Listening to my cell phone, I heard, "Sam, something's happened to Bitsey."

Kate's voice sounded strung out with fear. "She collapsed and can't get up. She's trying, but her back legs won't work."

"Can you keep her quiet and get her to stop struggling?"

"I'll try. She's in the living room...wait."

I heard the phone hit the Formica counter-top next to where it hung on the wall.

I stopped the Ford on South Main. I'd been heading to Quizno's for a turkey bacon and Swiss hero. I drove another hundred yards and pulled into the lot of a pharmacy to hear what Kate had to say.

A minute later, she came back.

"I brought her into the kitchen. I'm sitting on the floor with her. She's quiet."

"Did she fall on the stairs or jump off a chair and hurt herself?"

"No, she just stood up after lying on the floor, took a step and collapsed."

"Do her eyes look okay?"

I waited a few more seconds for her to answer.

"I guess so."

"Has she had her pills this morning?"

"Yes."

"Give her two more Prednisolone."

"She's only supposed to get one a day."

"I know, but she can have more. I think her joints are not working. The steroids should help. They can't hurt her. Put the pills in peanut butter, and see if she'll take them while I'm on the phone."

The dog took the pills without argument, seemingly glad to get the treat of peanut butter.

"Keep her quiet while I'm on the way home. Call the vet, and tell them we're coming. Tell them it's an emergency."

* * * *

Ronald Holt, DVM, was in his mid-forties, about six-five and at least two-hundred-and-fifty pounds. His hair always needed combing, and his short reddish-brown beard showed many flecks of gray.

Kate, Bitsey and I waited in one of his examining rooms, Bitsey lying quietly on a stainless steel table.

Holt entered the room via the back door. His light blue, short-sleeved clinical smock showed clumps of cat hair and smears of doggy smoots.

"Hi," he said in a deep, almost booming voice. He showed a look of concern for his long-time patient. "What's happened to Bitsey?" He scratched below her right ear.

Kate explained, and I added my two cents.

"She perked up after two Prednisolone?" he asked.

"Yes," Kate said. "Less than ten minutes after I gave her the pills she was up and able to walk."

"Sometimes old dogs have hip problems. It's more prevalent in large dogs, but the little guys get afflicted, too."

"She's lost her usual appetite," I said.

"For how long?"

"Three or four days."

"Is she eating anything?"

"After the first day of not eating dog food," I said, "Kate made her chicken and rice soup. She ate that, but she doesn't take all the treats or care about the table food we normally give her."

He spent ten minutes examining the old Scottie.

"She seems to have lost all vision in her left eye and has diminished sight in the other. She's probably ninety percent deaf. The idea of her responding to the Prednisolone makes me think the steroids you're giving her daily for arthritis may be masking something more serious."

Kate looked at me, and I looked at Ron Holt for a more detailed explanation.

"I don't want to alarm you, but if you don't mind, I'd like to keep her for a day or so and run some tests."

I nodded. "Sure, do you what you have to do. Any ideas?"

"A couple, but I want to check a few things before I come up with a plan. That work for you?"

"Sure," I said.

Kate nodded.

"Can I bring her blanket for her to sleep on?" Kate asked.

"I'm sure it will make her more comfortable," he said. "Stop in any time you want. She'll be happy to see you. While you're not here, Jamie will take good care of her."

Jamie, his young kennel assistant, always showed a genuine fondness for Bitsey.

Chapter Twenty-Four

I waited for Vinnie Falcone outside the restaurant where one of the female employees had been raped and murdered. El Jibarito is one of the best Mexican eateries this side of Gallup, New Mexico, but we didn't come for a ration of frijoles and rice.

Vinnie pulled up driving John's old electric blue Saturn.

We entered the restaurant after walking past a modernistic, metallic sculpture of six mariachis that stood on the sidewalk.

"Buenos dias, amigos," the young host said. "Table for two?"

I showed him my badge. "Si, senor," I said, "a table for two would be nice—all the way in the back of the dining room. Please tell Alberto we need to see him. It's police business."

"Of course, amigo. Follow me, por favor."

We walked through the dining room, past tables and booths. It was still early, and only a few people had arrived prior to the noon lunch crowd.

We passed the waiter's station and the open portal to the kitchen where the staff picked up their orders. Someone must have ordered fajitas because I heard the sizzle of hot meat and vegetables hit an even hotter iron skillet.

The seldom-used banquet room in the rear of the restaurant appeared as dark as a moonless night. We waited in the arched doorway while the host flipped a wall switch. Overhead lights brightened a room containing another two dozen tables, enough to accommodate more patrons than I ever saw in El Jibarito at one time.

"Have a seat, amigos. I'll get Alberto for you."

157

Alberto Mendez managed the restaurant for the Pacheco family who owned this business and another restaurant in Knoxville. Alberto looked around fifty and acted as smooth as Ricardo Montalban.

"Buenos dias, amigos," His subdued expression betrayed his mood. "Are you here about poor Maria?"

"We are," I said. "Do you have a few minutes to talk?"

"Yes, of course, but I've already spent much time with Senor Stallins."

Alberto's thick, dark hair had a liberal sprinkling of gray. He wore brown slacks and a yellow guayabera.

"We're not with the sheriff's office, but I think we have a few ideas that may help them find the woman's killer."

He shrugged. "I hope so. It is very bad business, no?"

I nodded. "I'm sorry to ask you to repeat your story, but please tell us what you know."

"Maria is not a waitress," he said. "I know you come here often. You must have seen her before."

I nodded.

"She just sets up and clears off the tables. You know, brings out taco chips and salsa and water before the orders are taken. She doesn't speak much English."

"And what do you know about last night?"

"Like every night, we close at ten. We had no customers that late, but some of us remained. Maria was one."

"We'd like to speak with everyone who was here."

Alberto nodded. "The last anyone saw of her was when she went out back to take trash bags to the dumpster. That was just before ten. No one remembers seeing her after that. I locked up at ten, but she was not here. I thought nothing of it because it was late, and we had no customers. I thought she had just left. She's young and...well, maybe not so responsible."

"Did she leave a jacket or purse or anything behind?"

"No, we found nothing. I think she keeps a wallet and keys in her pants pockets. Her car was parked closer to Food Lion. The night manager there found her before they closed at midnight."

"Do you know the Food Lion manager's name?"

"No, I'm sorry."

Vinnie asked, "Did she work with a group of waiters or waitresses, or does she just service the tables when the customers show up?"

"Maria handled the right side of the room. She works with three servers."

"Would she speak with customers at all?" Ask for drink orders or anything?" I asked.

"As I said, she speaks little English. If someone could speak Spanish she would converse with them."

"Can we see the three servers who worked with her last night? We'd like to show them a photo."

"You may, but only two are here now—Lupe and Seviero. The other waiter, Juan, comes in at one o'clock and will work late."

I had asked Bettye to print off an Alabama DMV photo of Telford Bone. I added five more photos from our rogue's gallery to make my photo lineup legitimate. When you offer a potential witness a photo array, you try to get six shots of people similar in appearance. Believe me when I say we keep precious few mug shots on hand even close to Bone's appearance.

"Before you get the servers," Vinnie said, "will you look at these pictures?"

I placed the stack of six on the table.

"And tell us if you recognize anyone here."

Mendez used his index finger to smooth down the right side of his dark mustache, and then he flipped through the pictures. The third one he looked at was Telford Bone. He stopped and tapped the photo.

"I know this man was here last night. He is a curious-looking man, no? I remember him."

"Look at the other photos, please. See if you've seen any of those men," I said.

He shook his head. "No, just this one, I'm sure. He is most odd."

I nodded and smiled. *Odd* sounded like an understatement.

"Thank you," I said. "Would you ask Lupe to come over?"

Mendez disappeared toward the main room. In two minutes a short, dark-haired Mexican woman in her thirties walked to the table."

"Lupe?" I asked.

"Si, senor."

"Sit down, please. I'm Chief Jenkins, and this is Detective Falcone. I think we may be able to find the person who killed Maria, but we'd like you to look at some photographs."

"Si, senor. Poor Maria, it is very bad."

"Tell us, Lupe, if you have ever seen anyone from these pictures. Please look at them all."

Bone was now the forth photo in the stack. She set him aside and completed looking at all six.

"I saw this man, senors. Last night, he ate here late, maybe eight o'clock or a little later."

I loved her accent.

Two sombreros, one black and one maroon, both embroidered with silver bullion thread, hung on the wall behind Lupe. A small Xapotec blanket made in garish colors filled a space between the hats.

"Why do you remember him?" Vinnie asked.

"He is…different looking, senor. And he spoke Spanish. Pretty good Spanish. I waited on his table. I remember his order—two margaritas and chili verde."

"Did you see him talking with Maria?"

"I did. Maria was young and pretty. Many men tried to speak with her. Not many men speak enough Spanish to have a conversation. This man could speak with her."

"Did you hear this conversation? Did you hear his Spanish?"

She shrugged.

"Could you tell where he may have learned to speak Spanish? In what country? Mexico, Guatemala, El Salvador?"

"No, senor, I am sorry."

"Did Maria mention him?"

"Not to me. If Maria was to pick a customer to flirt with, senor, this man would not be one of her favorites."

"Thank you, Lupe," I said. "Would you ask Seviero to see us, please?"

I saw El Jibarito carved along the top slats of each chair's backrest, painted in colors as bright as the blanket hanging on the wall.

Seviero turned out to be Alberto's nephew. He was a good-looking young man in his mid-twenties who spoke with no accent. I assumed he was at least a second generation American.

Vinnie and I posed many of the same questions and asked him to look through the photos. He looked at all six and went back to pick out Telford Bone.

"He was here last night. I saw him. Hard to forget someone so ugly."

"Did you see him pay particular attention to either Lupe or Maria?" I asked.

"Lupe is a nice woman," he said, "but she's not pretty like Maria. This man spoke Spanish to Maria. He hit on her. Maria was very shy. She gave him his salsa and chips. That's all."

"That's it?" I asked.

"When she served another table, I saw him call her over. He asked for more salsa. Maria told me he gave her the creeps so I brought him the salsa. He didn't need any more. He still had enough. He was just...you know, trying to get her near him."

"Any idea where he learned to speak Spanish?"

"Not Mexico. Central America, maybe. I'm not great at spotting accents or idioms."

"What time do you think he left?" I asked.

"We had a few people eating then. I guess it was close to nine. I'm not certain."

"When did you last see Maria?"

"We were all moving around, trying to get cleaned up so we could close at ten. Everybody does something. I think she carried garbage bags out back."

"Did you see her come back in?"

"No, I left with the others at five-to-ten or so. It's not unusual for someone to take out garbage and if it looks like everything's cleaned up, for them to just keep on going. I wish I had waited to see her leave, man. This is bad. She was a nice kid."

"Thanks for your help," I said.

"You guys think this ugly one killed her?"

"We're not sure."

"That guy looked like a pendejo to me."

161

"I think you've got that right, amigo. Thanks."

* * * *

As soon as we got back into my car, I called Bo Stallins' cell phone.

"Bo, you in the office?" I asked.

"Yeah, what's goin' on?"

"Wait for us. We'll be there in less than ten minutes. It's important."

"I'll be here."

A few minutes later, Vinnie and I walked into the sheriff's CID squad room.

"Did you catch a rape-homicide last night?" I asked.

"Yeah, li'l Mexican girl from the restaurant down the road."

"We've got a pretty fair idea who did that. You interested?"

"Since I ain't got any better lead ta foller, yeah. Whatcha know?"

I realized Bo Stallins had yet to meet Vinnie.

"I'm afraid my manners are currently up my butt, gennel-mens," I said. "Bo Stallins, this is Vinnie Falcone. Vinnie's a detective from the department where I used to work. He's down here for a visit and decided to tag along while I'm doing some real po-leece work."

"Personally, when I go on vacation I like the beach. But, Vinnie, if y'all like ta hang with this guy, I guess that's okay. Good ta meet ya."

"Good ta meet you, too. How's it goin'?"

Bo nodded. "Real fine, thanks. So what do you'uns know about this rape-homicide?"

I tossed the Alabama DVM photo on his desk, followed by a manila folder with copies of what we knew about Telford Bone next to it. The El Jibarito menu I found at the motel slid away to the side.

"Whoa, that's my boy, ain't it? This booger looks like a few miles o' bad road in that picture, don't he?"

"Oh, yeah, he's a good-lookin' troop," I said.

"A'sides from the obvious reasons, why's he on your hit parade fer this li'l offense?"

"Sit down, relax, and we'll tell you all about the secret life of Mr. Telford Bone."

Vinnie and I told Bo Stallins what we had learned about Bone. Vinnie took care of what the NCIS agent told him, and I relayed a cryptic and abridged version of Irv Kauffmann's portion of the epic.

"And who told y'all about the gub'mint suspectin' him o' bein' guilty o' all those sex crimes in the foreign countries?"

"I can't tell you anymore about that," I said with a shrug. "I guess I should say I'm not at liberty to say."

"Uh-oh, but whatever you heard got your curiosity up, and then there's what NCIS told ya."

"Sort of. Maybe the other way around."

"You ain't makin' this any easier fer me."

"Trust me, I know what I'm doing."

"Weren't it you who said never trust anybody who says *trust me?*"

"Did I say that? Well, maybe. Just find me this guy or his Hummer. Once we've got him in custody, I'll make a call, and we'll get lots of assistance. I might even be able to get you some DNA to compare. You'll be able to write off a case and will never have to worry about getting a conviction."

"You're makin' me think I don't want ta even ask any more."

"Yeah, that's not a bad idea. Bo, as we used to say back in the days when you were just a little boy, 'Go with the flow.'"

"Lord have mercy."

Chapter Twenty-Five

It was 3:30 in the afternoon, and I felt like banging my head against the office wall. I spent almost an hour in a Mexican restaurant, a good restaurant, not some border-rat's cantina. We should have eaten there, not just talked about the murder of a poor young bus-girl. After talking with Bo Stallins at the sheriff's office, Vinnie and I did a little more of the investigating that takes up time but nets you very little.

I still hadn't eaten lunch. Missing lunch never bothered Vinnie, and I kept thinking, when he did eat, he never cleaned his plate. I had a headache, wanted a drink, thought about my dog being terminally ill and how a friend might disappear out of my life.

All that seemed intricately woven around a world-class turd named Telford Bone who was guilty of God knew what and obviously instrumental in the half-assed blackmail scheme designed to embarrass and annoy me. I felt beyond annoyed and depressed when Stan Rose walked into my office.

"Hi, anything new?" he asked.

"Where would you like me to start?" I growled. "Some new things are not police business, but how about our man Bone most likely raping and killing a Mexican girl last night?"

"I heard about that. You think it was Bone?" Stan looked surprised.

"I'd like to say yes with certainty, but I'm only ninety-nine percent sure."

"And you know this because?"

"Don't ask."

He looked at me like I was a mental patient explaining my recent alien abduction.

"Alright," I said, "I got a call I can't tell you much about. Bone is suspected of numerous similar things…elsewhere. All the victims fit the same profile—I think. You already know what Vinnie found on Bone going back to his Marine Corps days."

"What do you plan on doing?" he asked.

"If we can latch on to his body, I can turn him over to the Feds. I'll call Ralph Oliveri, and he'll call someone else, and the Feds will rid us of the troublesome Mr. Bone."

"You know, you're right. I shouldn't ask."

"I told Blount County he was a good suspect. Bo Stallins knows what to do. They'll be looking for him with some enthusiasm."

"Let's hope they get lucky."

"Everybody here called every PD in the phone book and any cop they personally know," I said. "If anyone spots Bone's Hummer, we'll get a call."

"Good…good." Stan rolled his eyes.

"I guess you've got more to say?" I said.

"You don't want to hear it, and no offense, but I don't want to tell it. I'll handle it. You having coffee?"

"I could have a cup."

"What do we have today?"

"Bettye asked for something flavored, so I mixed regular Columbian with Montana huckleberry."

"Any good?"

"If you mix it half and half, I think so. Straight huckleberry is like a dessert."

"Okay, I'll try one."

"Good. Try it. You'll like it."

"Who used to say that?" He asked.

"Forget it…you're too young."

"You're making me feel older."

Bettye walked away from her desk and stood in my office doorway. "Sam, Lenny Alcock's on the phone. He says a cop he knows thinks he found Bone's Hummer at a motel up on 129."

Bettye switched the call to my phone. PO Leonard Alcock told me he called an Alcoa city patrolman asking him to keep an eye open for Telford Bone's black H2. The Alcoa cop in turn mentioned it to a Knox County deputy who drove the sector that adjoined Alcoa PD's area. That afternoon, the deputy called the Alcoa cop who called Lenny, telling him that a chrome-laden, black Hummer with Alabama plates sat outside a fleabag motel on US 129 in South Knoxville.

"You know the Alpine Motor Lodge?" Lenny asked.

"Not off-hand. What is it near?"

"Jest north of the Food City on 129. Right on the highway, they's a gun shop, a tattoo place and a couple more stores in a li'l strip mall. Go north another hunnert yards, and the motel's on the left, across from Hardee's."

"Okay, I know it. Is the car there now?"

"Was fifteen minutes ago."

"Who's the Knox County cop?"

"Guy named Bernie Waggoner. Don't know him personally."

"You have a phone number?"

"I do. You ready ta copy?"

Lenny gave me the number. I called. Officer Waggoner was sitting across the road from the roach motel watching the black Hummer. We saddled up and headed toward the motel.

"You see a driver for that vehicle, officer?" I asked as Stan and I drove north on US 129. John and Vinnie sat in the back seat.

"Couple minutes ago, an ol' boy walks out o' the mo-tel, stops at the Hummer ta git somethin'. Then he walks across the road and picks up somethin' at Hardee's and then somethin' else at the gas station convenience store. He's got a second floor room in the buildin' facin' the highway."

"Can you hang in there until we get to the motel?"

"Yes, sir. I'm a'hangin'."

"Thanks. We're ten minutes away. Gray unmarked Ford. Four of us."

"Sounds like y'all have plenty o' he'p, but I'll stick around anyways."

We arrived at the Alpine Motor Lodge. I parked next to the office, my car blocked from view by an old, ten-foot, C-band satellite dish, long obsolete, but one that had never been hauled away.

"John, you and Vinnie walk around back. He's supposed to be in the building parallel to the road, second floor." I got two nods. "Vinnie, you carrying a gun?"

"I could locate one if I need it."

"Good. I'll get a key from the office."

As those two walked around back, Stan moseyed along under the overhang of the second floor and waited next to the stairway near the Hummer's parking spot.

I entered the office to find a tattooed man of about fifty sitting behind the check-in counter. Large sweat stains under the arms darkened his red tank top. Curly brown and gray hair covered his bare shoulders and emerged from the low-cut neck of the shirt. He wore his hair pulled back in a ponytail and had a Fu Manchu mustache and a gold earring.

I showed him my badge. "I'm with the police department," I said, not telling him which one. "What room is the driver of that Hummer in?"

"207. Why?"

"Give me your spare key to 207."

"What's up?"

"Are you working for the public defender's office?"

"Do what?"

He scratched inside his right ear with the top of a cheap pen. A tattoo of a cartoon man with a big foot and the phrase 'Keep On Truckin'' decorated his forearm.

"Give me the key, and come with me."

"Whadda ya want me fer?"

"I don't want you anywhere near a phone while I walk up there. And I want you to knock on the door, and say something. Ask if his TV works."

"I don't think I gotta he'p ya."

"Don't believe everything you think, sport. You either come with me, or I'll leave you cuffed on the floor until the morning man comes in."

He finally decided that agreeing with me was the way to go.

Stan and I stood on either side of the door to room 207. Dr. Fu Manchu, the desk clerk, knocked on the door.

167

"Mr. Mincy, this here's Eulis from the front desk, Is yer TV workin' okay?"

Stan looked at me and mouthed the word 'Mincy' as if it were a question. I shrugged, not knowing if Bone made up another alias or who Mincy could be. We received no response from within the room, but I heard the TV playing.

"Try again, Eulis," I said in a whisper.

"Mr. Mincy, y'all in there?"

"Yeah, wait a minute, Goddamnit. I can't hear what yer sayin'."

The security chain slid off the door and rattled on the hollow painted metal. A dead-bolt turned. I pushed Eulis aside and drew my revolver. Stan already had his Glock out.

When the door opened a crack, Stan kicked it, and I pushed my way in. The force of Stan's kick knocked a short man down. He lay on the floor slightly dazed. I moved to the back of the room to check the bathroom while Stanley rousted the little guy.

The bathroom door had been open. I entered and pulled the shower curtain aside. The room was empty. No Telford Bone.

"No one here," I called to Stan, then stuck my head out of the old-fashioned, double-hung, rear window and saw John and Vinnie below me. "We're clear up here. Come on up."

The small man sat on the bed. Stanley stood over him still holding his Glock.

"Who are you?" I asked.

"Dalton Mincy," he said.

"What are you doing with Telford Bone's Hummer?"

"I don't know what yer talkin' about." He spoke with what could have been an Alabama accent.

"Stand up," I said. He hesitated. "I said, stand up." I grabbed him by the shirt and pulled.

He was a solid little guy, about fifty-years-old, wearing a beige dress shirt and brown slacks. Three bottles of Bud Light sat on the nightstand, one open. A Hardee's bag lay flattened out on the bedspread, a burger and orders of onion rings and French fries sat next to it.

Doctor Phil was on the tube talking to a man and women. The guy looked sad, while the woman answered Phil's question and cried at the same time.

As Dalton Mincy got to his feet, he assumed a passable version of a martial arts stance.

"Don't mess with me, man, I'll use Aikido on you," he said.

I looked at Stan who smiled, and then I focused back on Mincy. "Did you eat an extra bowl of stupid this morning?" I asked before snap kicking him in the groin.

After Mincy went down on both knees groaning and crying, I helped him up and sat him on the bed.

"Careful you don't sit on your food, Dalton," I said. "Let's talk about Telford Bone and his Hummer, okay? And no bullshit this time."

"Man, what the hell'd you go and do that for?" He held his crotch, doubled over sitting on the edge of the bed.

A framed picture, looking something like a Thomas Kinkaid knockoff, hung on the wall above the bed. The shade on a wall lamp over Mincy's head sat at a rakish angle.

"Telford Bone, where is he?" I cocked the hammer of my Smith and Wesson and put the muzzle against his temple.

"Whoa, man. Jesus, I'm a private detective. You ain't gotta treat me like this."

"Might be easier to tell him what he wants to know," Stanley said. "He's usually an even-tempered guy until somebody acts like a smartass. Then he sorta goes apeshit. Wanna try again?"

Mincy began blinking rapidly. "I don't know where Bone is. I'm just gonna drive his Hummer back ta Alabama."

"You're sure about that?" Stan asked.

All of a sudden, I felt a spark of memory. "I know you, you little prick." I grabbed Mincy by the throat and pushed him prone onto the bed, on top of his burger and fries. "I saw you at the Crown and Goose. You had the cell phone, you miserable little shit." I tightened my grip on his neck. He locked both of his hands around my wrist as I squeezed. His legs twisted up and down.

I looked toward the doorway. Eulis Fu Manchu, the desk clerk, stood there looking at me. John and Vinnie stood in front of Eulis taking in the scene within the room. Bernie Waggoner, taller than anyone else, stood in the background in his navy blue uniform.

169

"Get back to the office, Eulis," I said, "or I'll throw you and your customer off the balcony."

Bernie Waggoner spoke up. "It don't seem like y'all need any more assistance from me. I'll jest take Eulis here downstairs. Y'all have a good evenin'."

I focused back on Mincy. "You little piece of horseshit...where's your goddamn cell phone?"

"In my coat pocket," he croaked. "Je-sus, don't kill me."

"Somebody get me that phone."

Stan picked up the brown suit jacket and retrieved a cell phone from the pocket.

"Here ya go, boss." Stan held the phone at arm's length.

"John, hold your gun on this bastard, and if he moves an inch pull the trigger."

John and Vinnie moved over to the bed. Vinnie held his Glock loosely in Mincy's direction. John helped the little man sit up as he sputtered and coughed.

"Sit up, shorty," John said. "You're all red. Got a blood pressure problem?"

Mincy elevated his body, swinging his short legs over the side of the bed and onto the floor.

I took the cell phone from Stan and looked at Mincy. Ketchup and French fries stuck to his back. His burger lay on the mattress next to the onion rings, everything squashed flat. I spent a few seconds looking at the phone, unable to do anything more than look.

"Stanley, goddamnit, how do I retrieve any photographs this shithead took?"

"Let me see it, boss, It should be simple enough."

"Easy for you to say."

Stan pushed a few buttons, and a photo appeared on the phone's small screen.

"These are his photos? Recognize anyone?" Stan raised his eyebrows.

I looked at a picture of Rachel and me standing next to her Lexus, her kissing my cheek.

"How do I see what else he's got in here?"

Stanley took the phone. "Let me do it." He backed up through seven more photos, all of Rachel and me at the Crown and Goose."

"Hold onto that. It's evidence," I said and went back to stand next to Dalton Mincy. "Okay, you sawed-off little shit stain, where's Bone?"

"I swear, I don't know."

I grabbed him by the throat again.

"Stop, stop, stop!" His voice sounded somewhere between a gasp and a croak. "Okay, okay. I don' know where he is, but I switched cars with him, and I'm supposed ta meet him back in Birmin'ham."

"What kind of car did you give him?"

"A silver '04 Impala."

"What's he up to?"

"I don't know. He was paid to go after that girl and her roommate. Then he paid me to foller you. That's how I got yer pitchers."

"You sent the pictures to Boyd Williamson?"

"Yeah, Bone told me what to do."

I smacked the side of his head, and he fell back over on the mattress again. I didn't think I hit him hard enough to make him fall.

"Don't hit me, and I'll cooperate," he said. "Come on, man. I'm not fighting you here."

"I've got you for felony coercion now. And I suppose you didn't know Bone was a federal fugitive? But who cares? You're his accomplice. Think about all that felony hard time and how many of those big animals in the slammer are gonna have their way with you. Do you think I really have to be nice to get your cooperation?"

"Whoa, whoa, wait a minute. Let's make a deal here. Telford Bone ain't nothin' ta me. Cut me some slack, and I'll he'p ya however I can."

"Good. A wise choice," I said. "Stan, cuff him, and get his gear together. We're going back to the barn. John, you and Vinnie drive the Hummer back."

"Okay, Boss," John said, with a big grin. "See, Vinnie, just like the old times."

"Lucky me," Vinnie said. "It's almost impossible for me to get into trouble working in polygraph. So, I come down here to the sticks, hang out with you guys and get indicted. Cool...and very nostalgic."

171

Chapter Twenty-Six

Dalton Mincy sat in the back seat of my Ford, Stanley and I in the front. I swung onto the cloverleaf from 129 and merged onto the Pellissippi Parkway heading toward Prospect. I found myself pushing ninety on the almost deserted stretch of highway. I looked in the rear view mirror and didn't see John, Vinnie or the Hummer. I slowed down to sixty-five.

Stan said, "I hope you've noticed that I didn't ask about those pictures."

"Yeah, thanks."

"Can I assume they're germane to what we're doing?"

"Yeah, good guess."

"Will you ever tell me?"

"Sure, but let's deal with him first, then I'll explain."

"Just checking."

I left the Pellissippi, turned left on Broadway and took the back roads to Prospect.

* * * *

"Sit down, Dalton." I pointed to a chair next to one of the desks in the squad room. Stan cuffed him to the steel ring attached to the side of the desk.

"Okay, little feller, here's where we are," I said.

He interrupted. "You think you can quit makin' remarks about my height?"

If I were only five-three, I'd be sensitive, too. His problem, not

172

mine.

"The next time you speak before I ask a question I'm gonna smack you in the head with one of these chairs. Understand?" He hung his head, but said nothing.

I let it go.

"You're not in a position to flap your mouth, mister. Sit back, listen, and learn your fate. Right now, you're under arrest for coercion and/or extortion for taking those pictures and sending them to Boyd Williamson with the demand for me to back off the Dallas Finchum investigation. What you did was a felony. You'll be our guest for a while."

He began to speak. I remembered the little worm sitting in the pub playing with his cell phone. I wanted to smack him...several times. I didn't.

"Shut up," I said. "I'm not finished, and you need to hear more. As soon as I sort out where you fit in with Telford Bone, I'll be charging you as an accessory to hindering prosecution and something else, too. Those are more felonies. You're going to jail—for how long depends on you."

"I want a lawyer," he said.

"What makes you think you can have a lawyer?"

"I'm an American, Goddamnit. I'm entitled to a lawyer."

"Guess again, asshole. Your buddy, Mr. Bone, is suspected of selling arms to terrorists. You're his accomplice. Maybe you've got a one-way ticket to a US Army base in Cuba. We'll see. It depends on how much more you piss me off. I can make a phone call and get you express check-in to the Arab wing of The Guantanamo Bay Super 8. Bone is wanted for other international crimes, too. So far, you're doing your best to protect him. I'll hand you over to the FBI or the DEA or somebody else with a few initials for their name, and you may disappear forever. Or, you can knock off the smartass act and think about your future."

"You're bluffing."

"Okay, you sawed-off runt, listen closely. As far as I'm concerned, you're also guilty of all I described plus the rape and murder of a Mexican girl that we're after Bone for. If the Feds ever release you, we'll want you back for that. Are you interested in shutting your mouth and listening a little more?"

"Rape and murder?"

"Yeah, last night. Have you got an alibi?"

"Yeah, I was…uh…in the motel."

"With whom?"

"Uh…I was alone, but…uh, the desk clerk musta seen me come in, and—"

"Sorry, sport, you lose. No alibi. No hope."

"Whoa now, I—"

"I told you, Dalton. Shut up and listen. Ask yourself, how much do I owe Telford Bone? Do you want to play it like Gordon Liddy and do lots of hard time to protect Bone, or do you want to throw yourself on the mercy of my court and make a deal?"

"What are you offering?"

"The big thing you have to remember is Tennessee's lethal injection for the rape-homicide."

"I tol' you I didn't have nothin' ta do with that."

"Who cares," Stan interjected. "This is Tennessee. He's a police chief, and you're a shithead PI from another state. I don't even know why we're talkin' with this guy, boss. Throw him to the Feds, and wait until they finish with him and *then* charge him as an accessory to the rape-murder and all the other things that sweeten the pot."

"That's a good option, Sarge. We can give him to the Feds and see if sharing a cell with a camel-humping terrorist makes him more inclined to deal with us small-town cops. So, Dalton, my friend, go ahead and clam up, and we'll consider you just another fucking Arab."

"I ain't no A-rab."

"Okay, have it your way. I'll call the Feds, I'm sick of arguing with you." I picked up a phone. John and Vinnie walked into the squad room and stood looking at Mincy with an appropriate stare designed to rob the little guy of any comfort he may have felt from being inside a public building.

"Okay, okay, wait," he said. "I ain't seen Bone since I gave him my car—honest."

"Where was he going?"

"He didn't tell me."

"Where is he staying?"

"I don't know."

"I believe you need to come up with a positive answer, or I'll make that phone call."

"Oh, man! Whaddaya want me ta say?"

"When he hired you what did *he* say?"

"He wanted me ta follow you and see what you were up to."

"And you took the pictures. He recognized the woman and thought you hit the jackpot."

"Yeah, he recognized her and told me how to find her husband. The man's in the phone book."

"And you knew this was all to keep us from going after Dallas Finchum?"

"He told me we would be helping out a cop."

"Very noble of you, moron. I'll have the local FOP lodge give you an honorable mention. Now, how about Bone's assault. Did you punch him up to make it look like two Prospect cops did that?"

Mincy dropped his eyes and hesitated before answering.

"Talk now, or I might start…"

"Yeah, yeah, he asked me to hit him. I thought he was crazy to go that far, but he was payin' so I figgered, what the hell."

I bent over and got closer to him, only inches from his face. "Are you willing to put all that in writing for me?" He paused again, formulating his words. I stood up waiting for his answer.

He looked up at me, scanned the room, looking at each of us. Dalton Mincy appeared concerned about his future. "Will you keep me from going away for this terrorist business?"

"Am I going to learn that you were in a few Latin American countries recently?"

"I ain't never been outta this country. Shoot, I love America."

"Okay, one statement for no Feds. Deal. Now I want to know how Billy Ray Finchum knows Telford Bone."

"I ain't got a clue. Bone called me. Hired me cause we worked t'gether in Birmin'ham once't before, and then I done what I tol' ya. I ain't got no idea about no Billy Ray Finchum. I never met the man."

"What about the Mexican girl?"

"I don't know nuthin' about that neither. I *work* with Bone. I don't

175

socialize with the man."

"Alright, let's start writing, and I'll get an ADA down here to see how far we can let you slide."

* * * *

The on-call assistant district attorney was a young black man named Shelby Johnson. Thirty minutes after I called, he walked into Prospect PD. We sat in my office and talked, while Dalton Mincy enjoyed the hospitality of the Prospect lock-up.

"So, you really just bluffed him into making this statement?"

"Yes and no. First, I'd like you to give copies of this to Captain Barkens at the Sheriff's office. That will get him off my back, and he'll leave my two men alone once he really believes the accusation Telford Bone made was false. Next, I need you to keep what I'm about to say confidential."

"I can't guarantee that until I hear what you have to say."

"Not good enough. If you ever repeat what I tell you to anyone, I'll lose my memory. No one I speak of will ever corroborate what I've told you, and you'll not only look like a jackass, but you'll be on the hit list of every Federal officer you come into contact with—forever."

"Okay, point taken. I hear you can lose the Mr. Nice Guy act very easily."

"Bone is unofficially wanted by the Feds. If I get him into custody and make a phone call, in less than twenty-four hours, he'll disappear. It's that simple, and I can't tell you anymore." Shelby made a face and squinted at me, evincing a little disbelief.

"I *can* tell you," I said, "that based on what I've recently learned about him, I'm ninety-nine percent sure he's your man for the rape-murder behind El Jibarito the other night."

"And you know this how?"

"It's his MO, from his time in the Marines in Beaufort, South Carolina to more recent times in other countries. He's a psycho serial sex offender who's graduated to killer. Believe it. It's all documented, but no one has enough proof yet to arrest him."

"So what do we do with Dalton Mincy?"

"Whatever you want. I'm happy to have his statement to exonerate my two cops. With a conviction, he'll lose his PI's license. He can do a little jail time if you've got a spare room. Offer him something a public defender will agree to, and let Dalton think he's gotten the big deal of the day."

"You still don't know how Bone and Billy Ray Finchum tied up."

"Yeah, not yet, but that's my problem. It's not insurmountable, just a little time consuming."

"Okay, up to you."

"Book him, Danno. He's all yours."

* * * *

I left work a few minutes early and stopped at the vet's office before they closed up at five o'clock. Kate had been to visit Bitsey earlier that day. I knew that when I found the poor old dog lying listlessly on her favorite plaid blanket.

The vet's assistant opened the cage door, and I scratched Bitsey's head, getting a weak but affectionate wag of her tail. Our old Scottie didn't look very good.

"I ran the tests today."

I turned and saw Ron Holt standing over me. I scratched Bitsey again, began to stand and felt a familiar pain in my left leg. It took a few seconds to straighten up.

"I used to have trouble on cold, wet spring days," I said. "Now it's spring twelve months a year."

"There's a lot of that going around," he said, almost smiling.

"How's she doing?" I asked.

"I wish I had better news."

"That bad?"

"I found a good-sized brain tumor that's in a spot making it inoperable."

"Can medications do anything to…?"

"No. As I said, the steroids mask the problem, but they don't cure it. There's nothing that will shrink a tumor like this. Her kidneys are also beginning to fail. I'd say she'll have full renal failure in a day or so."

"I hear what you're saying, and I feel helpless because I can't do anything myself. But I can afford to buy you whatever you need to do what I can't."

"I'm sorry. There's really nothing to do. It's just her time."

"Is she in any pain?"

"Not yet. Once her kidneys go, she'll have lots of discomfort. And I'd have to start an IV to keep her hydrated if we don't do something tonight. She won't eat or drink."

"Tonight? Like right now?"

"Now would be best for her."

"My wife would like to be here."

"Sure, I'll wait."

Chapter Twenty-Seven

"I'll call the man who does animal burial arrangements," I told Kate while she poured her second cup of coffee.

I sat at the breakfast table, in front of me a bowl of cereal and a slice of toast.

"Where do you want to bury her?" she asked.

"In the grove, under a dogwood tree."

"That will be nice. Does the man make a coffin?"

"I think he uses a child's coffin. They have them in fiberglass."

"I'm glad she has her blanket with her."

"Yeah, me, too," I said. I wanted to change the subject or put on a pair of dark glasses. A few more remarks like that last one and my mascara would start to run.

"The guy we picked up yesterday had the pictures I spoke of in his cell phone. I'm charging him with something else, and he'll cop a plea. There'll be no court case, no problems, and you won't get embarrassed."

"Have you told your friend yet?"

"No, not yet. She called me the other day, and I haven't spoken to her since. Her husband didn't take all this very well at all. He wants them to leave Knoxville."

"Oh, my."

"She's taking a job with a station in Chicago. He'll relocate his business up there."

"That's a little drastic, don't you think?"

"I do, but that's only because I know he's got nothing to worry about."

Kate made no comment.

"He doesn't, and neither do you. Are we straight on that?"

"Did you love her?" she asked.

That question surprised me. "She was my friend. I love you. You create so many complications in my life I couldn't take a chance and have another woman as more than a friend." I smiled. "If I had a real girlfriend that you knew about, I'd only feel safe if I sold every gun I owned."

Kate didn't respond to my humor.

"I do love you, Sammy. Do you know that?"

"Yes, ma'am, I know."

She stood up. "Can I have a hug?"

"Of course you can." I did the appropriate thing.

* * * *

After an intense overnight shower, my rain gauge showed a little over one inch had fallen. The trees dripped as I walked out of the garage toward my unmarked police car parked in the driveway turnaround. The cold front that caused the rain brought cooler temperatures and clear air. Everything smelled fresh and clean. Birds flew around landing on branches and disappearing into dense cedars and Leyland cypress trees. The sun angled up at about forty-five degrees in the eastern sky.

I had a lot to do that day. Least tasteful of my tasks was to arrange to have my dog buried in dense clay, soil I've always thought was only a hundred years away from being solid rock. From my office, I dialed a number Dr. Holt had given me. The vet arranged to have Bitsey picked up at his office by the man who would bring her home. I called to arrange a time and give the man directions.

I telephoned Kate and told her the man would be there at 5 p.m. and after digging the grave, we'd bury Bitsey at 5:30 or thereabouts.

I clearly remember many relatives or friends dying or being killed. I never remember feeling as sad as I did when that dog died. Perhaps it was only a function of my age, but I believe that my exaggerated sadness came on because I always looked at her as one of the toughest and most loyal individuals I'd ever met. She was a true stand-up guy and my good friend—irreplaceable.

Bettye walked into my office and dropped a few folders on my desk and then stood there looking at me.

"Sammy, you look so sad again. What's wrong?"

I looked at her for a long moment, wanting to neither discuss it nor lose my composure. "We had to have Bitsey put to sleep last night."

"Oh, Lord have mercy, poor little Bitsey. Oh, good Lord, I'll miss her." She sat down, took off her glasses and pulled a tissue from her pants pocket. "Oh, now look at me, sittin' here a'cryin' like an old woman."

I tried not to look at her or listen to what she said. I picked up my glasses and put them on, but I had nothing to read.

"Oh, Sammy, darlin', I'm so sorry."

I nodded, tried a smile and said, "Thanks."

"I used to just love it when you brought her to work. She was such a good little dog."

"Yeah, the best."

Bettye looked closely at me. I think she understood. "I won't ask you to talk about it. I know how you must feel."

"Yeah, I guess you do. And I guess you and I can't sit here too much longer, or I'll have to borrow a few of your tissues."

"Okay, darlin', I understand. You just let me know if you need me to do anythin' for you."

"I never got the chance to tell Bobby John to call every cop on the job to try and locate the guy he stopped on the night Bone claims he and Junior beat him up. Now, thanks to Dalton Mincy, kung fu private eye, Bobby's off the hook, and no one has to bother. I'm glad it worked out for our two guys.

Bettye nodded and left, and I got up, shook off some of the funk I was in and poured a cup of coffee. I felt so sorry for myself that I grabbed two Entenmann's doughnut holes from the box John brought in that morning. I popped one in my mouth and took a sip of coffee too hot to drink.

I tapped in the main number at the Sheriff's office, and the operator answered.

"Captain Barkens, please," I said.

He answered on the second ring.

"Clifford, Sam Jenkins. Good morning."

"Good mornin' to you, sir."

"Yesterday we picked up a man at a motel in South Knoxville who was in possession of Telford Bone's Hummer. Among other things, he told us he didn't know where to find Bone, but they swapped cars, and Bone is now driving a silver '04 Impala with Alabama plates. Our guy also signed a statement explaining that it was him who caused the physical injury to Bone—at Bone's request—intentionally setting up the two Prospect cops."

"Lord have mercy. Bone had someone beat him up?"

"The man's name is Dalton Mincy. Shelby Johnson at the DA's office has the statement. You can read all about it or interview Mincy at the pre-trial confinement cells."

"I'll be damned. Did he say much about who hired Bone or his local connections?"

"He just mentioned Bone's connection with the Finchums. I'll work on that angle today."

"I guess you will. I'll get a report out right quick exoneratin' your two men, and I'll be askin' for a warrant for our Mr. Telford Bone for falsely reportin' an incident."

"I'm glad to hear that. I've told Shelby the whole story. Perhaps he can help somehow."

"But this defendant wouldn't give you any more information about how Bone hooked up with Billy Ray Finchum?"

"I've got a few things to look at in that area, but so far there's nothing definite."

"Well, good luck to ya."

* * * *

It was one of those days when I just couldn't get going. I lacked ambition, had few good ideas and just didn't feel like working. Ronnie and the Council were still dragging their feet. Since he represented my closest connection with the City Council, I thought I'd ruin his day by telling him about the conspiracy to blame two members of his palace guard of wrongdoing. The attempted coercion of Boyd Williamson was none of Ronnie's damn business.

I phoned Trudy Connor for an appointment and learned the mayor was meeting with the budget director all morning.

Five minutes after I hung up, Rachel Williamson called.

"Hi," she said, "Are you busy?"

"Nope, I've been sitting here waiting for you to call." After saying that I thought it may have sounded sarcastic.

"I guess I should have called you back sooner. I'm sorry I had to run the other day. I committed to do a couple of PSAs, and they were ready to do the taping. I'm sorry."

"I figured you'd call when you had the chance."

"You don't sound...good. Is something wrong?"

"Yes, a good friend died yesterday."

"Oh, I'm so sorry. Someone close?"

"Yeah, very."

"I'm so sorry, Sam."

"Thanks. I guess you're busy making arrangements for your move."

"I'm trying. There's a lot to do."

"When's your last day at the station?"

"A week from Friday."

"Wow, quick."

"Yes."

"No reason for me to watch the news any longer."

"Oh, Sam." She sounded genuinely sad.

I didn't immediately have something else to say. She did.

"Can I see you before I leave?"

"Sure." I thought about us having lunch and being photographed. "But before we discuss that, I have to tell you that yesterday we caught the guy who took the pictures of us and sent them to Boyd. I've got the cell phone he used. I arrested him for something else, and he's accepting a plea bargain. There will be no trial. Tell your husband no one will ever see the photos except me."

"How did you ever find this man?"

"Just good old-fashioned po-leece work." No sense letting the girl go to Chicago knowing I just stumbled onto Dalton Mincy, the little worm.

"You're something else, Jenkins."

"Thanks for the compliment, Mrs. Williamson. I did my best because you had a vested interest in the outcome."

"I know you did, Sammy. Thank you—very much."

"So you think you'd like to have lunch before next Friday?"

She gave no immediate response.

"That's what got us into all this trouble," she said.

"Yeah."

"I don't think lunch would be a good idea."

"What do you have in mind? A motel along the Interstate?"

"Oh, stop." She managed a laugh.

"Okay."

"Are you still alone at lunch time?"

"I can be. I'll get rid of John if I have to."

"That sounds awful."

"I'll tell him to get lost, not kill him. He'll understand. I won't tell him why I'm banishing him for an extra hour." Is one o'clock tomorrow okay?"

"I think that's fine," she said. "I'll see you at your place."

"Yes, ma'am. Don't be late."

Chapter Twenty-Eight

A few minutes after Rachel hung up Bettye walked back into my office.

"Sam, I just got a call from Donnie's coach. My li'l soccer player fell in the wet grass and twisted his ankle. He's okay. The school nurse looked after him, but he won't be able to get home on his own. Can I go and pick him up and get him comfortable at the house?"

"Sure you can. Need help with anything?"

"I'll call if I do. But I don't think I'll have to take him to a doctor. It sounds like just a little ice will fix him right up. John says he'll keep an eye on everything while I'm gone."

"Okay, kiddo. Call if you need something."

"Thank ya, darlin'. I will."

* * * *

Twenty-five minutes later, John Gallagher yelled at me. "Boss! Get in here! Listen to this."

I went into the outer office to find John next to the radio and Vinnie sitting on the edge of his chair.

"John, what the hell…?"

"Quiet, Boss, listen!" He pointed to the radio.

I heard Bettye's voice. "Now take it easy, Mr. Bone. Just tell me what you want, and please don't hurt my boy."

"What I want my beautiful, blonde sergeant, is you. But y'all haven't been very friendly even though I've tried my best ta be nice to ya."

185

I felt a wave of anger rise within me and began to grind my teeth.

"I just came to the school to pick up my son," Bettye said, her voice full of stress. "He hurt his ankle. Let me take him home, and I can go to lunch with you."

Good girl, I thought. She's giving us all the information we need.

"Well, ya see, Sergeant Lambert, it's more than lunch I'd like. And I'd appreciate it if ya don't take me for a fool. Do I look like I'd believe you'd come back if I let ya take your kid home?"

We heard Donnie squeak out an *ouch*. And then Bettye spoke again. "Please, Mr. Bone, don't hurt him. Please take that gun away from his head."

"Oh, don't ya worry, pretty lady. I won't hurt the little feller, long as you an' me can get along."

"Okay, please promise to leave him alone. If you won't let me take him home, let him go here, in the schoolyard. He'll just look like another little boy waiting around."

"Son-of-a-bitch!" I said. "That ugly prick has Bettye and the kid at gunpoint. She's said enough. John, start calling all the on-duty guys on their cell phones. Have them go to Prospect Middle School ASAP. Then call everybody off-duty and get them to respond. Vinnie, let's go."

I ran back into my office and opened my top desk drawer. Inside, next to the bottle of Scotch was a snub-nosed Chief's Special, my off-duty gun. I put on a rain jacket and dropped the little .38 into my pocket.

The situation was easy to understand. Bone held Bettye at gunpoint inside her car. She must have used her knee to key the microphone that hung on the console next to the radio in her police department Explorer.

I hoped that Telford Bone didn't notice the little red light on the radio console had illuminated, indicating that their conversation was being transmitted over our network.

The Prospect Middle School was only six or seven minutes from the municipal building. I made it in three. My tires squealed as I swung clockwise through the parking lot.

I spotted Bone's borrowed silver Impala and Bettye's white and blue Explorer about the same time a marked Prospect cruiser came wheeling in on my left.

I parked my car blocking both vehicles and bailed out, taking cover behind my open driver's door. The driver's window of the Explorer was open.

"Bone," I called out, "this is Sam Jenkins. Tell me what we can do to make this go away."

"Well, hello there, Chief." He spoke like we were old friends meeting in the park. "Ain't no reason for all the fuss. Sergeant Lambert and me were just havin' a little git t'gether here. Maybe y'all might want ta take a walk over, and we can discuss the situation."

"Bettye, are you alright? Is little Donnie alright?" I waited, assuming Bone would have to okay her speaking.

"Yes, Sam, we're fine. You be careful coming over here."

"Now, Chief," he said, "y'all heard our sweetie here is okay, and so is her li'l brat. Now you walk over here. Keep your gun holstered now and your hand away from it, and we'll talk. There's not much I'll be wantin'."

I unzipped my rain jacket, took the Chief's Special out of my pocket and held it in my left hand. I cocked the hammer and placed the gun alongside my leg.

"Vinnie," I said, "you walk up to the right rear of the Explorer. I'll go to the left to get him on that side of the car. I'll be near Bettye in the driver's seat. As I talk, edge your way up. Keep your gun on him, and respond accordingly."

I didn't look for car numbers, but the marked car I saw earlier sat thirty feet off the Explorer's left rear fender. Someone took cover behind his left front wheel and rested a gun over the hood.

"Gottcha, boss," Vinnie said, acknowledging my plan.

I stood up with the little .38 held close to my left leg and out of sight.

"Telford, I'm walking up to you now. Roll down your window so we can talk."

"Come ahead, come ahead, ol' buddy. No funny bidness, and no fast moves, or I'll be forced ta kill li'l Donnie here first and then hurt Miss Bettye real bad."

"Okay, I hear you. I understand. We're just talking here."

I walked slowly to the driver's side of the Explorer. I kept my right hand near my gun and wanted Bone to see me doing that. My guess was

Bone thought he held all the cards and totally controlled the situation. With luck, he'd concentrate on sticking it to me and wouldn't notice the gun I held on my left side.

When I got to within two feet of the car, the left rear window rolled down.

"Well, howdy now, Sam. Y'all don't mind me callin' ya Sam, do ya?"

"No, call me anything you'd like. I'm here to talk."

"Well, good, real good. Seems like I got most o' the high cards, don't it? I don't much care how many o' Prospect's finest shows up, cause I kin get off a couple o' rounds quicker than y'all kin do much o' anythin'. Now, why don't ya take your hand offa that ol' revolver your wearin', Sam? It's time for y'all ta listen and do what I need."

"Okay, Telford, it's your dime. Tell me what you want."

I let my right hand drop to my side.

"It's real easy," he said, his voice still conversational, without a hint of anger or stress. Telford Bone sounded like more of a psychopath than I figured. "Miss Bettye, Li'l Donnie and me're gonna drive outta here in my Chevy. When I git where I wanna be, I'll let the kid go. Then Bettye and me will keep on drivin'. Then somewheres else I'll let her go, but not before I'm ready. I'll be wantin' some in-surance, ya know. If I see any po-leece cars or any helicopters, I jest may have ta shoot 'er. I got no problem killin' women and got no problem bein' on my own, so jest keep that in mind."

"Yeah, okay, I hear you. How about letting the boy go now as a gesture of good faith?"

He laughed loudly, an exaggerated, theatrical laugh. His long teeth made him look like an amused donkey.

"Where'd y'all get that line, Sam? From hostage negotiatin' 101? Nosir!" His voice rose noticeably. "The boy ain't goin' nowheres."

He grabbed a handful of Donnie's sandy hair and put the muzzle of a Beretta 92, 9mm automatic against the boy's head.

"How about I kill the boy now as a gesture of how I mean bidness?"

I noticed the hammer of the Beretta wasn't cocked. Bone had to double-action the gun to fire a first round. It didn't require a great deal of effort, but it wouldn't happen immediately, and the gun couldn't go off accidentally. Obviously, Vinnie saw the same thing. He slapped the right side of the Explorer. Surprised by the sound, Bone turned right to look and saw Vinnie's Glock pointing at his head. Donnie pulled away when Bone slackened his grip and sunk into the foot well in front of his seat. Bettye pulled as far away from Bone as possible. He turned back to me, the Beretta now pointed at Bettye.

"Well, well, well now," he said, again showing me his teeth. He fingered the little patch of hair under his lip and said, "So, ya got me surrounded. I suppose they's even more o' yer men here by now. Don't matter much though, does it? I still got Miss Bettye in my sights."

I didn't plan on letting that imbecile take Bettye or the kid anywhere, and it's tough to negotiate with a psycho. Like it or not, I had to do something positive and soon. I hoped my first idea would be a good one.

"You know, Telford." I smiled myself, "this reminds me of an old Burt Lancaster movie. Remember one called *The Gypsy Moths*?"

Bone tilted his head in confusion and seemed to be intent on listening.

"Old Burt was a sky diver," I said. "When he found out he was dying, he wanted to make one last jump. During his freefall, we see Burt get a big smile on his face. He decided to make it the ultimate experience. He never pulled his D ring and—splat!"

That bit of nonsense caused him to wrinkle his brow and look at me through those reptilian slits he'd call eyes.

"You know what *that* reminds me of?" I asked genially.

Bone sat there about to speak, his tiny mouth open. But he hesitated. I knew he had listened to what I said, but saw no relevance in it. He looked from me to Bettye. He elevated his pistol a little, pointing it now at her head. She looked back over her shoulder at him. Donnie reached across the transmission hump to touch his mother's leg. Bone turned his stare back on me.

I looked straight into Bone's eyes, smiled as I tilted my head a little and said carefully and slowly, "Telford, as my old daddy used to tell me, a-wet-bird-doesn't-fly-at-night."

When I said the word *night*, I snapped the .38 up to almost shoulder level and shot him in the face.

Bettye screamed. Donnie called out, "Ma!"

The noise of the short-barreled gun firing plus-P ammunition into the car's interior was deafening. A two-foot flame shot from the muzzle of my little five-shot revolver. Bone dropped the Beretta and sank onto the rear seat.

"Vinnie, get the boy out!" I yelled.

A cop named Johnny Rutledge ran from behind his cruiser and stood near the Explorer, his Glock pointed at the rear window.

I opened the driver's door and grabbed Bettye by the arm, pulling her to me. When she was safely out of the vehicle, she hugged me. I had no time to comfort her. I let her go to check if Bone was dead.

"Hang in there, kid. I'll be right back." I left Bettye and opened the rear door of the Explorer. Still pointing the little S&W with my left hand, I reached in to take the Beretta that lay close to Bone's hand. By all appearances, he looked dead; no chest movement, his eyes were open and vacant. I saw and heard no breathing, and only a little blood oozed from the small hole in his head.

Vinnie already stood next to me holding Little Donnie by the hand. Bettye grabbed her son as I placed two fingers on Bone's carotid artery to feel for a pulse. Bettye pulled the boy to her and hugged him tightly. I pushed Vinnie aside and dragged Bone from the vehicle, waiting for a dead man to move.

Johnny Rutledge changed position and trained his pistol at the man on the ground.

As Telford Bone lay on the blacktop, I looked at the hole that entered his skull about an inch southeast of his left eye. A trickle of blood continued to ooze from the hole.

"Whaddaya doin', Sam?" Vinnie asked, knowing I shouldn't contaminate a shooting scene.

"I don't want this bastard to bleed out in her car, Vinnie. That's all."

"Jeez-us-Christ!" he said, shaking his head. He holstered his pistol. "Hell of a shot, Sam, hell of a shot."

Rutledge relaxed and stood there, the Glock dangling in his hand.

I stuck the Chief's Special into my waistband, turned to Bettye and put one arm over her shoulder and my other hand on Donnie's back.

"Everything's okay, guys. You're okay now."

Bettye put her hand on the back of my neck and pulled me close, touching her forehead to my shoulder. I felt Donnie clutching my leg.

Lenny Alcock and Harley Flatt walked up next to us. Bettye let go of me. Harley looked at Bettye, then me. Lenny took Rutledge with him to create a guarded perimeter and keep any civilians from getting close to us.

"Everything here okay?" Harley asked. "Miss Bettye, you okay? The li'l boy okay?"

Bettye nodded and looked like she wanted to speak, but no sound came out.

"Boss, y'all okay, too?"

"Yeah, Harley, we're all fine. Got a radio with you?"

"Yes, sir, right here. Whatcha need?"

"Hang in here a minute." I turned Bettye to face me. "Betts, take Donnie, and sit in my car."

She nodded and loosened the grip she had on my arm. I turned to my right. "Vinnie, sit with Bettye and her boy."

Vinnie nodded and led them to my Ford.

I watched other marked Prospect cars pulling into the school lot. Cops in and out of uniform helped form a perimeter around the scene following the instructions Alcock gave them. Major incidents in a public venue always draw a crowd, and I needed the gawkers who showed up to stay away from immediate area.

"Harley, give me your radio." I took the small portable and spoke to the troops. "Prospect one to all Prospect units responding to the middle school. Slow down. I say again, slow down. Situation resolved." I took a breath and stated, "Be advised—no police personnel were injured. Everyone is okay. Anyone who continues to respond, remain outside the scene perimeter. Anyone in uniform, stay on the road, and wait for an assignment from Prospect headquarters. Prospect one, out." I handed the radio back to Harley.

"You want me to start the county boys rollin', boss?" he asked.

"No, hang on for a bit. I've got to make a phone call or two."

I pulled the cell phone out of my jacket pocket and noticed that Stan Rose had walked up next to me. He stood there, hands on his hips, wearing a Lakers T-shirt and blue jeans, looking very large.

"Hey," I said.

"How ya doing?" he asked.

"I'm getting there."

"What do you need?"

"Make sure some of the guys protect the immediate scene, and everyone else keeps the public away. Have someone put up the tape now. Then check on Bettye once in a while. I've got to use the phone."

"You've got it."

He walked away, and I punched in Ralph Oliveri's cell phone number. As I waited for him to pick up, I noticed a young boy, no older than Donnie, on a bicycle with small wheels. He slowly rode around the perimeter of the shooting scene, looking interested. A few adults must have walked out of the school and milled around just beyond the police line. One woman held a cell phone in her hand. I thought she might be recording the action.

Finally Ralph answered.

"Are you in the office?"

"Sam? Yeah, I've been here all morning."

"I need you to get to a computer right now. Can you do that?"

"Man, what is it with you? I need, I need. Am I on the Prospect PD payroll or what?"

"Save your complaints for the next time I buy you lunch. This is serious stuff. I've got a real time problem working against me here. I need you to get up your liaison link to the CIA."

"What?" No one could have made one word sound more incredulous.

"You heard me. Bring up that link. And when you do, I'll give you a code to type in. That should explain everything."

"How do you...? Never mind. Hang on a minute."

Good old Ralph—he has faith. I heard keys clicking.

"Okay, I'm there. You know if I access this with a code word, I'll get an inquiry and have to answer it. This is serious shit. There are no tests here."

"Alright, before you type, let me explain something. I was asked to take a man into custody, then call Knoxville FBI and follow this procedure. I've got the man now. Only there's one slight alteration in plans. He's not in custody…he's dead."

"Do I really want to know about this?"

"You've got to know about this. I didn't intend on killing this guy, but it ended up that way. I need a little help here, buddy."

"You killed him?"

"It's a long story, but only an ACLU lawyer might question my justification here."

"Are you okay?" He sounded concerned.

"Yeah, I'm good. No cops hurt."

"I have a feeling that typing a name into a computer isn't all you want."

"It's not all I need. This guy was destined to be whisked away by you and delivered to a couple of spooks who then would do God knows what with him. Probably something that comes under a facet of the Patriot Act."

He groaned.

"Now I've got a dead body," I said, "and need to know if the Agency wants a team of local forensics people playing with their corpse."

"Jesus Christ, Sam! How do you get yourself into these things?"

"I'm lucky?"

"Alright, what's the magic word?"

"Funny you should say that. Try *Mandrake*."

He typed the eight letters.

"Okay, that registered," he said. "Now I have to wait for instructions."

"Good. Here's the poop they may want to know. I'm at the Prospect Middle School. The subject's name is Telford Bone, aka Calhoun Grant. He's DOA, shot during a legitimate, armed hostage situation. Bone is also suspected, by me anyway, for a rape-homicide in Maryville that occurred the other day. That should get you some interest."

"The screen says they want a phone call. I'll have to get back to you."

"Use my cell number."

"Okay, give me a few minutes."

I looked back toward the school buildings. The kid on the bike rode in figure eights in the teacher's parking area. He didn't seem to be troubled by the commotion. At least a dozen more people from inside the school had joined the woman with the cell phone and the crowd began to spread out, everyone wanting a better look. A middle-aged couple with a little Yorkshire terrier on the end of a leash stopped walking and joined the crowd of interested bystanders.

I walked over to my car and sat in the front passenger's seat. I nodded at Vinnie and turned to face Bettye. She put a hand over the arm I rested on the seat back.

"Thank you, Sam."

I nodded. "That was good thinking back there, lady. Real sharp to key the mike with your knee. I'm proud of you. You saved your son and yourself."

"I think you two had something to do with that," she said.

I shrugged. "It's over now. Hey, Donnie, you okay?"

The kid slumped in the back seat with his head on Bettye's shoulder. She held his left hand in both of hers.

"Yes, sir, I'm okay."

"What do you say to Sam, Donnie?" Bettye asked.

The boy lowered his eyes and said, "Thank you, Sam."

"It's okay, kid. Now I want to hear from your mother. You okay, too, Mom?"

"Sure, Sammy. I'm okay. I'm just startin' to feel like you."

"What do you mean?"

"I need a drink."

Vinnie laughed. Then my phone rang.

"This is Ralph," I said. "Excuse me." I stepped out of the car.

"What's up?" I asked.

"It seems our friends are grateful, but no longer interested in retrieving Mr. Bone...or Grant. They request fingerprint confirmation, so they can cancel their notice of interest and make the appropriate notifications. Other than that you're on your own."

Fool that I am, I felt shocked. "You're kidding?" I should have known better.

"Afraid not."

"I've got a ten pound can of worms sitting on my counter with no help coming?" I didn't expect an answer. "As far as I know, half the petty politicians in this county are involved with the people who brought this bastard here, and my big choice is to let the Sheriff's men investigate my shooting?"

"I wish I could help you."

I knew he did.

"How about you guys act as a shooting team for me?"

Ralph had no immediate answer.

"Ralph, you still there?" I sounded a little sarcastic.

"Part of the instructions I received, and apparently these have been approved by the Bureau, is we have no interest in Telford Bone, and we may take no part in your incident. Sorry."

"You can never find a Fed when you need one."

"It's not me, Sam."

I heard genuine concern in his voice.

"Yeah, I know. Okay, I'd love to stay on the phone and chat with you, Ralphie, but I've got a body here on the ground. Thanks for your help. Oh, and do me one more quick favor."

"What's that?"

"Before you log off your liaison link, give Mandrake a message for me."

"What now?"

"Two words: Fuck him. Ciao, buddy."

I made another phone call.

"Sara, this is Sam Jenkins. I need Irving. It's important."

"I'm sorry, Mr. Jenkins, but he's out of the office at a meeting."

"Is he in your building or reachable by telephone?"

"I believe so, but I can't interrupt him at the moment."

"Tell him I just killed the man he called me about, and his people have hung me out to dry."

"Please don't say any more on the phone." She spoke quickly and efficiently. "Hold the line for one moment."

While I waited, I watched the kid on the bike riding circles around the scene again. He stayed clear of the other pedestrians and never got too close to the police line, but he reminded me of an Indian in an old western movie circling the wagon train.

Bureaucracy moves slowly. In about three minutes, Irv Kauffmann came onto the phone.

"Sam, you may speak freely now. We're on a secure line. Tell me what happened."

I did and left him with no doubt that the boys or girls of Mandrake were not on my Hit Parade.

"What you heard was, of course, current information. We can't retrieve dead bodies in a case like this. You seem to be on solid ground with the use of deadly force to resolve a hostage situation. It should be handled locally."

"I'm left with a corpse and the only alternative to investigating this myself, which is far from kosher, is to have the county detectives do the work. They will no doubt ask many questions, and I still will not have an answer to the musical question—who really brought Telford Bone to Prospect?"

"I don't quite see your point."

"Your desires have been satisfied. Mine are riddled with gaping holes. I'm potentially stymied by local politics. At least one of those local politicos is considered a loose cannon by others of his ilk. I did you a favor. Now help me clean up your mess. I need you to make a phone call for me, and grease the skids for a little unconventional operation."

"Such as?"

"Call a US congressman named Jimmy Dillworth. You know of him?"

"Yes, we've met."

"He's already on board with this to a minor degree. Have him do several things. First, call a local commissioner named Claude Webbster and have him cease and desist any contact with or assistance to one Billy Ray Finchum."

He interrupted me. "Billy Ray is his legal name?"

"Lots of them down here."

"Hmm."

"Next, contact Calvin Pitts, the District Attorney General for Blount County. I'll be seeing a grand jury for killing Bone. I can assure you the shooting was justified. Have Dillworth instruct the DA to accept my report without utilizing another law enforcement agency to investigate.

196

Have a DA's investigator audit the case to insure my account is plausible and to keep me honest. But I want to know that he won't give me any crap about unusual procedure."

"You're asking a lot, old friend."

"Remember my words? I'm cleaning up a mess that is as much yours as mine."

"Let's hope the congressman is willing to jump on board our little boat and not sink you."

"I'm confident he will, but I'll take steps to insure that."

I didn't give him time to respond. "Lastly, have him tell the DA that when I bring in other defendants for conspiracy and political corruption, play it straight with me. No slack or good ol' boy discounts for the bad guys. Does all that sound reasonable and doable to you?"

"I'm not the one to decide that. You say Dillworth has prior knowledge of other incidents relative to this?"

"He does."

"I'll make the call."

"Thanks."

Yet another phone call was necessary. *And I wonder why my life is never simple.*

"Judge, Sam Jenkins. I'm at the scene of a shooting. The matter we've been discussing turned ugly. I'll explain everything in due time. Can you do me a favor?"

"Of course, Sam. Anything you need."

"Jimmy Dillworth will be getting a phone call from a government man named Irving Kauffmann. Dillworth may know him. He'll ask Dillworth to intercede in matters here in Blount County. Dillworth can explain them to you. Please insure the congressman makes a genuine effort to do what's necessary, or the embarrassment brought down on local people will be considerable."

"Can you talk now, Sam?"

A black Lincoln navigator pulled up to the police perimeter. Ronnie Shields got out. Stan Rose jogged up to him.

"No, sorry. I've just had to kill someone. I'm going to have to get a crime scene unit and medical examiner here quickly and quietly and investigate this incident myself. That's one of the things I'll need

Dillworth to clear for me. I'll call you back as soon as I can. I also wanted to ask you about your inquiry into the connection between Telford Bone and Billy Finchum."

"I don't have much to tell you there, but we can discuss that later. Don't worry, Sam. I trust ya. I'll call Jimmy."

"Thank you, sir."

Stan escorted Ronnie over to my car.

"Good God, Sam! That man over there's dead."

Sometimes I marvel at my mayor's astute observations.

"He is. I killed him."

"What was he doin' here?"

"Trying to sow some wild oats, but I turned him into shredded wheat."

Ronnie gave me a look, obviously not pleased with my attempt at gallows humor. "He was holding Bettye and her son at gun point," I said to clarify.

"Good Lord. Is that Telford Bone?"

"It is."

"Can't you do somethin' with him? Cover him up or somethin'?"

"We're about to call for the medical examiner and crime scene people. They have things to do before we can touch him or have him moved."

"Is Bettye alright?"

Glad he thought to ask.

"Both she and her son are shaken up but okay. They're sitting right behind us in my car."

"I didn't notice them with that dead man layin' over there."

"Stick your head in the car, and say something to them."

I began to lose patience with Ronnie Shields at that moment. I looked at Vinnie and gestured for him to roll down the back window.

"Lord have mercy," Ronnie said, looking at Bettye. "I'm so sorry somethin' like this had ta happen. Are you two alright? Do y'all need anythin'?"

Sure, Ronnie—a couple of corn-dogs and large cups of sweet tea.

"No, sir, we're fine," she said, "thanks to Sam and Detective Falcone here."

"Well, if you need anything, time off or...anything, you jest let me know."

"Thank you, Mr. Mayor. I will."

"Betts," I said, "I'd like you two to take a ride to the hospital. Donnie can have someone look at his ankle, and if you'd like, both of you can see a doctor and talk about what just happened. Now's the time."

"Oh, Sam, I don't know that I could put up with sitting in an ER right now. I'll take care of Donnie myself. He's not hurt badly, and I'm fine, really. I'd just like to go home."

"I'd say please, but I understand what you mean. I'll get you a ride."

I asked Stan to arrange for one of the cops to drive them home and stay for as long as she wanted.

"When you've got Bettye taken care of, call crime scene and an ME's wagon. Do it by phone. Call them directly. Don't go through the duty officer. I don't want this on the radio in case some hungry reporter is listening to a police scanner. I don't want the press here."

"Okay, boss," Stan said.

"Sam, we're gonna have ta put out a press release sooner or later," Ronnie said.

"Why?" I asked. "I think this should be kept as quiet as possible. This is too complicated to explain without major embarrassment and jeopardy to what remains to be done."

"Sam, look at all the people watching us. Is that wise?"

"I'm going to handle this whole thing myself. I'll make it short and sweet. Then I'll finish up all this Finchum crap as quickly as I can. Right now, I don't need county dicks and reporters crawling over me. Officially, Ron, we were never here."

He gave me a strange look.

"Are we tryin' ta cover up somethin'?"

"You know better than that."

"You said you'd do the shootin' investigation yerself? Is that ethical?"

I guess there are camels and then there are camels. After having to euthanize my dog and then kill a man, Ronnie Shields dropped a straw onto the back of my personal camel that almost caused the proverbial break.

When I get angry, really angry, people tell me the tips of my ears turn red. I'd like to think that steam comes out of my ears, but that's not true. My blood pressure is usually one-ten over seventy—that's a good thing. That morning, taking my blood pressure would only have scared someone. But I've had lots of practice controlling my emotions, and I did just fine.

I took a deep breath and let most of it out. "Mr. Mayor," I said, "you and I have to take a short walk."

He looked at me with confusion. I looked over the roof of my car toward the teacher's parking lot. The kid on the bike pulled up next to Johnny Rutledge. The kid asked a question. Rutledge chased him away. A man I recognized as the school's assistant principal was attempting to muster his troops from the crowd and herd them back into the building.

"Just over there," I said, "so we can have a private word."

"What's wrong, Sam.?"

I walked away, and he followed.

"I hope you can see how upset I became when you questioned my ethics."

"Sam, I didn't mean to imply..." He held up both hands as a conciliatory gesture.

I held up one to stop his noise. "Forgive me, but I'm just a little miffed. I've had a bucket of shit dropped on me by all the petty politicos who think they can scare me like a professional mobster. They sent a couple of thugs to try and intimidate everyone I was concerned with. I locked up one of those hoods and killed the other. There are people who have to answer for their parts in all this. No one will prevent me from accomplishing that. And I would suggest you keep your deputy mayor far away from me. I can't stand that guy on a good day. Can you imagine how I'd deal with him today?"

"I hope you realize I thought of you when I told him not to come here with me. I know you two don't get along, but I think he means well, Sam."

"I doubt that, Ronnie. I think he's the eyes and ears of the chairman of the County Commission. And I have no doubt that as soon as you and I discuss something about this case, he runs to a phone and reports to

Uncle Micah. I wouldn't be surprised if those two weren't in cahoots with Claude Webbster, Billy Ray Finchum and anyone else who wants to throw monkey wrenches into our gears."

The mayor looked utterly shocked at my accusation. "You really believe that?"

"I do. And if I learn that either or both of that pair is complicit in this, I'll nail their balls to a tree along with all the overt players. The end result will be very useful. People will be punished, and those who sit by and watch that happen will learn that fucking with me is a fool's errand. So talk to those *other people* about ethics."

"Sam, I...I jest...I guess...I'd better get back to the buildin'. I won't contact the press until y'all are ready."

I scowled.

"Or not. And, Sam, I...I'll see ya later."

I nodded and let him go.

In time, two teams of county crime scene investigators arrived and processed the scene. They photographed everything, drew technical sketches, dusted the interior of Bettye's Explorer for Bone's fingerprints, inventoried his personal property and tagged and bagged the 9mm Beretta he had used. Finally, one man rolled a set of fingerprints from the corpse.

I surrendered my Chief's Special to Investigator Jackie Shuman so a TBI ballistics man could match a fired round to the bullet in Telford Bone's skull.

Before they finished, I turned my attention to Doctor Morris Rappaport, the attending pathologist. His assistant, as usual, was Earl Ogle.

"Sam, you said you're going to investigate this yourself?"

"Yeah, Mo. It's something I have to do."

"You just shot this man. I'm not questioning your reasons for doing something a bit unconventional, but speaking as a physician—and there are some who think I'm still qualified to attend to the living as well as the dead—I suggest you give yourself a break. Too much stress, my friend, at our age isn't always good."

"All this is very complicated, and I appreciate your concern," I said, "but wasn't it Robert Frost who said, 'I have miles to go before I sleep?'

That's me today."

"Ah, Robert Frost, yes. Wasn't he a Vermont farmer?"

"I think he farmed in Massachusetts. He was a full-time poet in Vermont."

"A full-time poet. I should be so lucky. My point is, Sam, if you can't get someone to do this for you, then do what you have to do, and go home. Have a drink—but not so much, and relax. Tomorrow is another day. Then finish what you started."

"I'll get to that relaxing right after I bury my dog."

"Oh, Sam, I'm sorry. Be careful here, boychek, there's nothing worth ruining your health."

"Thanks for the advice, Mo. I've got to start a few people writing their statements. Give me a call when you're doing the autopsy."

* * * *

A small, dark blue Chevy pick-up sat in my driveway when I got home. I looked in the dogwood grove and saw two men, both dressed in khaki work uniforms, occupied at the spot I had designated for Bitsey's grave. One dug with a long-handled spade, and one sat on the ground next to a light green fiberglass child's coffin. I parked the Ford and walked over.

"Hello," I said.

"Mr. Jenkins, is it?" the one digging said. He was short with what looked to be bleached blond hair. He wore wrap-around shades with orange, mirrored lenses. A Tennessee surfer, perhaps.

"Yeah, how are you?" I offered him my hand.

"Doin' fine, sir. Sorry for ya loss. We'll be ready here in mebbe a half hour. Didn't figger they was so many roots and the so'l would be so hard. I wanna git down least four, five feet, and it'll take me longer than I 'spected."

"That's okay. No hurry. Would you like something to drink? Soda? Water? A beer?"

"No, sir, we're fine. I'll holler at ya when we's done."

"Thanks."

Thirty minutes later, the same man knocked on the front door. He removed his glasses and told me he was ready. Kate and I followed him

202

back to the grove.

The two men lowered the coffin into the grave with straps. Kate dropped a mixed bunch of daisies, late iris and rhododendrons onto the coffin, and we each said our silent good-byes.

Kate cried and walked back to the house. I did my best to look like the stoic Indian chief. I wrote the man a check, thanked him and accepted his condolences.

Neither of us felt very hungry that night, but we picked over a couple of frozen dinners in relative silence. Later we each drank a little too much, and I admit that for the first time in more than thirty years, I got drunk before I went to bed.

Chapter Twenty-Nine

The next morning, I walked into the office and noticed there was no joy in Muddville.

Joey Gillespie worked the desk. Stan had arranged his reassignment. The day before, when I drove to Bettye's house to take her statement, I insisted that she take time off.

Ten minutes after I arrived, John and Vinnie came in. In Bettye's absence, I made the coffee. The New Yorkers drank coffee. Joey chose a decaffeinated Pepsi from the soda machine.

Over coffee in my office, we talked while Joey listened for the phone and radio.

"For us to get to the bottom of this," I said, "we have to learn how either Claude Webbster or Billy Ray Finchum tied up with Telford Bone."

Vinnie asked, "You still believe this Mincy character not knowing the connection?"

"It's plausible. If I was Bone, and I hired a bottom feeder like Mincy, I wouldn't share my connection with him. He didn't need to know. I think Bone would recognize that concept. Mincy was an employee, not a partner."

"You want us to take another run at Mincy today, Boss?" John asked.

"It couldn't hurt. He's here until his trial on the conspiracy thing. Get Shelby Johnson to give him a pass to anything else he admits to—within reason, and he can just go for his part in beating Bone and framing our two guys. He thinks he's going to skate on the coercion of

Boyd Williamson, but tell him I'm starting to get in the mood to revoke his deal for that charge. That's not true. I really don't care much about those pictures, but he doesn't know that. Also, I doubt Bone used accomplices in his sex crimes, so Mincy should be clear with that. See what you can do."

"You got something in mind yourself?" Vinnie asked.

"Yeah, I'm going to work on Bone's past history with Southern Air Transport. I know someone local who may be able to help with that."

Vinnie set his coffee cup down on my desktop with a slam. "Okay then. Me and the Irish fool will go to the jail. You gonna call us about lunch?"

"Let me see what I get accomplished. I'm in a shitty mood, so you may not like my company."

They both offered their own forms of sympathies on the loss of my dog. Cops, and these old-timers especially, don't often get very conciliatory over personal loss. I understood that, and it was okay. I had work to do. Once I finished that, I'd look for time to screw off at lunch.

* * * *

I drove north out of the town center, over the Crystal Creek Bridge and turned right on Sevierville Road, heading northeast. In another mile and a half, I turned again into the interior or flatlands of our jurisdiction. I passed cattle grazing on scrub grass, horses milling about in pastures and a llama farm.

On a flat open plain, with the foothills of the Great Smoky Mountains in the background, I turned into the parking lot of the Prospect Air Park. I hadn't been there in months.

As I approached the Administration office, a low, prefab, commercial building, I read the sign which said Prospect Aviation and Air Park, C.A. Goodhardt and A.A. Goodhardt, owners. C.A. was Lieutenant Colonel Charlie, USAF retired, and A.A. was his daughter Amelia, the loveliest pilot and aviation mechanic I'd ever laid eyes on.

Charlie was my age. He had retired from the Air Force in 1998 and several years later bought and restored the Air Park. Amelia was now pushing forty. She flew a bright red bi-plane, drove a Jeep Wrangler and had once helped me solve one of the most bazaar cases of my career at

Prospect PD.

I climbed the three wooden steps to the Admin office and opened the door. Behind the customer counter, two desks, assorted file cabinets and computer gear took up the left third of the building. To the right, a waiting room with uncomfortable-looking seats, a couple of vending machines and a Formica topped dinette table with four kitchen chairs filled the rest of the interior.

Charlie Goodhardt sat behind one of the desks. Still thin enough to fit in the cockpit of a fighter-bomber, Charlie had gray hair a little longer than a crew cut and a likable smile. He looked up when I closed the door and the weather-stripping made a sucking sound.

"Hello, Sam. What are you up to these days?"

"Whaddaya say, Charlie? Got a minute to give an old Army grunt some Air Force information?"

"Sure. Want to swap war stories and other lies?"

"Maybe something a little more technical. What do you know about Southern Air Transport?"

Before Charlie could answer, the back door opened, and his daughter entered. She walked over behind the counter and looked at me with expressive dark brown eyes and a slight frown. I've never met a woman more suited to be a blue jeans model. Amelia wore a pair of pale blue Levi's that looked like they were made to fit no one else. She stood with her hands on her hips, the sleeves of her dark blue denim shirt turned up on her forearms. In a tomboyish way, the woman was gorgeous.

"Hello, stranger," she grumbled.

"Hi, Amelia. How are you?"

Things are bad when a much younger woman can come close to intimidating a middle-aged tough guy.

"Better now that I know you're not dead. It's a good thing I didn't wait on the runway for you to take that ride in my bi-plane. The gasoline would have turned bad by now."

"Gee, I'm sorry. We've been pretty busy lately. You know how it is—crime never sleeps."

I tried out my shy little boy smile on her, the one that says how could you ever be mad at me? I noticed Charlie grinning.

"Okay," she said, "I guess you're forgiven, busy big-time hero cop like you."

Then she gestured with her finger for me to come closer to where she stood.

I touched my chest with an index finger. "Who me?"

She nodded.

"You look like you want to hit me."

"Come here, and find out."

I did, and she leaned over the counter and kissed my cheek.

"It's nice to see you again," she said.

"You, too." Her dark brown hair fell well below her shoulders. "You look good...more like Charlie's granddaughter."

"Or yours, mister."

"Yeah, I guess only your old man and I get older-looking."

"I never really thanked you for that bottle of wine," she said. "We loved it. I wanted to buy another until I found out how much you paid for it."

"You helped me find the kidnapped cow and made dinner for me. I wanted you to have a bottle of something nice. Just my way of saying thanks."

She was softening up. I flashed another smile for good measure.

"It was nice. I had to fight Charlie to get my half." She gave me a big smile. Hers outclassed mine by miles.

"Sounds like a domestic squabble. Want me to send a patrolman?"

Charlie, probably tired of me flirting with his daughter, interrupted. "What do you want to know about SAT?"

"You probably won't hear much about it on the news, but a man was just killed here in Prospect after a hostage situation. This is all very hush-hush, so please keep our conversation confidential."

"If you're asking about SAT," Charlie said, "I figured it might be."

"What conversation?" Amelia smiled. I assumed an Air Force brat knew how to keep her mouth shut.

"This guy was a former SAT employee turned criminal. He'd been hired by a local man for all the wrong reasons, and I'm trying to find out how those two got connected. Right now, I'm seeing nothing apparent where a local man might have found a hard case from Alabama."

"Sounds like something newsworthy. Should I try and guess why it's being hushed up."

"That shouldn't be too difficult given all the factors. After the shooting, the *company* who would normally be a source of info on SAT and their former employees decided to take their phones off the hook."

"Sounds typical. You had to do the shooting?"

"Yeah, lucky me."

"You had to kill someone?" Amelia asked.

"I'm afraid so."

"I hope none of your good guys got hurt."

"We were all lucky."

"I'm glad," she said.

"Yeah, me, too," Charlie said. "You think SAT may be the connection to your man?"

"The only other thing might be the Marine Corps in an indirect way, but that was even longer ago, and a lot more people to check through."

"Yeah, but they say, 'Once a Marine, always a Marine.'"

"Even a crazy jarhead would steer clear of the guy I'm investigating."

"SAT attracted some hard cases looking for exciting work," Charlie said, "and they were a close knit group. When I flew with Special Ops, out of Hurlburt Field in Florida, we ran across those people and their planes often enough."

"Do you personally know anyone who worked for them?"

Charlie shifted in his chair and nodded. "As a matter of fact, I do. A young captain who worked for me at Hurlburt finished his Air Force time and took a job with SAT flying re-supply to the pro-American military down in Central America. When SAT went out of business in the late-nineties, he opened his own little air service. As far as I know he's still down in the Tampa area."

"Can you check with him?" I asked.

Charlie nodded.

"Ask him if he remembers a guy who called himself either Calhoun Grant or Telford Bone. Bone was his real name. He was a tall blond guy, not very good-looking. If he ever saw him, he'd remember. Also, does he know any former SAT personnel in this area? Maybe these ex-flying spooks have reunions or something, and that's the connection."

"A person is actually named Bone?" Amelia asked.

"He was."

"Hmm, sorry."

"Was this guy Bone a pilot?" Charlie asked.

"No, cargo handler or loadmaster or whatever. Probably flight crew rather than ground personnel. That's what he did in the Marines."

"I'll try to track down my man today and give you a call back."

"I appreciate that."

I was about to leave when Amelia asked, "Should I gas my plane, Mr. Jenkins? You ready for that ride?"

"I didn't spray my hair this morning. If I flew in an open cockpit, I'd look frightful when I did my detective work. Can I ask for another rain-check?"

Her feigned scowl changed to another big smile. "Sure you can, but it won't last indefinitely. If I get tired of waiting for you, I just may find myself some old Navy veteran who wants a ride."

"I had hoped your father taught you better. But that gives me a reason to come back. I don't want some ex-squid ruining your life."

* * * *

I arrived back at the PD just before Gallagher and Falcone walked in after interviewing Dalton Mincy at the county lock-up.

"How'd you guys make out?" I asked.

Vinnie shook his head and sat at John's desk.

"No luck, Boss," John said. "We double-teamed him, tried offering him something, but he didn't give us squat. We think he's probably telling the truth. I even tried using *reverse psychiatry* on him."

Vinnie looked at me and smiled. Joey Gillespie looked at me and frowned.

"How did you do that, John?" I asked with a straight face.

"You know, Boss—reverse psychiatry. It's like you use on kids. You tell them you don't care if they tell the truth or not. You get tough and make them think you would rather not hear what they have to say. You know, like you don't need what they've got. Reverse psychiatry. It's an old trick. I'm surprised you haven't heard about it."

209

"I live and learn, John."

At quarter to one, I told John and Vinnie to go to lunch. I expected Rachel to walk in soon.

"You want anything, Sam," Vinnie asked. I declined.

"I think the Boss's girlfriend is coming to see him," John said.

Wisely, Vinnie chose to listen and not comment.

"Isn't that right, Boss?" John couldn't let it go.

I guess if he'd known it was the last time I'd see her he may have shown some mercy. Or maybe not. Gallagher can be a real pain in the ass sometimes.

"Yeah, in about fifteen minutes. Now get out so you don't scare her away."

"Did you know the Boss had a girlfriend, Vinnie?"

"Come on, stupid. Let's go to lunch."

John stood there grinning.

"Okay, she's a friend," I said. And she's a woman, not exactly a girlfriend. Keep breaking my chops, John, and you can spend your lunch hour in a cell. Did I mention it's time for you to get out?"

"See ya later, Boss. Don't do anything I wouldn't do."

"Piss off, John!"

Vinnie waved as they left. John laughed.

Ten minutes later Rachel arrived.

"Hi," she said, standing in my doorway wearing a black pin-stripe suit with a white tailored blouse and a single strand of pearls. I'd seen the outfit before and liked it.

"Hi."

"Are you doing okay?"

"I can remember better weeks."

We sat in the guest chairs. I told her a few things she didn't know.

"And none of this is for publication?"

"Not yet, but you've got another week. I think I'll have something you can use pretty soon."

"You know, at this point, I really don't care."

"Short-timer's attitude?"

"I guess."

"Yeah."

"This is awkward, isn't it?"

"A little. I'm going to miss you."

"I'll never forget you, Sammy."

I nodded.

"I really hate this," she said. "I don't know if I'll ever see you again."

I felt one of those lumps in my throat. Lately, they'd been a recurring problem.

"Who knows?" I said. "I hope you find a nice place to live, that you work with good people and enjoy life."

"We've really been pretty good together, haven't we?"

"Maybe the only cop and reporter who ended up liking each other."

"I guess we could drag this out, but…that's not good, is it?"

I shook my head. "Probably not."

"You know, I've kissed you, but you've never kissed me."

"I see you're not wearing lipstick. Is that for a reason?"

"You're pretty observant."

"It's my po-leece training."

I stood up, so did she.

"I think we can fix that," I said.

She dropped her purse on the floor. I put my hands on her shoulders, bent over a little and kissed her on the lips. A long gentle kiss. I opened my eyes; Rachel's were still closed. Her hands felt good on my sides. I put my arms around her, pulled her closer and kissed her again, just as long, but a little harder.

When I let her go she said, "Wow, I think we've been missing something." A single tear ran over her cheek.

"Yeah, all that time we've been behaving ourselves has been misspent."

"Silly us."

I got a vision of the Foothills View Motel and changed the subject.

"You got a haircut," I said.

"You like it?"

"You look beautiful."

"Thank you."

"My pleasure."

"I guess I have to say good-bye."

"You can. I have a problem with that."

"What do you mean?"

"I've never been able to do that. I mean, I can't say the words. They just won't come out."

"Oh? Then how's this?" She grabbed my shirt, pulled me down and kissed me again—very passionately.

"That said a lot."

"Good."

That lump in my throat came back. I thought I may have developed an allergy to emotion and was going into anaphylactic shock. Rachel wiped another tear from her cheek. She also hadn't worn her usual amount of eye makeup.

"I love you, you know," she said.

"I thought you did, and even though we've avoided discussing it, the feeling is mutual. We just can't do much about it."

"Yeah, I guess. When did you know?"

"Probably from the first day," I said.

"Me, too."

"It took me fifteen minutes or so. You wore a low cut T-shirt and a short skirt that day. I guess it started off as lust."

"Oink."

"I knew you'd say that."

She smiled, brushed away the tears that trickled down her cheeks and took both my hands in hers.

"If I don't leave now I'll go to pieces."

"It's not going to get any easier."

"No." She stood on her toes to kiss my cheek for a last time. "Good-bye, Sammy."

I wasn't exaggerating when I told her I couldn't make those words come out. I never could. If I tried, I would have… Well, I don't know what I would have done. But I had to say something. And parting on a light note came to mind.

I thought I'd let one of her favorite characters speak for me. "So long, doll-face. If you ever get back this way again, look me up. I'm in the Yellow Pages under gumshoe."

"So long, Bogey," she said. "I'll remember that." Then she pointed at me with her index finger and let her thumb fall like the hammer of a gun.

As she walked out, I thought about that famous scene from Casablanca, but Humphrey Bogart wasn't standing on that Moroccan runway, I was. And it wasn't Ingrid Bergman and Paul Henreid walking toward a waiting DC-3, it was Rachel and Boyd Williamson. The icing on the cake was when Dooley Wilson began singing *As Time Goes By*. Rick Blaine and Ilsa Lund would always have Paris, but Rachel and I would have to settle for Knoxville.

Chapter Thirty

Mo Rappaport stood over a stainless steel counter in the autopsy room. Sitting on the counter, an electric knife sharpener hummed as the grindstone whirled around on its axle. Mo slid what looked like a six-inch kitchen knife over the spinning stone. I think a doctor would call it a Liston knife. Sparks flew to the sides with each pass he made. His short curly gray hair needed a brushing, as it always did. He wore a rubber apron and had the sleeves of his white dress shirt rolled up above his elbows. I'd never seen Mo wear scrubs.

When he finished sharpening his shiv, Morris sliced a sheet of scrap paper almost in half. Satisfied with his test, he turned to me and smiled. Morris always looked like a satisfied worker. He seemed to like his job. I seriously doubted anyone would take up the practice of dissecting other human beings by mistake.

"Sam, hello. I was expecting you."

"Greetings, Dr. Cyclops. Nice of you to invite me."

"Dr. Cyclops." Morris turned on a bigger smile. "George Zucco played him. I remember. Not the best movie. When I was a kid, I liked Wolfman films. I was a big Lon Chaney fan."

"A much better man than his little kid, Dick."

"Ahh, the sound of bitterness. But I think they spell their names differently"

I didn't care how they spelled their names and paid no attention to my orthography lesson.

"That's a real scalper you've got there, Mo."

"Yes, it is a good knife—carbon steel. I hate stainless. You never get as keen an edge."

"Uh-huh."

Two naked bodies, both subjects of previous post mortem examinations lay on gurneys pushed up against the wall to my right. A black man and a white woman. Each had a story, but I wasn't interested.

"Some doctors, especially young ones," Morris said, "are short knife men—scalpels mostly. I happen to be a long knife man."

"Isn't that what Crazy Horse said about Custer?"

"Ha! You're funny, Samilah. I've always said that."

"Thanks, I'll tell my agent you think so when I ask for gigs on the Borscht Belt. I'm tired of this police job."

Mo reactivated his nostalgia-inspired smile. "I loved the Catskills when I was a kid. Did you go, too?"

"Every summer. It was Natty Bumppo's favorite place, you know."

"Who? Natty sounds Jewish, but Bumppo, I don't know."

"Scotch-Irish, maybe. No one is sure," I said.

He looked at me, waiting for a smile. He thought I was kidding.

A young man in green surgical scrubs hosed down one of the exam tables. A diluted red stream disappeared down the small drain hole in the surface of the stainless steel. Most of Mo's professional world was stainless steel, that and the pale green ceramic tile on the walls and the floors.

"Your body, Telford Bone, is up next. Earl will bring him in," he said. "You're the only one viewing the post?"

"Yeah, lucky me."

"How many have you seen, may I ask?"

"Less than you, but I guess only Boris Karloff has done more."

"Ahh, your humor again."

"Yeah, I'm a barrel of laughs. I love your company, Mo, but I hate autopsies"

"Why? You see one, you see them all. Well, not really, but that's true for the layman, I suppose."

"I get your point, but, no offense, they stink."

"Ahh, yes, most people say that. Don't you use Vicks or smoke cigars to mask the smell?"

"I tough it out and have bad dreams."

215

* * * *

"Hey, boss," Vinnie said, "You had a phone call while you were out—a Lieutenant Colonel Charles Goodhardt. Said he has information for you. Want his number?"

Someone found an old card table and set it up next to John's desk for Vinnie to have his own space and make himself at home. A few folders and a couple of yellow pads lay on the top. He looked like he belonged.

"I have it, Vin. Thanks."

He winked.

I stepped into my office, tossed my sport jacket at the guest chair and missed. It was the chair where Rachel usually sat. I shook my head and left the coat where it fell. I tapped in Charlie's number at the Air Park.

"I got lucky," he said. "That guy I told you about was on a short run and called me right back."

"One of the few lucky things I've seen lately."

"You were right. Those old SAT guys do have reunions. They time them to coincide with the big Special Operations Association convention in Las Vegas each year. Have you ever been?"

"I'm not much for reunions or association meetings—ti-ti bullshit, GI."

"I hear ya. Anyway, this guy did some looking for me and came up with a name, Vance Caudell. Guess where he's from."

"I'm terrible at guessing games."

"How about Knoxville?"

"Hot dog."

"A few more interesting things. My friend thinks he remembers your pal as Calhoun Grant. How does the description *big ugly pear-shaped blond guy* sound?"

"Right on the money."

"You might make me a detective for what I tell you next."

"You never know. Prospect PD is like the Marines. We're looking for a few good men."

"Caudell flew 130s in and out of the hot spots—El Sal, Guatemala,

216

Nicaragua. Calhoun Grant was one of his regular crewmen."

"Sherlock Holmes, eat your heart out."

"I called a friend at the FAA for you, too. They have Vance Caudell listed as part owner of Tenn-Air Cargo Service."

"Are you going to tell me where they're located, or do you want a drum-roll first?"

"I'm too modest. Right here in the new cargo area at McGhee-Tyson."

"I'm watching all these pieces falling into place. You must be a whiz with jigsaw puzzles."

"Maybe I have a new career?"

"Sorry you didn't work with OSI?"

"No. I liked being a birdman."

"I guess I'd better pay Mr. Caudell a visit."

"Need tactical air support?"

"Wow, an airborne detective. I'll parachute onto the runway and attack his office."

"Just like the old days?"

"Almost."

"Anything else I can do for you?"

"Accept my sincere thanks."

"Anytime."

* * * *

I called Stan Rose and Harley Flatt in early. Those two and John, Vinnie and I drove fourteen miles to McGhee-Tyson Airport in two cars. I led the way, turning off Alcoa Highway onto Wright Road and then into the rear entrance of the newly developed south cargo area. Tenn-Air wasn't difficult to find. One large hangar served as the business center for the company. Two small, regional jets sat on the runway sporting Tenn-Air logos.

The large hangar doors were closed. We parked on the side of the building near a pedestrian door marked Office. We waited, while John and Harley walked around back to watch for quick rear getaways.

The office seemed typical for something in a small airport, but not as neat as I associate with airline facilities or airports in general. We found no one present in the office. There were no name plates or documents telling us Vance Caudell was associated with Tenn-Air.

I looked through the glass in a door that separated the office from the hangar floor area.

A third small jet sat parked on the expansive indoor concrete.

I looked closer at the plane. A small flatbed cart stood next to the fuselage. A trap door in the plane's side stood open, and a man appeared to be working, half inside the fuselage.

"You're an ex-Air Force guy, Stanley. What's he doing?"

"Could be anything. That may be a storage area, but I think some of these small jets have their fuel tanks running alongside the hulls like that. It's hard to say."

"Vinnie, walk over to the left. Keep an eye on him, but look for someone else on the starboard side."

"Starboard? Aren't we technical?"

I ignored him. "Stan, walk ten or fifteen feet to my right. I'll approach him straight on. Let's do it quietly. If he's guilty of something, let's not give him a heads up."

We had to cover at least fifty feet of open floor to reach the plane. We were still twenty feet away when the man took a dark blue gym bag from the fuselage. He seemed totally engrossed as he laid that and a socket wrench on the flatbed.

Vinnie's leather sole loafers made more noise than I wanted, but the subject didn't look toward the tapping.

The hangar had the hollow sound and feel of those large industrial buildings with little or no insulation. A faint smell of petroleum products tainted the air.

"Police officers," I called out. "We'd like to speak with you."

He turned around quickly to face me and looked startled. Actually, he looked embarrassed, like he had just been caught doing something wrong.

"Jesus, you scared me," he said.

"Are you Vance Caudell?' I asked.

"That's me, and you are?"

Caudell wore a khaki jump suit with the company logo embroidered onto the breast. He stood about five-ten, medium weight and had that look of an adventurer about him—someone who may have gone out with Brenda Starr.

"My name's Jenkins, Prospect Police. This is Sergeant Rose."

"What can I do for you?" He offered us a smile.

Stan stepped close to the fuselage and looked into the open compartment.

"Isn't that a fuel tank you just took a panel off?" he asked Caudell.

"Ah...no. It's a storage area. I had some tools inside." Vance lost the smile.

"I've seen enough aircraft to know a fuel tank when I see one. Mind if I take a closer look?"

"Yeah, as a matter of fact, I do. What's this all about?"

"Right now, Mr. Caudell," I said, "It's about you creating a suspicion that you've got something to hide. You said the wrong thing. Why'd you lie?"

"Who says I'm lying?"

"A guy who knows a lot about airplanes. Step aside, and let him have a look. As far as I'm concerned you may have a weapon in there, and our safety is in jeopardy."

"Hey, you can't—"

"Yes, I can. Hush, now. You hear that?"

He looked confused.

"That's the sound of nobody caring what you think." I drew my revolver.

"Hold on now. This is my property."

"Turn around, and put your hands against the plane—assume the position."

He did, with a little too much familiarity for the drill.

Stanley slid the partially open panel away from the exposed fuel tank.

"I guess you could say he had a weapon close by." Stan extracted a well-worn M-16 assault rifle from the dry fuel tank. He worked the action, saw that no round sat in the chamber and laid it on the flat bed next to the gym bag. "Look here...he's got a couple more inside."

"Okay, Mr. Caudell, handcuff time," I said.

Vinnie walked around from the rear of the airplane, saw the M-16 and said, "Hello, what's this? Automatic weapons?"

"Keep your gun on Mr. Caudell, Vincent, while I hook him up."

"Certainly, sir. I assume he's a dangerous operator."

By the time I had double locked the cuffs, Stanley had taken out three more assault rifles. They were all well-used, at least fifty percent of the black parkerized finish worn off of the metal.

Stan and Vinnie looked closely at the weapons.

"These are the real deal," Vinnie confirmed. "Three place selector switches."

"Strike one," I said.

"Hey," Caudell said, "I can explain those."

"Sure you can," I said. "But it was foolish of you to have left the zipper open on your luggage, Vance. Makes it easy to look inside."

"You know damn well that zipper's closed."

I shook my head. "I'm sure that argument is something a judge has never heard before."

I unzipped the canvas bag. Inside, I found a seven-by-nine inch Zip-Lok plastic bag stuffed with white powder. Beneath that was a kilo brick of what I assumed was marijuana. Vance didn't look like he needed more than two pounds of oregano. And beneath that was a loaded 9mm Browning Hi-Power.

"Well, sir, I guess you were either shopping to make yourself the life of the party, or you pick up a few things on your trips to help offset the overhead of doing business. Would you care to sit down and chat with us about that?"

"I want a lawyer."

"You'll probably need one or two. Vinnie, will you open the back door and let our two colleagues in? We'll need help searching this plane. It's big."

"Okay, okay, hold on," Caudell said, "I'm not supposed to tell anyone this, but I work for the government."

"Sure you do, Vance. Just like Austin Powers, international man of mystery. Try that spook crap on someone else," I said. "Stanley, do you have an impound sticker to slap on this plane?"

"I never leave home without one."

"Good, we'll start with this one, and after we get a warrant for the two outside on the runway, we can take those out of circulation, too."

"What the hell are you talkin' about?" Caudell asked.

"It's about asset forfeiture, sport. You transported what I believe to be illicit drugs in this vehicle. I have the option to seize it and give it to my friends, the Feds."

"You can't do that."

"Sure I can. I learned all about that long ago. It was my first big break as a cop. I found two marijuana seeds in an E-Type Jaguar. I knew it was paid for, so I seized it and gave it to the district attorney. After that, I was one of his favorite guys. Can you imagine how cool I'd be to own my own airplane?"

"I'll be your crew chief," Stan offered.

"Can I have a ride?" Vinnie asked.

"I just happen to know an extremely lovely pilot. Gents, I think we're in the airline business."

"Isn't there something we can do about this?" Caudell asked.

"There's always some wiggle room in life, Vance, ol' buddy. As they say around here, life's simpler when you plow around the stump. All you've got to do is say the magic words."

Stanley, John, Vinnie and Harley Flatt now stood behind me watching the spectacle.

"This may take a long time, Vance, but we can start by getting comfortable in your office and answering a few quick questions."

"A long time? How long? I've got charters to do. Pilots will be here to take these planes out. I don't have a lot of time."

"I'll let you call someone who can rearrange your schedules. These planes aren't going anywhere. So, the quicker you think and the more you say will be to your benefit."

"We gotta make this quick. I could lose tons of money here."

"You had four automatic weapons in your possession, obviously with intent to re-sell them. If for one minute, I thought you had some terrorist in mind as a customer, I'd have to call the FBI or Homeland Security and watch them flex the Patriot Act. Are you beginning to see how important cooperation is?"

"Okay, okay, let's get started."

* * * *

Vance Caudell admitted knowing Telford Bone. He further admitted introducing Bone to an airport fireman named Billy Ray Finchum who needed a *persuasive* man-for-hire to help solve a problem his son was having. *Small world, huh?*

Billy Ray, who had always been around the day-to-day airport operations knew Caudell well enough, but that pair got tied together for the purpose of finding this man-for-hire after another fireman named Willie brought Billy Ray to Tenn-Air specifically for that purpose.

Caudell had the right connections and accepted a small finder's fee for assistance in procuring the services of Bone, the so-called private investigator.

We locked the Tenn-Air building and left Harley Flatt to guard the two planes on the runway. I notified the Airport Authority, US Customs agents and the airport police and then made a visit to the airport fire department.

A man in his fifties sat behind a desk in the small office next to the large garage bays that housed the fire apparatus. I had no problem drawing an inference when I saw the name plate *Willard Barkens* on the man's desk.

"Hello there," I said. "Are you the man in charge?"

"I'm the house man. The lieutenant's in charge, but he ain't here right now. I guess ya could say the real man in charge is the chief of safety, but he's got an office at the police station."

"I noticed your name plate. Are you related to Clifford?"

"Yessir, he's my brother. You know him?"

"Yeah, I'm from Prospect Police. I'm working with Clifford on something at the moment. He seems like a good guy."

"Yep, he's my big brother. Prospect Po-leece, ya say?"

"Yeah, I guess I'm not too popular with one of your lieutenants right now."

"Ya mean Billy Ray?"

"Uh-huh. I need to see him. Is he the lieutenant on duty?"

"Comes in tonight."

I thought I'd try a little fibbing to establish a few things a guy like

Willie Barkens might not tell me if I used the direct and honest approach.

"Last time I spoke to Billy Ray he mentioned having a friend in the Sheriff's office. I wish I had known Clifford was the friend he was talking about. Who knows, that may have made things a lot easier for all of us."

"Shore, Billy Ray knows Clifford. He didn't tell ya?"

"Well, listen, I've got to go and see Billy Ray. Thanks for your time."

* * * *

"Chief, Miss Menzies from the DA's office called," Joey Gillespie said. "She asked if you'd stop down and see her soon as ya kin."

"Thanks, Joey. I'm going to call Bettye and see how she's doing and then grab a sandwich and head down to the Justice Center."

"Say hello ta Miss Bettye fer me, boss. I hope she's doin' aw right today."

"I'll tell her you said so."

Joey looked more like a Dublin footballer than an American cop. His red hair shone from some slick hair tonic, and his face had what I'd call the map of Ireland all over it.

"Hello, Sam," Bettye said. "I'm glad you called."

"Everything okay at home, Betts? Little Donnie's ankle getting better?"

She didn't answer immediately. "Yes, everything's okay, I guess. Li'l Donnie is doin' fine. I expect him to go back to his summer soccer camp next week."

"How are you doing?"

"I'm fine, darlin'. I miss all you guys at work."

"We miss you, too. The boys need their den mother back here."

"Uh-huh."

"Betts, you don't sound good. What's wrong?"

"Oh, I'm just a little tired. I guess this business had more of an effect on me than I thought."

"I hope you're telling me the truth, lady. If you need anything, if I can do anything for you, just call. Please."

I will, Sammy, I promise. But don't you worry none. I'm okay.

223

How's everything coming along?"

"We're just about wrapped up. It turned into the biggest can of worms I've ever seen in such a little place. You won't believe who's involved. But I think in a day or so it will be all squared away. I'll tell you all about it when it's over."

"Good. I'm anxious to hear everything."

"Moira Menzies wants to see me, so I guess I'd better get ready to listen to her kvetching."

"Kvetching?"

"I'll teach you a new Yiddish word when I explain things. Take care, Betts. Gotta go."

"Bye, Sammy."

* * * *

I sat in an uncomfortable armchair in Moira's office in the Justice Center. She sat behind her desk.

She made a face, tossed a pencil onto the desktop and said, "You sure can pull strings when you need to."

"Never for personal gain, Moira. When I call in my horsepower, it's for the good of all humanity. That's written in the Superhero's Handbook."

"Sam, I don't believe I've ever met someone with more of a smart mouth than you. Do you always try so hard to get on people's nerves?"

"How can you say such a thing? Surely, you know my deeds are just, and my heart is pure."

"What I know from personal experience is you're generally a royal pain in the ass."

"I appreciate all your kind sentiments and love to hear you say all those nice things about me, but can we get down to business?"

"I've been *ordered* to cooperate with you. What I'd like to know is can we work this out to create the smallest possible explosion?"

"Of course, I'm not hard to get along with." I admit, I enjoyed myself a little too much at Moira's expense. "Okay, let's do a little recapping, and I'm sure you'll see we're really on the same page."

Moira rolled her eyes and gazed up into the stratosphere. "I can hardly wait."

"Dalton Mincy is still sitting in pre-trial confinement. We have him for obstructing governmental administration and for complicity in beating Telford Bone to falsify the assault charge Bone leveled on my two cops. He's already given a statement admitting all that and that Bone told him he was hired by Billy Ray Finchum."

She nodded while I spoke.

"So do whatever you want with him," I said. "How about charging him with simple conspiracy and cut him a deal?"

Moira's college diploma and law school degree hung on the wall behind her desk. She faced a window that overlooked the jail.

"When I spoke to Mincy he mentioned something about photographs and how you confiscated his cell phone," she said. "His lawyer jumped in and told me that wasn't relevant to any of this. Mind telling me what that's all about?"

"Nothing much. The lawyer's right. It's not worth mentioning."

"Then why do I think it is?"

"Maybe your woman's intuition is in high gear? It's better to forget about that, just like you should forget all the business at Tenn-Air which I turned over to the Feds. Customs is happy to cut Vance Caudell some slack in return for the statement he gave me implicating all the local players. Caudell may end up being an all-star informant for the Feds in things outside our scope of interest. And I have no place to store the three small jet planes I confiscated. The Feds, on the other hand, can use those as leverage to keep Caudell on the string for who knows how many good cases."

"Okay," she said. "Mincy is not a problem. Both he and his lawyer are ready to roll over for their best deal."

"All that brings me to Billy Ray Finchum," I said. "I'd like an arrest warrant charging him with something good."

"What do you have in mind?"

"Since you want this to be low profile, and I want to cooperate and make your life easy…"

She shot me a dubious look with her big baby-blues.

"How about a couple of things he can cop to that won't break the bank and will allow you to get him out of your wavy blonde hair quickly?"

"I'm listening."

"How about conspiracy to commit coercion? Billy Ray solicited Bone to intimidate Dorie Asher and Laura Hensley. And accessory to falsely reporting an incident? Without Billy Ray, Bone would never have accused my two cops of assault. Considering how complicated his life could be, not to mention the potential legal fees, if this stretches out in court, I think he'll jump on a deal strictly as an economic alternative."

"And you're not looking for blood? You won't oppose a plea bargain and maybe probation?"

"I'm with you here," I said. "Let's make this go away."

"What else?"

"You've got two cops who've done bad things. I think if you allow Charlie Dietzen to retire and go away quietly, he'll admit to what he did and roll on Clifford Barkens. Tell Barkens you'll give his little brother, Willard, a walk for introducing Finchum to Caudell and getting Finchum closer to Clifford, who arranged for Dietzen to falsify young Dallas's polygraph report. All that would only cost Clifford his job. If Clifford retires, he avoids any criminal or administrative charges which may lead to loss of his pension and possible jail time."

Moira sat there shaking her head. She shrugged and picked up the pencil she previously tossed on her desk

"Cops are easy when you've got their private parts in a vice," I said. "He'll take the deal and just go away, too."

"How do you keep all this straight in your head?"

"Years of practice. I think the last maneuver will make Joe Don Hartung pleased—no scandals in his shop."

"Uh-huh."

"The only one I can't tie directly to all this foreign intrigue is Claude Webbster, who probably started the ball rolling back when Dallas Finchum was arrested for rape.

"I'm sure the people in Hamilton County, who are as guilty as sin of assorted counts of misfeasance and malfeasance, won't rat him out unless I get totally frustrated and dump this whole thing on my buddies at the FBI."

"Do what?"

I grinned like the village idiot. "I just wanted to be sure you were listening. I have no reason to do that if we iron this out locally. I'll see if I can deal with Claude in a more clandestine manner."

"Yeah, right. I can hardly wait to see how that plays out."

"Don't sound so bitter. This will work out smashingly all around. I have no doubt that once I tell the Prospect City Council what's happening, they'll shake their collective asses and sign off on terminating Dallas Finchum's probation with the PD."

"And you not only get to arrest Billy Ray, but you send him the message that it was a big mistake to screw with Sam Jenkins."

"Gee, I wish I'd thought of that."

"I'll have your warrant ready by ten o'clock tomorrow morning. Do we have anything else to discuss?"

"Yeah, I like your suit. You look great in police-car-blue."

Chapter Thirty-One

At quarter to ten the next morning, a DA's investigator named Cletus Dunn walked into my office. Dunn had been the officer detailed to submit the backup report on my investigation of the Telford Bone shooting.

"Sam, you doin' aw right today?"

"Hello, Clete. How's it going?"

"I got an arrest warrant for ya. Figgered I'd deliver it instead o' you havin' ta drive in and pick it up."

Clete looked like a typical, old squad dick you'd find in any department on the planet. He was about fifty, but could have been younger…or older, but I doubted that. He always wore a sport jacket and tie and acted with an air of confidence only gained by having your shit together.

"Thank you. I appreciate that."

"I figgered I'd deliver a message to ya from Moira, too."

"What's she need?"

"She's kinda concerned how you'll handle the warrant. Kinda afraid ya mean ta break Finchum's ass and hold him till after arraignments are over and make him spend the night in a cell."

I laughed. "Tell Moira her fears are unfounded. Like everyone else, I want this all over as quickly as possible. I can't afford any more gray hairs over Billy Ray Finchum or anyone else involved in this fiasco."

"I hear that."

"There's no doubt I owe Billy Ray grief for many of his actions. He tried to jam up a couple of my best guys. Because of him, I had to kill

228

Telford Bone. That's no loss to the rest of the world, but it was something neither Bettye Lambert nor I needed."

Clete nodded. "Uh-huh."

"But tell Moira not to get her knickers in a spin. I'll behave myself and have Billy Ray in for arraignment long before the judge takes off at 3:30."

"Moira's not a bad sort, Sam. She's jest kinda serious-like about her job, is all."

"I know that, Clete. If I didn't think she'd take it the wrong way, I'd invite her to lunch. Sort of like a peace offering."

"Mebbe ya should ask her."

"Probably not. I know my audience, and I'm lousy with small talk. Maybe I'll send her flowers."

"There ya go."

"Thanks for everything."

"You bet."

* * * *

I didn't take any back-up with me to execute the warrant on Billy Ray Finchum. I drove to the Yorkshire Dales subdivision in Prospect where the Finchums lived, parked my car on the street and walked up to a good-looking two-story brick house with a leaded glass front door.

"Whaddaya want?" Billy Ray asked after he opened the door.

Billy seemed to have a great and un-varied wardrobe. Just as he did at our meeting outside the mayor's office, he again wore one of his blue fireman's T-shirts and blue jeans.

"I have an arrest warrant for you," I said with little enthusiasm. "You have to come with me. After I process the arrest, I'll take you to court, and you'll probably be home on bail this afternoon."

"You're a piece o' work, Jenkins," he said. "You ruin my boy's life, and now y'all are—"

"Hold on, and stop acting like an ignoramus. I'm not going to argue or debate anything with you. I came here myself instead of sending two uniformed cops to drag you away in cuffs. That was out of courtesy to your son. You understand that?"

He didn't reply. Nor did he ask me what he was being charged with.

"Look, I don't like you," I said, "and I'd love to embarrass you however I can, but I do like your kid, and I don't want to make things more difficult on him or your wife. So let's just take care of this. Have your lawyer meet you in court, and you'll be rid of me."

He gave me a look I would have taken pleasure in wiping off his face with a cement block. "Don't fight me. This is going to happen."

"Kin I at least tell my wife what's happenin'?"

"Yes, but I'm coming in with you."

He turned and walked away without comment.

I followed him into the kitchen. We found Dallas and his mother sitting at the table. Dallas held a glass of orange juice, and his mother played with a cup of coffee. The breakfast dishes were all over the counter near the sink. Two other coffee cups were on the table.

"Man says I'm under arrest, Krista. Says I gotta go with him. Call Robbie Blanchard, and tell him what's happenin'."

Dallas stood up. "Chief, do ya have ta arrest my father?"

"I'm afraid so, Dallas. Your father got involved with a couple of bad people who did some real serious stuff."

"Can't you forget about him if I come in and resign like you asked?"

"Dallas, you're a nice kid, and I'd do you a favor if I could, but I can't agree to that. A judge issued an arrest warrant. You know what that means. And it's too late to resign now. None of this is going to go away."

"Please, sir, isn't there something I can do?"

"I'm sorry, son. This isn't the end of the world. Your father will be home later today."

Billy Ray needed to stick in his two cents. "Sit down, boy, and save your breath. Ain't no talkin' with him." He put a wallet into his back pocket and a wad of bills and loose change into the front. "Okay, I'm ready. You gonna cuff me?"

"Let's walk outside."

At the edge of the road, I opened the car door for him and delivered a brief message. "You're under arrest. You have the right to remain silent, use it. I don't need any more of your wise mouth, so shut it. Thanks to you, I had to kill a man. So don't think it would bother me if I had to blow up your ass, too. The law is very clear. If you try to escape from custody, I can shoot you. Don't tempt me."

Billy Ray remained silent for the trip to Prospect PD. Once in the squad room, he answered the questions I asked to complete his arrest report without any additional smart remarks. He waited quietly, while I finished the arrest package, fingerprinted and photographed him and then he was driven to the Justice Center by two of the duty patrolmen.

* * * *

Twenty-four hours after I arrested Billy Ray Finchum Joey Gillespie walked into my office.

"What's up, Joey?" I asked.

He hesitated. "Boss, I jest sent Lenny over ta the Finchum place. Mrs. Finchum called, said Dallas done shot himse'f."

"Shot himself? Is he hurt badly? Is he alive?"

Joey shook his head. "No, sir. She says he's dead."

"Jesus H. Christ! Where's John?"

"Him an' Vinnie's over ta the garage talkin' with Earl."

I threw a small phone book I'd been looking in across the room. "Goddamnit! What the hell did he kill himself for, Joey? Stupid, goddamn kid. Je-sus Christ."

"Whaddaya want me ta do, boss?"

Joey didn't look either very happy or confident he could handle the situation.

"Just hang in there. I'll pick up John and go over to the Finchum's. Is the mother alone?"

"I suspect so."

"I'll call you and tell you what we need. Don't do anything until I say so."

* * * *

I picked up John Gallagher and Vinnie Falcone who had been shooting the breeze with Earl Biggins, the city mechanic. The three of us pulled up behind Lenny Alcock's cruiser at the curb in front of the Finchum house.

We found Alcock and Krista Finchum sitting in the kitchen waiting.

I nodded to Lenny and spoke to Krista. "Mrs. Finchum, I'm very

231

sorry for your loss." She nodded. "Where is your son?"

"In his room."

"Stay here, Vinnie. Lenny, take us."

We walked down a hallway, took the stairs to the second floor and entered a bedroom approximately twelve-by-fourteen feet. Dallas lay back on the bed, his right arm dangling off the mattress. A stainless steel, snub-nosed Smith and Wesson revolver lay on the floor next to the bed. Before entering the room, I handed latex gloves to both Leonard and John.

"Y'all see this?" Lenny asked, pointing to a handwritten note lying on the night table.

I picked up the note, put on my glasses and read what represented Dallas Finchum's last message to the world.

'Dorie, Chief, Mom, Dad and everyone at PPD, I'm sorry for the problems and things I've caused you all. I'm truly sorry. I meant no one harm or embarrassment." He signed it, "Your son and friend, Dallas."

I took off my glasses, placed the note back on the nightstand and pinched the bridge of my nose with my thumb and forefinger. "Poor fuckin' kid."

We were all silent for a few moments, and then I spoke again, "I'd like to do something, if I can, but you both have to agree to it." I looked at John and then Leonard.

"Whatever you want, Boss." John spoke quickly. I believe he knew what I was thinking.

Lenny said nothing.

"Listen to me first, and then decide."

I took a quick look around the room. It seemed spotless, almost too clean. A desk under the window. A laptop on the desk. A small TV on a roll-around stand, the cable and electric plug connected to the wall. A mirror over a dresser and a single framed print by a local artist on the wall. There were no dirty socks on the floor. No photographs of family or friends on the walls or in frames anywhere else. No UT football posters. The whole place lacked personality. It almost looked as if Dallas was afraid to express himself for fear of offending someone, perhaps one of his parents. It wouldn't be difficult to guess which one might be hard to please.

"Nothing we do will bring Dallas back," I said. "But if we say he died accidentally, then people won't think he killed himself because he raped a girl three years ago and went unpunished. Screw his old man, but his mother doesn't need any more grief after losing her son. You two have to be comfortable with this before I tell the mother what I think."

"Like I said, Boss. I'm good with this," John said without hesitation. "The kid was a cop, so anything you want."

Okay, John," I said. "Lenny, what do you think? It's your call. I'm open for your opinion, and whatever you say is fine with me."

"Shoot, Sam, I don't know. You think we'll git caught?"

"No one's going to catch us. If I call this an accident and go without asking for an autopsy, then that's what it is—as long as his mother goes along with it."

"Aw, Sam, I don't know."

"I'm only suggesting it because I liked the kid. When he worked with us, it seemed that everyone liked him. He did a good job. For a short time, he was a good cop."

"I know," Lenny said. "He was a good boy."

"His father screwed everything up with his half-assed plan to get his kid off the hook. I guess the kid felt too much pressure with the rape charges, and after the old man got arrested, he may have blamed himself. Who knows? Look, I'm not trying to strong-arm you, Lenny. If you like the idea, okay. If not, that's okay, too."

"I guess it makes the kid look better, don't it?"

"It does, and calling it a suicide won't make him any deader."

He looked at John and then at me. "Ain't like nobody killed him." He hesitated, ran a hand through his dark hair and shook his head. "Okay, I'm in."

I nodded, picked up Dallas's note, folded it in half and placed it in my jacket pocket. "I'll go and talk with the mother," I said. "You guys wait here."

Downstairs, Vinnie Falcone sat silently at the kitchen table. Krista Finchum busied herself drying a few dishes. She wasn't a particularly attractive woman, but maybe years ago she had been. She looked to be in her late-forties, with dark hair done in a style too old for her actual years.

"Vinnie," I said, "Do me a favor, and go out to the car and listen for the radio."

He looked at me questioningly.

"Give us a minute," I said.

He nodded and left.

"Mrs. Finchum, there's nothing I can do to bring your boy back. I'm sorry he chose to do this."

She looked at me silently, waiting for me to continue.

"I have the discretion to call this a suicide or an accident. Dallas left a note upstairs. There's no doubt that he intended to take his own life."

She had been dry-eyed when I arrived, but my remark started her crying.

"I liked your son, Mrs. Finchum. I liked him a lot. I'm sorry things that happened in the past have brought all this trouble back to you."

"Are you feelin' guilty over him killin' himself?" she asked.

I could have smacked her for that, but I tried again.

"This isn't on me, Mrs. Finchum. A woman complained about being raped by your son. I gave him the benefit of the doubt, but everything led me to believe that a night of simple romance between two kids went terribly wrong. I had to stick up for the victim. Maybe you should talk to your husband about hiring criminals, and maybe your brother, too, before you accuse me of anything. They started a landslide trying to outwit the system. That all started three years ago."

She wiped her eyes with tissues she had in her pants pocket.

"I'm sorry. I know all that," she said. "I know Billy Ray got carried away. He just couldn't abide Dallas being called a rapist. He believed his son."

"This isn't the time for me to outline all the things Billy Ray and Claude may have done that were in violation of law. What I had in mind was for Dallas…and to help you. If you agree to it, I'd like to say that Dallas accidentally shot himself cleaning his gun. Would you like me to do that?"

"Why would you do that for me?"

"I told you, I liked your boy. I think, aside from one big mistake years ago, he was a good kid. And he was one of my cops. That's all."

She thought for a moment. Then she blew her nose and nodded her head. "Yes, sir, I suppose that would be better. Can you tell me what he said in the note?"

I took out the note and read it for her. It caused her tears to increase, a real human waterfall. I suggested that she sit and brought her a glass of water while she calmed down.

"Okay then, you and I will keep this as our secret, and your boy won't be seen as having killed himself."

She nodded and began to cry again, this time with less intensity.

"Have you called your husband yet?"

"No, sir, I was waitin' for y'all ta get finished. I knew he'd only cause a fuss if y'all were here."

"That sounds like a good idea. You should *not* tell Billy Ray Dallas took his own life. That may be a difficult thing to live with alone, but your husband doesn't look like the kind of man who could write that off easily. Save him and yourself more potential heartache, and let it stand as an accident."

And keep him from blowing the whistle about sticking my neck out for you and your kid.

"I'll be through in just a few minutes," I said. "Then I'll have a police photographer stop by. Please wait until I tell you to call Billy Ray."

She agreed, and I walked back upstairs to Dallas's room.

"If you two want to go downstairs, do it now. I'm going to look around and see if I can find a cleaning kit. If I do, I'll set it out and make it look like he was cleaning a loaded gun when it went off. You two don't have to stay. You'll have plausible deniability."

"I'll help you look," John said.

If I killed someone and said, 'Oops,' John would ask if I wanted him to fetch a shovel.

"Lenny?"

"I'll stay."

"Okay, Lenny, you play chickie. Make sure no one comes up here."

It took us less than ten minutes to find a cleaning kit in a plastic box. Dallas had stashed it in the bottom drawer of his nightstand. I took out the aluminum rod, screwed on a bronze bore brush and put out a few cotton patches on the bed next to a cleaning jag. A bottle of Hoppe's #9 solvent lay in the box waiting for someone to swab out the bore. It was that simple. I left the folded suicide note tucked inside my jacket pocket.

I called the Sheriff's office on my cell phone and asked for a crime scene investigator to take photographs and a gun-shot-residue test on Dallas' hand. That test would go a long way toward convincing me Dallas had indeed pulled the trigger without help from a family member.

In fifteen minutes, Investigators Jackie Shuman and David Sparks walked into Dallas's bedroom. After a short conversation, they spent twenty minutes doing what I requested.

"Sam," Jackie said, "I'll holler at ya when I git the pitchers printed and the reports done up."

"Thanks," was all I said.

"John, go on outside and keep Vinnie company for a few minutes. Lenny, go back on the road if you'd like. Or take lunch or take the rest of the day off—whatever you want."

"Mebbe I'll jest ride around a bit."

"Okay. Not a bad idea. Tell Joey you're still out of service. See you later, and thanks."

Back in the kitchen, I spoke again with Krista Finchum. "You can call your husband now."

"I'll do that," she said.

"One of us has to stay with Dallas until he goes to the funeral home. I think we both agree it shouldn't be me if Billy Ray is coming home."

"Maybe so."

"I'll leave Detective Gallagher here with you. Would you like him to call a funeral director?"

"Yes, sir. That would be fine. Thank ya."

I explained to John what I needed, asked him not to get into an argument with Billy Ray when he arrived home, and I drove Vinnie back to the PD.

"What was that all about?" Vinnie asked.

"Just something to save the mother a little extra sorrow and to make the kid look better in the papers."

"Do I really want to know?"

"Think about it. You're a smart boy. You'll understand. If you want, ask John. We've never known him to keep his mouth shut."

"Why do I think you're takin' one hell of a chance?"

"I like the extra tension?"

* * * *

I spent an hour typing a preliminary report on my computer. I printed a copy, saved the file on a disc and decided that Ronnie Shields should share in the moment.

"Did you hear about Dallas Finchum's death?" I asked Trudy Connor, who as always acted as the sentinel, guarding His Majesty's outer office.

"Yes, sir, just a little,' she said. "That's such a shame. He was such a nice-looking boy."

I've never really been able to figure out what makes Trudy tick. She's fifty-something, unmarried, well-dressed and from all accounts and opinions, an excellent worker and an almost likable person. My big complaint: her clothing smells of cigarette smoke. I'll bet if I followed her, I could catch her sneaking a smoke behind the dumpster.

I nodded. "I have to tell him about it." I grabbed hold of the knob on Ronnie's door.

"Mr. Jenkins, please let me announce you." She spoke with a plaintiff look.

I had no good reason to act contrary with Ms. Connor. I relented, nodded and allowed her a moment of formality.

She picked up her phone and buzzed the maharaja.

"Y'all can go in now," she said. "And thank you." She gave me a tiny smile.

I nodded again, returned the smile and began to enter Ronnie's command center when Darnell Means stood and started walking around his desk toward the double oak doors.

"Are you going somewhere?" I asked.

"I'm following you into the mayor's office."

I wanted to kill him.

"You and I need to have a word."

"About what?"

"Trudy has work to do. I don't want to disturb her. We'll talk outside."

He didn't seem in the mood for a fight and followed me into the hallway.

"What?" he said.

"You and I had a conversation not long ago, and I thought we came to an understanding. As you remember, I possess information that could embarrass you and possibly ruin your political life."

He interrupted, "How many times are you going to repeat that?"

"As often as necessary to get you to walk on the opposite side of the street when you see me coming."

He folded his arms across his chest, giving me a display of negative body language. "I've done nothing more than give the mayor a few reasonable suggestions."

"Hogwash," I said. "Look, I have no doubt that you're conspiring with your Uncle Micah to do whatever you can to impede my investigation and make me look bad."

"You're paranoid."

"You're dishonest.

He tried to interject something, but I stopped him. "And don't give me any crap about being careful in what I say. I frankly don't give a rat's ass if you think I'm guilty of liable or slander or any other form of political suicide. I intend on bringing everyone complicit in this case to task for their conduct and make them pay one way or another. If you and Micah Blevins want to be part of that pool, keep sticking your noses into my business."

"I'm…we're…doing no such thing."

"Bullshit. Now here's my final warning. Do not try to involve yourself in this case. Do not assume you can listen to what I tell the mayor. You and I are finished. Period"

"I'm the deputy mayor."

"Who cares? If you follow me into his office, I will throw you out the window."

I left Darnell standing in the hall, smiled at Trudy Connor again and entered Ronnie's office…alone.

"I'd like to tell you about Dallas Finchum's death," I said.

"I heard, Sam. That was tragic, wasn't it?"

I sighed and felt my shoulders drop two inches. "Ronnie, what you heard was only a bit of the truth."

He wrinkled up his brow and looked at me with trepidation.

"Here's a copy of what I consider my official statement." I handed him two typewritten pages. "But I need you to know the truth, Ronnie. Dallas didn't die accidentally."

"What?"

"The kid killed himself—an intentional suicide. I have a note." I patted my top jacket pocket.

"What are you sayin', Sam?"

"I'm saying the world doesn't need to know that poor kid took his own life because his moron father created a living hell inside the kid's head with criminal acts and dirty politics."

I'd need two paragraphs to describe Ronnie's facial contortions, blinking and other involuntary antics after I explained that.

"Go back three years," I said. "If Dallas had been taken to task for the date rape, which could have been plead down to a misdemeanor sexual misconduct, he would have been on probation for three years and afterwards gotten on with his life."

Ronnie closed his eyes, much like a child would pull a blanket over his head to make a bad dream go away.

"But his politician uncle and politico, envelope-stuffing idiot of a father and I don't know who the hell else, jumped through hoops to squash the whole episode. But Dallas was never off the hook after that, was he?" I asked. "All that business got stored up in his head, eating away at him for years."

"He left a note?" Ronnie asked.

"I said that."

"Lord have mercy, Sam. You could get inta all kinds o' trouble for not reportin' a suicide."

"Sure, but that's my problem, not yours. Unless you want to flip me in to some stiflingly honest Internal Affairs investigator like Clifford Barkens. I just wanted you to know the truth."

"Sam, I just don't know what ta say."

"No reason to say any more. I'll just suggest we all keep an old adage in mind, 'Remember the past and build on it.' No one should make the same mistake twice."

He nodded several times while looking downward. It almost seemed like he was praying. Then he raised his eyes and looked at me.

"I see your point, Sam. I surely do. Thank you."

"You going to the kid's funeral?"

"Yes, I suppose I should."

"I agree. I'll send up the details."

Chapter Thirty-Two

"I've never believed in a charmed life before I met you," Moira Menzies told me as we again sat in her office.

"That's a fairly one-sided, subjective opinion."

"This all worked out almost as you predicted. And for the life of me, I can't understand why. We didn't exactly have a string of airtight cases."

"If you recognize who you're dealing with, it's not impossible to anticipate their reactions."

"That sounds very philosophical."

"Maybe I should wear a toga instead of a sport jacket."

No police-car-blue that day. Moira wore a moderately short, but still appropriate, black skirt, a red silk blouse and somewhere nearby, a matching jacket waited to complete her suit. For a girl of around fifty, Moira had pretty good figure and nice legs.

"Everyone jumped on their best opportunities," she said. "None of the lawyers objected."

"They were lucky. Each of them saw the gift you presented. We're not punishing any good people here, Moira."

"I guess not."

"You heard Dallas Finchum died?"

"Accidental shooting? He just *happened* to be cleaning his gun?"

Lawyers love to act like they know the *real* stories.

"Even before dying, he was one of the victims here, too."

"You're morose today."

"I could have done without the events of the last week. I guess I've been in a better mood."

"I heard your girlfriend is leaving Knoxville. I suppose you're sad about that?"

That remark really pissed me off.

"Do you enjoy playing the rollicking bitch with everyone, or do you reserve it only for me?"

My statement had the desired effect. Moira's eyes widened. She must have known she'd gone a bit too far.

"I shouldn't have said that, Sam. I'm sorry."

"Don't worry about it. Are we finished for today?" I stood up.

"No, give me another minute, please. I apologize. That was rude of me. I don't know why I said that."

I sat down again. Her statement had gotten the desired effect. "It's okay. Forget it. But, for your information, I do feel bad about her leaving. She's not going to Chicago for the right reasons. She's another one of the victims that came from the little melodrama we watched play out."

"Someday you can explain that to me."

"Someday."

"Can I ask you a personal question?"

I wasn't sure I wanted to explain myself, but I didn't rain on her parade. "Sure, I can always refuse to answer."

"I'm just being nosy, but you really liked her, didn't you?"

"I guess that was obvious. Yes, I did."

"Everyone thought you two were having an affair."

"I suppose I should be flattered people would think that. And if I were a typical guy who wanted a reputation as a lady's man, I would capitalize on it. But sorry to disappoint all those who congregate at the various water coolers of East Tennessee, we were just friends."

She tilted her head, made a face and conveyed the unspoken question, 'Are you kidding me?'

"Maybe *friends* isn't an adequate word, but there was no affair—in the traditional sense. So if you wanted the true poop from group, that's it."

"It's really none of my business—or anyone else's."

"That's correct. But if you wish to preserve your secret, wrap it up in frankness." I said, quoting someone, but I can't remember who. I stood up again. "Now, I have to get back to the farm."

She got an impish look on her face. "Two things a man cannot hide: That he is drunk and that he is in love." She had a quote of her own to throw at me.

I laughed and hit her with, "Attorneys and rogues are vermin not easily rooted out of rich soil." *I've got a pocketful of them.*

She laughed. "Get outta here, Jenkins."

"So long, Moira."

"Yeah. See ya, Sam."

* * * *

John and Vinnie sat in my office eating Chinese takeout from Wah Lum. While they monopolized my desk, I sat in a guest chair.

"Moira says everyone rolled over easy enough," I told them. "The two cops, Dietzen and Barkens, are going to resign in lieu of any kind of criminal or administrative charges. Mincy pled guilty to obstructing and conspiracy. He'll serve twelve months, and they're allowing him to do it in an Alabama jail. Billy Ray got a real sweetheart deal—five years probation for criminal solicitation. He only admitted that he *thought* Bone might try to intimidate the two girls on his behalf. Some shit, huh?"

John stuck a lump of chicken into his mouth and shook his head; Vinnie stopped in the middle of picking up a shrimp between his chopsticks and said, "Some shit is right."

"But because of all his attempts to cover up the truth," I continued, "Billy Ray's son is dead. It's hard not to see that as part of his punishment. Let's hope he lives with that thought for the rest of his life, the bastard."

"The kid's funeral is the day after tomorrow, Boss," John said. "There's a *remorial* ceremony at ten o'clock. You going?"

"Yeah, I think standing in the background might be appropriate. Put out the word so the guys know, will you, John?" He nodded. "And you may want to spell *remorial* with an extra M." I looked at Vinnie. "What do you think, Tonto? Is our work here done?"

"I guess so, Kimosabe. I suppose I had better call the airline and see about getting a seat home."

"You did a lot of good stuff, Vincent. We couldn't have worked this one without you. Thanks."

"Anytime. I even enjoyed working with John again."

"I know that's a lot to ask of anyone."

"Hey, I know you guys are talking about me," John said, through a mouthful of General Tso's chicken. "I pick up on all that, you know. I don't let any hair grow under my toes."

* * * *

I had only one more thing to do. I wanted to visit Jodelle and Dorie Asher.

I know most cops would disagree with the risk I'd take, but I wanted to tell Dorie that Dallas took his own life. I didn't see Dorie as the kind of person who would gloat over that fact, but I thought it might offer up an unspoken apology from Dallas for how he violated her years before and for never admitting his guilt. I guess I really wanted to give the kid a possibility of closing out an episode in her life I knew she had tired of living with.

When I called Jodelle Asher, I learned that Dorie would arrive home at about 5:15. I'd stop there on my way home.

* * * *

I told John to take some time off that afternoon and give Vinnie a sightseeing tour of the Smokies. Our big job was finished, and Prospect PD was back to handling the mundane calls of the tourist season.

If the state declared an official tourist season, did they intend to let the local hunters shoot them?

My chance of pondering other interesting questions was cut short when Bettye Lambert walked into my office.

I've always thought about Bettye wearing a police uniform to work with mixed emotions. Putting civilian clothes on a figure like hers would be like allowing me to look at a piece of artwork every day. Bettye wearing the less alluring khaki and green uniform issued to the Prospect troops keeps my libido in check and helps stifle the lust that could easily build up in my aging mind. But every so often, it seems I'm entitled to a treat.

My treat came from seeing Bettye's blonde hair down to her shoulders, her wearing a snug, deep purple, V-neck T-shirt and a pair of pearl gray slacks. It's very possible that there is no better-looking desk sergeant on the planet.

"Hello, Sammy," she said and sat in one of my saddle-leather tan guest chairs.

"Yi ya, Betts. How are you doing?"

She didn't answer, but rather touched the corner of her eye, looked away and then looked back at me.

"I have a problem at home, Sam." Things looked very serious.

"There's nothing out there I can't at least try to fix for you." I tried to cheer her up with a cautious smile.

"It's not just me. That would be easy. It's Donnie."

"Little Donnie? Is his ankle getting worse?"

"No, Sam. Not Li'l Donnie...my husband, Donnie."

"Tell me what's wrong."

"This thing with Telford Bone has him worried. He's upset and not very reasonable."

"He's afraid for you?"

"Yes. He mentioned that this was the second incident where I could have been hurt."

"I understand his concern, but—"

She interrupted before I could finish.

"You think you understand, but you think differently than he does. Donnie is an electrician. He's always been an electrician. He's never been a soldier, and he's not a policeman. Donnie doesn't understand violence."

She paused, long enough for me to look at her and think how incredibly lovely she looked. I thought back to the first day I met her. When she spoke again, I came back to the present.

"When something like that happens to you, Sam, and no one gets hurt except the bad guy, you think it was just another good day at the office. You run around and fix everything. No one else has to think about what to do, because you do it for them. Other people look at these tragedies differently. Some of the things you get involved in just scare the stuffin's out of other people."

That seemed like something she took a long time to formulate.

"So what has he told you?" I asked, fearing the worst.

"He's asked me to resign.

"What did you say?" I heard her, but I didn't want to allow that thought into my mind.

"Let me explain a little more," she said. "He asked me to resign, but he didn't tell me to resign. He said if I chose to stay he'd understand, but he'd leave me."

I looked out the window into the lobby. Joey Gillespie worked away, unaware how Prospect PD might change forever. I shook my head and wanted to scream. Instead, I settled for a muffled, "Jesus Christ."

"Sam, I have three children. The girls are grown, and after they finish college, they'll be off on their own. My son is ten. He needs a father, and Donnie is a good father. He's a good husband, too."

I knew what was coming. On top of everything else that happened over the last week, I didn't want to hear it, but as I once read in a novel where the protagonist kept repeating the line, "Fate is inexorable," I knew I was about to lose Bettye.

"I understand," I said. "You have to do what's best for you and the kids. I can comprehend that."

I just hate it when I act so understanding.

"I have to resign, Sam. I'm so sorry."

I felt that all-too-familiar lump starting to constrict my windpipe. I attempted to suck it up. "Hey, it's okay. You're more important than a little jerkwater police department."

Bettye slid her chair very close. She touched my cheek with her right hand. "I'm not talking about the department or the city, Sam. I'm talking about you. Don't you understand? I come to work, and I look at you and tell myself how lucky I am. I think about what a good guy you are and how much fun it is each day. I'm going to miss that. I'll miss you."

I blinked a few times and felt genuinely shitty. "I'll miss you, too, Betts. There's just no one who can replace you."

"I feel terrible doing this. I just hate it."

"It's not your fault."

"No, I mean putting this on top of everything else."

"Everything else is just police work."

"Not the police work, you big fool. Rachel left me a note, and I saw her on TV the other night. I know she's going to Chicago. I'm sorry, Sam."

"Rachel's making a career move. I hope she has good luck."

"Sam." She gave me a look.

"Rachel's a friend, Betts. You're my partner. Yeah, I feel bad, but I'm okay. You guys have to take care of yourselves."

"Your friend, Sam? Tell me she was just your friend."

"Okay, she was more than a friend," I said. "Just like you are a hell of a lot more than a partner. Does hearing that make walking out of here easier for you?"

"Oh, Lord have mercy, Sam! What are we going to do?"

"You're going to watch Little Donnie grow up, and you're going to be proud that you have three good kids. And they'll be proud of their mom and think of her as the prettiest ex-cop around."

"Donnie said something to me I don't think I can ever forgive him for."

"Nothing is unforgivable. What did he say?"

"He told me that even if I didn't resign I should stay clear of you. He said you're trouble, and if I didn't want Li'l Donnie growing up without a mother, I shouldn't have anything to do with you."

I thought that was an interesting observation, and I didn't have a clever answer to it.

"I don't know exactly what to say to that, Betts. Maybe he's right. Maybe times have changed, and my way of doing business doesn't work so well any longer. Don't fight this. Do what's best for you, and forget something he said in anger."

"I have to do this, Sam."

"Then just do it."

She took a .40 caliber Glock automatic and the sergeant's badge from her purse and placed them on the edge of my desk.

I nodded. "I'll take care of this for you, kiddo, but don't think that you're leaving without giving your boss a hug."

"I wouldn't do that, Sammy." Tears began running down her cheeks, and her hazel eyes appeared vacant and glassy. She stood up. I pushed my chair back, stood up and put my arms out. She let me embrace her. She returned the hug and held me tightly.

"Oh, my poor Sammy."

"Make sure you stop in every once in a while, Mrs. Lambert. And I'll expect some of those peanut butter cookies for Christmas."

Bettye looked up at me, grabbed the back of my neck and kissed me so passionately I saw stars.

"Where were you, Sam Jenkins, when…? Oh, damn you!"

Bettye turned, walked through my doorway and turned left, heading toward the back door. When it slammed shut, I winced. The lump in my throat could now be awarded old friend status. My head was clogged, and my eyes were on the brink of leaking.

I sat down in my swivel chair, took out a handkerchief and blew my nose. My head felt like it was about to explode. I opened a desk drawer and took out two bottles. From one I shook out a half-dozen Advil. From the other I poured two fingers of Scotch into my coffee cup. I washed down the Advil with Glenfiddich, sat back and closed my eyes.

Chapter Thirty-Three

Jodelle and Dorie Asher and I sat in their living room.

"Would y'all like some sweet tea or somethin', Chief?" Jodelle asked.

"No thanks, Mrs. Asher. I just need to take up a little of your time."

Dorie, as usual, looked subdued. Jodelle looked pensive, perhaps wondering what news I had for them.

"I'm sure you ladies heard that Dallas Finchum passed away."

They both nodded.

"I'm taking a chance tonight and hope I can trust you to keep what I say confidential between the three of us. I'm only doing this because I think that what I tell you here may be of some help to Dorie."

I looked at them for a long moment. The two women sat quietly waiting for me to continue.

"I reported Dallas's death as accidental. That wasn't true. He committed suicide. I believe everything, going back three years, became too much for him to live with."

Jodelle looked shocked. Dorie began crying.

"Why'd you not say he killed himse'f?" Jodelle asked.

"I know Dallas hurt your daughter terribly, Mrs. Asher, and nothing can change or diminish that. But for the time I knew Dallas, he was a good person. I didn't want to pile another heap of sorrow on his mother's shoulders. I don't think she had anything to do with any of the problems Mr. Finchum brought down on us all."

"This is all my fault," Dorie said, crying and twisting her hands in her lap.

"Dorie, you're wrong," I said. "You were a victim. None of that was your fault, and neither is this."

"No, no, you don't understand."

"What?" I asked, hoping she wasn't going to tell me she popped the round into Dallas's head and jumped out his bedroom window.

"Dallas and I had sex in the dorm that night, but he didn't rape me." After making her statement, she covered her face with both hands and sobbed.

It took me a few seconds to process that. I looked at Jodelle who said nothing, but she appeared more shocked than I did. Dorie sat there weeping, gently rocking back and forth. I reached for a box of tissues on a lamp table and set it down next to her on the couch cushion.

"Take a minute, Dorie, and when you're ready, tell me what you want to say."

"Dorie, darlin'," Jodelle said, "whattaya sayin'? Ya know that ain't true."

"Give her a minute, Mrs. Asher. Let's wait and hear what she has to say. Maybe she'd like a glass of water."

Jodelle didn't move.

"The water, please," I repeated. She got up and walked to the kitchen.

I looked at Dorie who tried to stop the tide of tears with a wad of Kleenex. She looked at me with red and swollen eyes and nodded. Jodelle returned, sat again and placed a tumbler of water on the coffee table. Dorie took a sip. I waited.

"I never wanted to bring this up again, Momma," Dorie began. "I was ashamed of what I did." She stopped to blow her nose and tuck the used tissues into her jeans pocket. "Everything was just as Dallas said. I wanted to have sex with him. I liked him, and that night everything was going right. Oh, Momma, this is all my fault. He wouldn't be dead if it wasn't for me." She began sobbing again.

Jodelle was about to say something, but I stopped her. "Mrs. Asher, let her talk. She needs to get this out. She has three years of guilt inside her."

Jodelle sat back, looking annoyed, and folded her arms across her chest.

"Dorie," I said, "how did you get the bruises on your thighs?"

"We were playing, Dallas and me. I made it tough for him so he'd, like, fight." She covered her eyes with a hand and sobbed. "I liked it rough."

"And how about the bruise on your cheek?"

"After we were finished and laying there, I wanted to do it again. I started playing again. I smacked him a couple of times and said, 'Dallas, you raped me.' I grabbed him, you know, down there, and said, 'I bet you're going to rape me again.' Then I started slapping him and trying to get him to do it again. I slapped him too many times, and he said, 'Cut it out.' And when I didn't, he hit me and got up." The tears began again, and she went after her eyes with a pair of new tissues. Between sobs she said, "He told me I was crazy."

Dorie drank more water, coughed and finally stopped sobbing.

"Why did you go to the police and the hospital?"

"Laura came back to the room and saw me. She got upset, and I didn't want her to know it wasn't real. I'm not proud of what I did."

"And when everyone in the hospital assumed you were raped, you didn't correct them?"

"Yes, and when those policemen gave me a hard time and made me feel…like I didn't matter, I got mad. I *do* matter."

"Yes, Dorie, you do. Everybody matters. What else happened?"

"I told Momma about it, and she got mad because I wasn't treated right."

"That's right, Dorie," I said. "You weren't treated right. Those policemen should be ashamed of themselves."

I didn't really need any more information. Everything I could think of would probably be true and asking would only be a waste of time. That can of worms had grown in size and population again.

Jodelle asked, "I guess ya got ta arrest her for somethin'?"

"This is a little shocking," I said. "I never expected to hear that. I don't know what I'm going to do." I paused.

Jodelle waited for an answer. Dorie cried.

"Dorie didn't do the right thing. There's no doubt about that. But neither did any of the other people who screwed around with a cover-up."

251

I didn't think giving a lecture on the statute of limitations for falsely reporting an incident would have been appropriate, so I tried a different tack that sprung into my mind.

"Nothing is going to bring Dallas back, but here's something to think about, Dorie. This has had a noticeable effect on you for the past three years. You feel it, as much as your mom, and I can see the effects on you. Now, more grief's been piled on your shoulders."

Dorie nodded and wiped at her eyes with a conglomeration of used tissues.

I shrugged. "I'm not going to force you to do anything, but think about how the damage to Dallas's reputation and keeping this secret for three years has damaged the way you feel about yourself."

Dorie looked at me with an intensity I didn't think she was capable of.

"You'll only be able to put this behind you if you unburden yourself of all the guilt you now feel. The people who caused the cover-up are being punished. One man is dead. One's going to jail, and others have had their lives ruined. You'll hear about that soon enough. Maybe everyone should hear that Dallas Finchum wasn't a rapist."

"You want me to tell everyone? Like how?"

"The woman your mother called at WNXX news, Rachel Williamson, has promised to hold off with any story until I said a broadcast wouldn't harm you or your case. She's my friend and won't do anything that would hurt you. Rachel's a very smart woman and a good, compassionate person. If you told her your story—from one woman to another—she'd do the right thing."

"I'd have to say this on TV?"

"Maybe not. Maybe a little. I don't know. You'd have to talk with her first. I believe that if you weren't happy with what she wanted to do, she wouldn't embarrass you." I shrugged again. "You don't have to do *anything*," I reassured her, "but I don't think living with this lie inside of you much longer will make you a very happy person. You have a long life ahead of you. Think about it and call me."

Chapter Thirty-Four

At 10:30 the next morning, Dorie Asher called my cell phone.

"Do I really have to go on TV and say that I lied?"

"I don't know, Dorie. But I can find out if Ms. Williamson would be willing to talk to you off the record. After you hear her suggestions, you can decide what you want to do."

"She's like a TV star. You can, like, just call her?"

"Yeah, I'll just call her. I told you…we're friends."

"And you'll let me know what she says?"

"Yeah, sure. If she agrees to an off-the-record conversation, I'll even drive you to the station. Then you two can talk in private."

"I guess it can't hurt to, like, ask."

"No, it can't. I'll call you back—soon."

* * * *

"Sam, I thought…," Rachel said.

"I know, we said… Well, you know what we said, but this is different. You still have a few days left, and I thought you may want to listen to a little business."

I explained what Dorie and I discussed.

"She wasn't raped? My God. And she's kept up that lie for three years? That poor man! He must have been so frustrated."

"And I didn't help any. I won't even mention all the crap his uncle and father went through to stage a cover-up. You know most of that."

"And the girl became a victim of the cover-up, if not the rape," she said.

"Right. I think she wants to clear the air, get it off her chest. If you can help her do that, everyone will end up knowing Dallas Finchum wasn't a sex offender who went unpunished."

"And you're doing this why?

"I have faith in you. I know you'll figure out how best to help both the girl and Dallas's memory. You're the TV pro."

"Thanks for the compliment. Wow, I hope I can live up to it."

"I know you will. All you have to do is speak with her off the record. When you formulate your plan, see how she likes it, and then let your conscience lead you."

"I won't betray her, Sam. Not her and not you."

"I know that."

"Good."

"She's off today. Can I bring her in? I'll just drop her off. You two keep your talk private."

"Okay, one o'clock at the station?"

"Works for me."

"I think we're back to parting company again."

"So it seems."

"Do you think you'd ever get to Chicago?"

"Who knows? I travel all over on business and pleasure." It was a convenient lie, but the best I could do at the moment.

She laughed. "Well, okay then."

"Yeah, okay then... Good luck, love."

"Oh, my dearest Sammy, to you, too."

* * * *

The drive to WNXX in Knoxville took forty minutes. Dorie and I did it mostly in silence. I felt uncomfortable and assumed she did, too.

I pulled into the side street where the large brick building that housed the station stood. I made a broken U-turn in the driveway of the employee's parking lot and saw Rachel's gold Lexus parked in the front row in her assigned spot. I stopped at the curb in front of the main entrance.

"I have to be somewhere soon," I lied. "I'll have Detective Gallagher meet you right here and drive you home."

"Thank you."

"Good luck, and remember, you can trust Rachel."

Dorie walked inside. John had driven Vinnie to the airport. I called and told him to continue north and wait for Dorie at the station.

Chapter Thirty-Five

John Gallagher stood on my right, Stan Rose on my left. We all wore suits, our badges suspended on the leather fobs that made up half our badge cases. Black elastic mourning bands stretched across our oval silver and gold shields.

In the crowd, closer to the group of people near the gravesite, were other members of Prospect PD. A few airport firemen also stood there in uniform. Someone, Claude Webbster or Billy Ray perhaps, arranged for a Sheriff's honor guard to stand at the gravesite. I felt content to stand in the background.

"Big funeral," Stanley said.

"More people than what came to my wedding," I said.

"Must be over two hundred," John observed.

A white and green sheriff's car with blue lights flashing escorted a white Cadillac hearse and a procession of four limousines from the public street up the blacktop lane inside the cemetery. At least three dozen privately owned vehicles followed the hearse. Two Sheriff's motorcycle officers picked up the rear of the motorcade.

The hearse stopped next to the canvas canopy that covered several rows of folding chairs. The open grave was situated just outside the canopy, and the pile of dirt taken from the grave had been covered with a blanket of green Astro-Turf.

Black-suited drivers and their assistants escorted Billy Ray and Krista Finchum and other close family members to the seating area. A minister in a light gray suit waited behind a portable pulpit.

"Some shit, wasn't it?" Stan said.

"Yeah, poor kid," I said.

"Who'da guessed?" John added.

As often happens, at even the best-organized funerals, a number of attendees didn't take their seats quickly. Others insisted on paying their respects to the mother and father before the service and clogged up the area around the pulpit. Still others milled around aimlessly and didn't get into acceptable positions. I spotted Darnell Means, Micah Blevins and Claude Webbster standing a few yards to the right of the main group talking intently, perhaps conspiring like the witches from *Macbeth*, but I couldn't find a bubbling caldron.

It seemed like an interminable amount of time passed before the minister could begin his program.

To my left, I heard, "John, move over a little, please."

I looked over as Bettye stepped up next to me.

"Hey," I said.

"Hey, yourself." She smiled.

I didn't want to appear obvious, but I turned a little more to look at her dark green, sleeveless dress—simple and very pretty. She wore her hair pulled up on the sides and fastened behind her head. The back hung lose to her shoulders.

"I'm glad you came," I said.

"I thought I should," she said.

I nodded.

"This turned into such a mess."

"There's more you don't know yet," I said.

"Will you tell me?"

"Sure, whenever you're ready to listen."

"I guess it would be okay for me to go to lunch with my ex-boss. I could listen then."

I wanted to caustically say, 'You better ask your husband first. He's thinks I'm a bad influence on you.' But I didn't.

"That would be nice. Tell me when," I said.

"Today's good." She put her arm through mine, squeezed and held on.

The minister tapped the microphone and heard he had amplification.

"I like your hair like that," I said.

"I know."

"How do you know?"

"I just do."

The minister began speaking. The amplifier squealed. He backed away from the mike a few more inches and continued.

Bettye came close to my ear and asked, "Did you give the mayor my resignation?"

I shook my head. "Not yet."

"No?"

"No, you have ten vacation days coming. No sense not getting paid for them."

"Thank you."

"And you're allowed sixty days leave of absence before I have to ask to fill your spot."

"You're going to wait?"

"Uh-huh."

"Why?"

I shrugged. "A lot can happen in seventy days."

She tightened her grip on my arm. "Can it now?"

"Sure. You get to know these things when you're a police chief."

"And what makes you so smart?"

"I'm the boss. I'm brilliant."

"Don't make me laugh at a funeral."

* * * *

At five after six Kate asked, "Do you mind if I put the news on?"

Over the last couple of days, I had been careful not to turn on the TV during the times Rachel's show was on the air.

"No, of course not." I put a bookmark into Joe Wambaugh's latest novel, dropped it on the lamp table and joined Kate on the couch.

After a few minutes of other news, Rachel led into her story by saying, "This morning Prospect Police Officer Dallas Finchum was laid to rest by his family and other police officers from East Tennessee. Finchum, not yet twenty-six, died from an accidental gunshot wound."

She was wearing glasses rather than the contacts she normally uses and a simple dark blue dress.

"Recently, Officer Finchum had been under investigation because of allegations that he sexually abused a young college classmate three years ago while attending UT Chattanooga."

The screen switched from Rachel to distance shots of the funeral procession and then the gravesite.

"The investigation was still ongoing when Finchum accidentally shot himself while cleaning his off-duty revolver."

Rachel came back, and the camera panned wide, showing her and co-anchor, Jack Larsen.

"This afternoon during an NXX exclusive interview with the woman who filed those charges, a woman who wishes to remain anonymous, I learned that she now recants her statement and admits that Dallas Finchum did not rape her."

The cameraman tightened up with a close-up of Rachel.

"The young woman told me that after engaging in rough sex, she had been seen bruised and looked as if she had been beaten. Embarrassed, she claimed rape. I'll repeat, she now states categorically that her allegation was not true."

Rachel flipped a page of notes and continued. "Prospect Police Chief Sam Jenkins listened to the girl's new information and stated for the record that her confession sounded credible. There will be no formal charges made against this woman because the statute of limitations on making the false report three years ago prevents that."

Rachel's partner then began a follow-up story on the toxic ash spill from the Watt's Bar Nuclear Power Facility.

Kate pushed the mute button on the remote control. "Did you tell her that?"

"Not exactly," I said. "After the girl told me, I suggested she talk about it and clear her conscience and Dallas's name all at once. I thought *that woman* might be the best way to do it."

"Her name's Rachel," Kate reminded me, speaking softly.

"Oh yeah?"

"Wouldn't the police in Chattanooga have to say they won't prosecute the girl for making a false statement?"

"Yeah, I interjected a little poetic license there. But what the hell, I'm the boss, and I didn't think anyone in Hamilton County would object to me speaking for them, especially since I have the option of handing over all my notes on their police shenanigans and political corruption to my friends at the FBI. If anyone questioned my right to say whatever I want, I'd have to make their cover-up public knowledge, and I'd embarrass the hell out of them."

"That sounds like blackmail."

"Actually it's coercion or maybe extortion. It's definitely official misconduct."

"You're bad."

"Worse."

"The statute of limitations on the false statement she made right here isn't up yet."

"Oh, Katsy, you're so smart. No, it isn't. But I'm the one with the discretion there, and because her mother sort of pushed her into making the statement to me, and she voluntarily told me she lied, and after living with that lie for three years, I'm allowing her to go free with time served—figuratively, of course."

"You make them up as you go along, don't you?"

"Sure, it's good to be boss."

"You're amazing, aren't you?"

"When I told Ronnie about this, he agreed to make the record of Dallas's suspension disappear."

"Isn't he *your* boss?"

"Yeah, but he's pliable. I didn't believe in the kid. I was wrong. I figure I owe him something."

"Didn't you say the law makes allowances for a policeman who's not always right if he's always reasonable?"

"I did."

"It was a nice thing to do for his parents, though."

"Screw his parents. His mother was okay, I guess. His father is a shithead and always will be. I did this for me...and maybe for Dallas."

"And maybe somehow he'll know."

"Yeah, right," I said sarcastically.

"Have a little faith.

"I'm just sick to death of this whole business.'

"You've had a rough couple of weeks."

"I guess. But I'll never admit that because I'm a world-class tough guy."

"Tough-guys can feel bad, too."

"So I've been told."

"Rachel is leaving on Friday."

"Uh-huh."

"And Bettye resigned."

"Uh-huh."

"Need a new girlfriend?"

"Nope, got one."

"Want her around more often?"

"I've always liked that idea."

"She resigned her job, too."

"Oh, really?"

"I resigned from the state library group. They'll have to find a new president for next year."

"Sure you want to do that?"

"I'm sure."

"Good."

"Are we okay here?"

"We've always been okay. A little glitch here, a little glitch there, but I'm okay if you are."

"I'm okay."

"Good."

"Want to open a bottle of wine before you put on the movie?"

"Sure. Red or white?"

"You pick it."

Chapter Thirty-Six

"Sam, what you've told me sounds like some kind of movin' picture with a convoluted plot. Hard to believe, isn't it?" Minas Tipton shook his head and set his lowball glass of Gentleman Jack on the lamp table next to him.

We sat in his living room, me on the striped sofa and he in a wingback chair. He with bourbon and me with scotch. I wore a tan sport jacket and brown pants, he a navy blue blazer, gray pants and a paisley ascot.

"What bothers me, Judge, are the problems people like Billy Ray Finchum caused my good friends. Their lives are changed forever because Finchum thought his political connections entitled him to more than the rest of us."

"I understand how you feel, Sam. I truly do. And I'm sorry those ladies were hurt. But those things can't be undone now. It's no consolation, but life is full of collateral damage, isn't it?"

"You're right. It's no consolation to them or to me. Back in my old neighborhood, we'd say it sucks."

Tipton laughed. "Many of us hillbillies would say the same, son. Believe it."

"I know nothing can be reversed, but it sticks here," I tapped a spot high on my chest, "when Finchum is going to skate through five years of probation."

"His son figuratively died at his hand, Sam. The knowledge of that will never go away."

"And my dog died because I told the vet to put her to sleep. I know how he feels, but you know what, your Honor? I don't give a rat's ass about him."

"I'm sorry for you, Sam. Believe me when I say that."

"I do. Thanks. How'd you like to do something to make me feel better?"

"What's that, son?"

"Get rid of Claude Webbster. He's the other bastard who started that ball of shit rolling downhill, and so far he's the one who'll walk out of this unscathed. He's corrupt. He pulls strings, not to get a job done, but for selfish, personal gain. Tell him to resign, or I'll drop a finished case on the FBI. They won't let him bow out gracefully."

The old judge raised his white eyebrows. "Claude's been around county government for a long time."

"Then maybe it's time for some new blood to take his place—clean blood. Claude's a piss-ant. He won't be hard to replace."

Tipton nodded thoughtfully. "Claude could be an embarrassment. You're right. It's not like we'd be takin' away his livelihood. He owns the plumbin' supply business." The old man sat there thinking, moving his lips around, nodding his snow-white head. "I'll talk to the county mayor. I'm sure he'll see it your way. And under the circumstances, I think he'll want to keep you happy—or at least satisfied."

"*Satisfied* is good. For him, *quiet* is better. Thank you."

Chapter Thirty-Seven

In the 1960s, during the Vietnam War, there was an expression prevalent among soldiers.

When a career NCO with only a double-digit IQ indelicately disciplined a soldier, when a twenty-year-old boy received a "Dear John" letter from a young wife who decided not to wait for his overseas tour to be over or when a group of men stood over the body of a fallen comrade, you would often hear soldiers say, 'It don't mean nothing.'

No one ever commented on the grammatical error, but no one ever truly believed the statement either. No matter how many times you said it or heard it stated, most everyone knew that if you told someone, 'It don't mean nothing,' it really meant a lot.

But soldiers or cops don't continue to do their jobs without a healthy sense of denial.

Those in the military who didn't take that approach or couldn't, often ended up with what we called a three-day Thorazine R&R.

So, after all these days of aggravation and personal grief, I was tempted to tell myself, 'It don't mean nothing,' and continue to march.

I didn't because I'm no longer a twenty-two-year old GI, and after trading quotations with Moira Menzies, I began to feel somewhat philosophical and examined how I felt.

It's been said that all the ancient Gaelic legends passed down by my ancestors revolve around love, land and loss. Falling in love is like a hurricane you can't escape; it hammers your coast and leaves your mental landscape forever changed. Hiding inside and looking out the window at the water and wind won't help. You're left with only two choices: play in the rain or evacuate. But flight never provides peace of mind and inevitably leaves you wondering how you can rebuild. I own a nice piece of property with beautiful woodlands and mountain views, and no reigning monarch is threatening to remove me to a foreign colony. That left the third option.

The American Heritage Dictionary defines *loss* as, "The condition of being deprived or bereaved of something or someone."

Roget's lists forty-six synonyms for the noun alone. Some of those are: deprivation, bereavement, forfeit, irretrievable, ruin, deterioration, decrement, waste and defeat.

None of those are happy words. I felt too old not to spend the rest of my life being relatively happy.

About loss, Sir Thomas Moore wrote:

> *All that's bright must fade*
> *The brightest still the fleetest;*
> *All that's sweet was made*
> *But to be lost when sweetest.*

Kate and I had been together a long time, certainly not fleeting. I always looked at her as the sweetest. She wasn't lost. Try again, Thomas.

Lastly, there will never be another Bitsey. Her death affected me like no other so far. But life went on.

Maybe it was time to grow up. I've always wondered what I should do when the time came.

I remembered Peter, Paul, and Mary singing:

> *Dragons are forever,*
> *Not so little boys.*

The same dictionary that defined *loss* also listed *can-of-worms*. "A source of unforeseen or troublesome complexity." That fits.

THE END

Author's notes:

A Can of Worms is based on two actual, but separate incidents. The first, the story of "Dallas #1," played out much like the beginning of this book.

Dallas #1 was hired as a police officer. Prior to the end of his probation, a complaint lodged against him for a prior date rape caused an investigation. This all took place in New York, not Tennessee. His case was simple and straightforward. He was guilty.

Simplicity left my life when my investigators ran into the corruption of a polygraph examiner, the compromise of an upstate district attorney and several police and security officers, and a politically active father who gave new meaning to the phrase *a can of worms*.

In the end, Dallas #1 was terminated without ceremony. He simply faded away.

"Dallas #2" was another story. He had not been hired, but rather scored high on his entrance test, but could not be appointed because of a pending criminal court case, a felony. He too had been accused of forcible rape, but in a neighboring jurisdiction.

The two officers investigating that alleged sex crime pressured Dallas #2 to confess and clear the air. Dallas #2 refused, claiming his innocence. At some point, the pressure and frustration overwhelmed the young man, and he took his own life. Subsequent to his suicide, the complainant admitted her exaggeration and his innocence.

Both Dallas #1 and #2 were real people who shall remain unidentified. Sam Jenkins and all the other boys and girls in and around the fictional city of Prospect are embellishments or figments of my overactive imagination. All except Bitsey who accompanied us through life for seventeen years.

About the Author

Wayne Zurl grew up on Long Island and retired after twenty years with the Suffolk County Police Department, one of the largest municipal law enforcement agencies in New York and the nation. For thirteen of those years he served as a section commander supervising investigators. He is a graduate of SUNY, Empire State College and served on active duty in the US Army during the Vietnam War and later in the reserves. Zurl left New York to live in the foothills of the Great Smoky Mountains of Tennessee with his wife, Barbara.

Zurl has won Eric Hoffer and Indie Book Awards, and was named a finalist for a Montaigne Medal and First Horizon Book Award. He has written four novels and more than twenty novelettes in the Sam Jenkins mystery series.

Author Links:
Author website: http://www.waynezurlbooks.net
Twitter: http://www.twitter.com/#!/waynezurl
Facebook: http://www.facebook.com/waynezurl

Other books by the author at Melange
From New York to the Smokies
A Leprechaun's Lament
Heroes and Lovers
Pigeon River Blues
A Touch of Morning Calm

Coming Soon!
A New Prospect